THE MAJOR'S CANDLESTICKS

THE MAJOR'S CANDLESTICKS

BY

GEORGE A. BIRMINGHAM

METHUEN & CO. LTD.
36 Essex Street W.C.
LONDON

First Published	.	.	.	.	April 25th 1929
Second and Cheaper Edition		.	.	July	1930
Third Edition (Cheap Form)		.	.	August	1931
Fourth Edition (Cheap Form)		.	.	March	1935
Fifth Edition (F'cap 8vo, Cheap Form)				1935	

THE MAJOR'S CANDLESTICKS

CHAPTER I

COOLARRIGAN CASTLE never was a castle. It was a dignified Georgian country house, fit to be inhabited by a man of moderate fortune. It was called a castle, because the Irish gentry in the 18th century, and indeed long afterwards, had a taste for the grandiose. They would have considered it beneath their dignity to live, as Englishmen of their class often do, in simple houses. Coolarrigan Castle, or House, stood pleasantly enough on one of the lower reaches of the Shannon, not far from Lisnamoe, a place well known to salmon fishers who go there year after year, attracted by the prospect of catching fish and the certainty of finding a comfortable hotel, a rare thing in rural Ireland. Even salmon fishers, keenest of all sportsmen, are not indifferent to the satisfaction which comes of a good dinner and a comfortable bed.

The fish are still there and can still be persuaded to jump at tempting flies. Fishermen, in the proper season, still flock to Lisnamoe and find that Eileen Costello, who has lately taken over the management of the hotel, feeds them satisfactorily. Revolutions affect salmon very little, and Miss Costello, though she takes an intelligent interest in politics, is far too sensible to let them affect her cooking. But Coolarrigan Castle is there no more. Not even a broken wall or a charred timber survives to show where it once was.

Before the war Coolarrigan Castle belonged to Mrs.
Aubrey and achieved a moderate fame among Irish
country houses. Its rock gardens were, admittedly,
the best in Ireland. During the war Mrs. Aubrey
died. The house and the rock gardens passed into
the possession of Major Kent. At the time of his
inheritance the Major, like many another ' dug-out '
officer, was serving his country by conducting drafts of
men from their English training centres to the base
camps of France. It was a thankless and exceedingly
unpleasant job, for though the Major was never seasick
himself the men under his charge invariably were,
violently and explosively, all night. His ship, a small
one and generally greatly overcrowded, was in a
disgusting state when she arrived at Le Havre. The
Major, though an earnest patriot and a good soldier,
was as glad as every one else when the Armistice came
and he was free to leave the Army for the second, he
hoped the last, time.

He had the choice of two houses to live in, his own,
Portsmouth Lodge, on the shores of Ballymoy Bay, and
Coolarrigan Castle. He chose the castle. Ballymoy,
the bay, the neighbourhood and the islands had lost
some of their delights for him since his friend Meldon,
the Rev. J. J. Meldon, accepted a parish in England and
left County Mayo. He was also influenced in his
choice by the fact that the land round Coolarrigan
Castle was singularly well suited for the rearing of young
horses. The Major was still deeply interested in the
breeding of polo ponies. Out of a pious regard for his
aunt's memory he kept the rock garden free of the
grosser kinds of weeds ; but the plants in it languished,
as plants often do when deprived of human love. The
polo ponies, on the other hand, flourished exceedingly,

and in 1921, three years after the Major settled there, Coolarrigan Castle had achieved a new reputation quite equal to that won by old Mrs. Aubrey's rock gardens.

1921, as some of us still remember, was a troublous time in Ireland. Irregular executions, which old-fashioned people still called murders, were common. The burning down of houses—always done with the best intentions and the loftiest motives—was commoner still. Most of the Major's friends went away, seeking security in such places as Bath and Dinard. The Major, though the neighbourhood became lonely, stayed on. There was no reason that he knew of for shooting him. Nor did he see how the cause of Irish independence could be advanced by the destruction of Coolarrigan Castle. Being a simple-minded man he assumed that politics, and even revolutions, were conducted on reasonable lines, and that he, an entirely inoffensive person, would be let alone.

He was mistaken. One Saturday night, a dark night in the middle of October, he was awakened by the glare of an electric torch turned on his face as he lay in bed. He opened his eyes, blinked a little, and then discerned behind the glare a masked man with a revolver in his hand.

' Who the devil are you ? ' said the Major.

He spoke with some irritation, natural and almost excusable irritation. No one likes being wakened suddenly from a sound sleep. Most people dislike having revolvers pointed at them when they are in bed.

The masked man did not answer the Major's question. Midnight marauders, who may very well turn out to be murderers, seldom explain exactly who they are. But though he did not say what his name was the man gave the Major some useful, indeed valuable, information.

'If you're not out of this house,' he said, 'in ten minutes it'll be the worse for you.'

'Well, I'm damned!' said the Major, this time more astonished than annoyed. 'You're the last man I'd have expected to be mixed up in this kind of thing.'

The face behind the flashlight was invisible because of the mask ; but the Major recognized a familiar voice, the voice of Michael Gannon, his head groom, a man of singular skill in the management of young horses. It would have shown great stupidity in the Major if he had failed to recognize the voice. He was accustomed to spend hours every day talking to Gannon about polo ponies, their merits and their failings, their diseases and the way to cure them.

'What on earth do you want to murder me for ?' said the Major.

He still clung to the delusion that there must be reasons of some sort for all actions, even crimes.

'Sure, what's the use of talking that way ?' said Michael Gannon. 'Nobody wants to murder you.'

He spoke in a friendly tone, almost apologetically. To show that he meant what he said he pointed his revolver at his own toes instead of the Major's head. But though friendly in spirit he showed himself a man of devotion to duty.

'But you've got to be out of this in ten minutes,' he said firmly.

'Why ?'

The Major was still inclined to argue, as simple-minded people are when faced with things which strike them as entirely unreasonable.

' Because the house is going to be burned,' said Michael Gannon. 'That's why, and it's why enough for you or any other man, so get up out of your bed now and be off with you.'

The Major got up. It seemed foolish to stay where he was. He slipped on his socks and a pair of shoes. A bare-footed man is always at a disadvantage whether he means to fight or fly. He took a thick dressing-gown from the chair on which it lay. Nights in October are often chilly, and a mist had been rising from the river since sundown. A warm dressing-gown is desirable, if not as necessary as socks and shoes. He opened the door of his room and saw another man who had not taken the trouble to mask his face, pouring petrol over the stair carpet. That convinced him that Michael Gannon had been speaking the truth. Some-body—presumably somebody very patriotic—really did intend to burn down the house.

' Why are you doing it ? ' he asked Michael.

' What is to be must be,' said Michael deliberately, speaking as a man does who had thought long and deeply over difficult problems.

' I wish to goodness,' said the Major, ' that you had some sense. What on earth is the use of burning down my house? Nobody'll be a bit better off when it's done. What are you trying to do, Michael ? What are you at ? What's the meaning of it all ? '

' The meaning of it,' said Michael, ' is this. Things has been the way they are long enough and it's time now for us to be yous and for yous to be us.'

Major Kent is not a quick-witted man. He thinks slowly, but he does think, and in the end his conclusions are usually sound. He recognized in Michael's first answer the theology which made Islam mighty and inspired the discipline of Cromwell's Ironsides—' What is to be must be.' The second answer was even more illuminating. It gave the complete philosophy of all revolutions. Coolarrigan Castle was to be burned down because it was written in the Book of Fate that Coolarrigan Castle should be burned. He himself was to be turned out in a dressing-gown and pyjamas because in the past he had been master and Michael Gannon servant. Now the time had come for a change of parts. Michael Gannon and his friends were to be on top. The Major and others like him were to be underneath.

Orators and even poets have said and sung fine things about liberty, fraternity, democracy and other pretty goddesses. Michael Gannon was an Irishman and therefore an uncompromising realist. His dawning class consciousness divided men into ' us ' and ' yous.' He saw that the chance had come of turning the one into the other and the inversion seemed to him desirable.

The Major walked down the petrol soaked stairs. Michael Gannon followed. With great politeness he held his electric torch so that its light fell on the steps and the Major could see where he was going.

' There's no need to be hurrying yourself,' he said.

' I'm not hurrying in the least,' said the Major.

With that cool gallantry which characterizes the officers of the British Army, he was retreating, since he had to retreat, in good order, without flurry or confusion.

' You've got ten minutes, so you have,' said Michael Gannon.

This was generous. Ten minutes had been the

original time limit and at least three had passed since the light first wakened the Major.

' And I needn't be telling you,' said Michael Gannon, ' that if there's anything you'd like to take with you there's no objection in the wide world to your taking it.'

There were a good many things which the Major would have liked to take with him. There was some china in the cabinet in the drawing-room. He had no idea of its value, but he knew that his aunt thought very highly of it. There were some old miniatures. There were several dozen bottles of very good port in the cellar. There was a Romney portrait. There was a set of chairs which—the Major was no expert in such matters—were supposed to be the work of Chippendale himself. There were other things, such things as accumulate and gather value in a house which has been inhabited for many years by the sort of people whom Michael Gannon called ' yous,' who in future were to belong to the ' us ' class, while their cherished possessions—— The smell of petrol was unpleasantly strong. Another marauder was emptying a tin of the stuff over the Chippendale chairs as the Major entered the dining-room. Why he went there he could not have told, nor why, on his way through the hall, he picked up a large fishing-basket which hung from a peg. You cannot put a Romney portrait into a fishing-basket, nor, even if the basket is unusually large, can you carry away twelve Chippendale chairs in it.

' Mind, now,' said Michael Gannon. ' You've no more than ten minutes. I'd give you half an hour if it was me that was boss, but the rest of the fellows that's in it doesn't care to be kept waiting too long.'

There was no chance of their being interfered with by

police or other supporters of the old order of society, so it was not fear which made them unwilling to delay. Simply the hour was late, or rather very early, 2 a.m. Some of the marauders had several miles to go in order to reach home. Being young men, they wanted as much sleep as they could get. It was a Saturday night, and every man of the party intended to be at Mass early next morning in order to receive the divine blessing on the work they were doing. In Ireland even murderers are most particular about hearing Mass.

There is a story told of a lady, a passenger in a great steamer which for some reason began to sink unexpectedly in the very middle of a wide ocean. The lady had gone to her cabin and was in bed when the disaster happened. Her husband, who at the moment was in the smoking-room, drinking whisky and soda, ran down to her. He told her to get up at once. 'You've got five minutes and no more,' he said. 'Collect everything you think you're likely to want in an open boat and then join me on deck.' The lady, like Major Kent, began by putting on her dressing-gown. Then she looked round her cabin. 'I'm sure to want a pocket-handkerchief,' she thought. 'Wherever I am I must want that.' She stuffed one into her pocket and walked round the cabin, thinking hard about what she was likely to want. It occurred to her that a pocket-handkerchief would certainly be useful. She put a second into her dressing-gown pocket. She made another tour of the cabin, thinking hard. Like a flash of inspiration it came to her that it would never do to go off in an open boat without a pocket-handkerchief. She seized a third and put it into her pocket. The minutes went by quickly. The lady's mind worked with frenzied rapidity and she acted on each thought that came to her. When, some hours later, the boat in which she and her husband sat was picked up by a steamer which had rushed to the rescue, it was found that the lady had salved only pocket-handkerchiefs out of all her store of belongings. But she had salved seventeen of them.

The Major was not a coward. No Major is. He had the coolness of a man inured to danger of every kind. But his mind, never a very brilliant one, was not at its best when he had been wakened out of a deep sleep at two o'clock in the morning. The news that his house was going to be burned down prevented deliberate and careful thought. He walked round his dining-room with the fishing-basket in his hand, till he came to the sideboard. He picked up a silver candlestick from it. That, he reflected, would be an easy thing to carry off and might be useful afterwards. He put it into his basket and walked on. In due time he came back to the sideboard and his eye was caught by the candlesticks which still stood there. He put another into the basket and made another tour of the dining-room. Why should his actions be described in detail ? When warned by Michael Gannon that eight of his minutes of grace had passed he walked out of his house with seven candlesticks in a basket ; seven out of the eight which had adorned his sideboard during the day and most of the night, which held the candles which lit his table while he dined.

The candlesticks were made of silver and had therefore an intrinsic value far above that of pocket handkerchiefs. They were old—so the Major's aunt had often told him—and were therefore more valuable than the metal of which they were made. They were also the work of Paul Lamerie. The Major had been told this, too, by his aunt, but he had forgotten it.   Nor, if he had remembered the name of that artist, would it have meant much to him.   He was not the kind of man who gloats over the value of candlesticks made by Paul Lamerie.   In old Irish country houses there are —or were before Ireland's war of independence—many things of great value.   Their owners were attached to them because they had belonged to their grandparents. They would perhaps have valued them more and would certainly have been more ready to part with them if they had known the price they would have fetched at Christie's.   The Major might have made an effort to save the eighth candlestick if he had known what each of them was worth.

His first impulse when he got outside was to go to the stables in order to rescue a few of the polo ponies.   His way was blocked by four stern men with revolvers in their hands.   The Irish patriot is quite ready to destroy Romney portraits, Chippendale chairs or Spode china. But he knows the value of horses and is most unwilling to burn to death a well-bred polo pony.   These particular patriots understood the value of horses so well that they did not mean to let the Major walk off with a single one.   He might have Paul Lamerie candlesticks if he liked.   They meant to keep the polo ponies for themselves.   They refused to allow him to approach the stables.   They made it quite clear to him that he must take the path which led to the river.

Dean Swift, while discussing the copper coinage of Ireland, said that one man in his shirt cannot hope to fight successfully against three men fully clothed and armed.   Major Kent did not read Swift, but he reached the same conclusion by the light of his own intelligence. One man in pyjamas and a dressing-gown cannot contend with four men who flourish revolvers. He took the path they pointed out to him. It skirted a broad lawn on which the mist lay densely. It plunged into a large shrubbery where the moisture, gathered on the leaves, wet the Major's dressing-gown as he brushed past. It led downhill under a grove of pines from which great drops fell heavily on the brown needles and fir cones which strewed the ground, and occasionally on the Major's head, which was bald. Among the pine trees the path ceased to be a path, and beyond the grove lay an open space of rough grass which reached down to the river and a boat-house. Here the mist grew thinner for a moment and was blown about in pale grey wisps by an errant breeze. The Major made for the boat-house, and as he reached it was conscious that the mist had ceased to be grey. There was a glow of colour in it, and turning round he saw that behind him the colour was brighter, orange and red.

He opened the door of the boat-house. On a slip, her stern just clear of the water, lay a boat. The Major laid down his fishing-basket, the candlesticks rattling as he did so, and pulled at the stern of the boat. She slid down. There came a roar of cheering and a rattle of shots fired, a mere *feu de joie*, for, now that the Major was gone, there was no one left about the house whom it would be desirable to shoot. Looking back through the door of the boat-house the Major saw that behind the trees the sky was aglow with light. His house, well petrol-soaked, was blazing. The cheering grew louder. More shots were fired. The major gave the sliding boat a final push, and, grasping the skirt of his dressing-gown, tumbled in over the bow. As he fell forward his right foot kicked the fishing-basket, and it fell over the side of the slip into three feet of water.

Being weighted with seven silver candlesticks it sank at once. The Major took no notice of it. Moved to fury by the blaze and the cheering, he forgot all about the candlesticks. He had not understood, even when he took them from the dining-room sideboard, that they were the work of Paul Lamerie.

The boat floated clear of the boat-house on the broad breast of the Shannon. The Major, shivering slightly, took the oars and paddled downstream.

CHAPTER II

ON an August morning in 1924 the sun shone brilliantly on the pleasant sea front of Weymouth. Along the beach bathing tents flaunted their gay stripes. Mothers sat sewing in hammock chairs while their offspring—an enormous number of offspring—dug in the sand and paddled in the tepid water. Blue-jerseyed fishermen tried to induce timid strangers to hire small boats by the hour. Vendors of ice-creams and toy balloons made their appeal. The agent of the Weymouth City Fathers, a bored man, went about collecting pennies from the mothers who sat in the hammock chairs. Donkeys waited patiently for the blows which their masters would shower on them when there were riders in the saddle. Cynical goats stood ready to drag tiny carriages about, wondering as they waited that men and children could be the fools they were. In the sea itself bathers disported themselves, many of them venturing so far from the shore that the water reached their waists.

Along the broad drive above the beach, charabancs, heavily laden with excursionists, made their way among the smaller cars with all the dignity of great liners going up the Solent among racing yachts. Girls in the shortest of cotton frocks and the pinkest of stockings paraded arm in arm. Gentlemen, in clothes which proclaimed themselves ' holiday suitings,' stood at the doors of hotels and restaurants with pipes in their mouths. An aeroplane flew low. A highly-powered motor-boat flashed across the bay and swept round in a wide circle amid a smother of foam. It was August in Weymouth, and August at its brightest and best, an August in what the local landladies called ' a good season.'

Along the broad parade came a large open motor-car of antique build. The grey paint on its body was cracked and stained. Its mudguards were badly dinted. Its hood, loosely folded and carelessly strapped, showed itself to be shabby and worn. Its horn, operated by a small boy who seemed to be sitting on the driver's knee, was never for a moment silent. Its engine made an incredible amount of noise, but, though noisy, it was a sound and efficient engine. The car went along the drive at about forty miles an hour. The drivers of charabancs cursed it audibly. An elderly gentleman, ambling quietly along in a two-seater, narrowly escaped a collision. He shook his fist furiously at the driver of the larger car. The girls in cotton frocks and pink stockings fled to the side-walks in frightened bevies. The gentlemen in ' holiday suitings' took their pipes from their mouths and stepped backwards towards their hotels. Two policemen, one at each end of the parade, took out their pocket-books and made notes of the number of the grey car.

But there was no venom in the way they made their notes, and the blasphemy of the charabanc drivers was quite pleasantly uttered. The flying girls giggled as they escaped. The gentlemen in the ' holiday suitings ' had the air of those who hold—and mean to impress upon the world—the great truth that boys will be boys. Only the old gentleman in the two-seater seemed really angry, and there was some excuse for him. His car had escaped complete destruction by less than half an inch.

The grey car was full, even a little over-full of small boys. There were eight of them in the back of it. There were four on the driver's left, and one, either sitting on his knee or somehow squeezed in on his right. Of the thirteen, twelve were cheering and waving their caps. The thirteenth was so completely occupied with the horn that he could neither cheer nor wave. All the world, even the police who regulate traffic, is tolerant of small boys at holiday time.

Even if the boys had not made their unfailing appeal to the heart of the crowd a glance at the driver of the car would have turned away much wrath. He was a clergyman. His collar, though dirty and a little limp, proved that. He had a shabby grey hat set far back on his head. He had a grizzled red moustache. He had bright shining eyes and an expression of reckless happiness on his face. It was plain that he was enjoying himself as much as any of his boys were. He waved an airy greeting to the policemen who made notes. He smiled in the friendliest way at flying girls. He shouted ' Steady on ! ' to the cursing charabanc drivers. He glanced amiably at the old gentleman in the two-seater. He glanced at him again, looking round, perilously, after he had passed. Then with a wild shrieking of tortured brakes he stopped his car with extraordinary abruptness. The small boys in the back tumbled over each other. The four on his left fell forward and hit their heads against the windscreen. The stomach of the boy with the horn was driven hard down on the knob of the gear lever.

The driver, the Rev. J. J. Meldon, once curate of

Ballymoy in Co. Mayo, shouted a greeting to the man in the two-seater who had shaken his fist.

' Hullo, Major ! ' he said. ' I never expected to see you here.'

Major Kent managed to pull up his car with two wheels on the side-walk and one mudguard scraping the running board of Meldon's grey car. He had another exceedingly narrow escape.

' Good God, J. J. ! ' he gasped.

' Don't swear, Major,' said Meldon. ' Even if you've no respect for the fact that I'm a clergyman, try to realize that these are choirboys. I can't and won't have their morals corrupted by the kind of language you learned in the barrack-room.'

All the boys cheered, except the one whose stomach hit the gear lever. He, poor child, had no breath left to cheer with. J. J. smacked him on the back with kindly firmness.

' Hop out, all of you,' he said. ' I want to talk to the Major.'

There was a scramble. Through the doors, over the sides, even over the folded hood at the back, the boys tumbled out on to the road.

' I might have known it was you, J. J.,' the Major muttered. ' Nobody else in the world would drive at such a pace in a car—' he looked at it with disgust—' in a car like that.'

' Now then,' said Meldon to the boys. ' Attention ! Form fours ! I mean to say, dress from the right and number ! '

The order was perhaps a little confusing. Perhaps the boys thought that drill was unsuited to a holiday. They gathered round their pastor in quite irregular formation, clutching at his coat and trousers.

'Major,' said Meldon, 'you're a military man Draw these boys up in a line. I never can remember the proper orders to give.'

A small crowd was gathering. The note-taking policemen, smiling agreeably, were standing near the cars with their pencils still in their hands. A large number of girls, happy after their escape from sudden death, giggled on the side-walk. Two charabancs had pulled up. Their drivers and their seventy-two passengers were gazing at the scene with interest. The Major looked round. He was a man who prized his dignity, disliked being the centre of attention, and, beyond everything, hated being laughed at.

'I can't, J. J.,' he said feebly. 'I really can't.'

'You mean to say you won't,' said Meldon severely. 'You're always coming down on other people, Major, for not speaking the truth. Even the most trifling inaccuracy when it's anybody else makes you irritable. But when it comes to telling the truth yourself you simply don't do it. You know perfectly well that you can drill those boys if you like. You can't have forgotten the only thing you ever knew, those silly old words of command. And yet you have the nerve to say that you can't draw up a dozen boys in a straight line.'

'J. J.,' said the Major pleadingly, 'don't ask me to do it. There's a crowd, and I really should feel such a fool.'

'Very well,' said Meldon, 'if you won't, you won't. But you can and will lend me a pound.'

The Major, who was still in his car, struggled to get at his trousers pocket.

'I'm afraid I've only got silver,' he said.

'Silver will do if there's enough of it. But don't

try to put me off with half a crown as if I was a girl selling poppies.'

' I'll give you all I have with pleasure,' said the Major, dragging at his pocket.

' There,' he said at last, ' that's all I have, but it's more than a pound. What do you want with it, J. J. ? '

' I want to give it to the boys,' said Meldon, ' so that they'll be able to hire boats.'

The boys cheered. Several people in the crowd cheered, too. The policemen, who are not allowed to cheer while on duty, looked as if they wanted to.

' It's all for your own good, Major,' said Meldon. ' If I don't get rid of these boys I shan't be able to go home to lunch with you. You wouldn't like that, would you ? '

' Of course not,' said the Major. ' I mean to say of course you must lunch with me, and dine and stay the night if you can. But—' he looked a little anxiously at the boys—' if you let those boys go out in boats by themselves they'll be drowned.'

A bearded boatman, scenting his prey from afar, left the beach and joined the crowd round the cars. He pushed his way through the giggling girls and addressed Meldon.

' That'll be all right, sir,' he said. ' You leave them boys of yours to me, sir. I'll put them out in boats, sir, if that's what they want. Just you trust me, sir. I'll see as how they don't drown themselves.'

' They will be drowned,' said the Major firmly, ' if they go out in boats by themselves.'

' Don't be absurdly fussy, Major,' said Meldon. ' It's totally impossible to drown a choirboy. You might hold one down for hours, with his head under water, and he'd come up smiling at the end, like a flea that you were trying to drown. You've no experience of choir-boys, Major, but I have.'

' Well, it's your affair, and I don't suppose it'll matter much if they are drowned. It would be a good thing to drown a few boys. There wouldn't be so many left to get under the wheels of cars.'

' Major, you forget that these are choirboys, the most valuable kind of boy there is.'

' England's far too full of boys,' said the Major grumblingly. ' The loss of a dozen or so won't be noticed, except by the parents, and they'll be glad. They've all got more children than they want. Must have. Just look at that ! '

He waved his hand towards the beach. It could scarcely be denied that there were enormous numbers of children. An eager member of an infants' welfare committee, when he looks at Weymouth on a fine August day, must realize that the saving of infant life has been carried a little too far.

' Just you trust me, sir,' said the boatman again.

It was not clear whether he meant, as he did at first, that he might be trusted to keep the boys safe ; or, having grasped the meaning of the Major's words, that he might be trusted to drown them all. Whichever he meant he got his wish and was trusted. Meldon handed over to him the one pound, three shillings and sixpence which the Major had produced. He gave a parting admonition to the boys.

' See that you get value for the money,' he said. ' The Major doesn't really hate paying up as much as you might think, but he does not like being stuck.'

The boys, determined to secure the last pennyworth of rowing, trooped down to the beach after the boatman.

Meldon stepped into the Major's car and sat down.

'Now then, Major, I haven't seen you for years and years, not since Coolarrigan was burnt down. Take me to your new house wherever it is. You have a new house, I suppose? From what I know of you I should think you're sure to. You'd never be happy without a house of your own.'

'I've got a sort of suburban villa out at Wyke,' said the Major. 'Not what I'd call a house. The sort of thing a retired greengrocer might live in.'

'Don't grouse,' said Meldon. 'It's an old habit of yours and you ought to try and conquer it. There are much worse things in the world than suburban villas. Take me to it at once.'

The Major considered his position. Two of his wheels were on the footpath. His front mudguard was pressed against the running board of Meldon's grey car. Most of the crowd had moved off to watch the boatman drowning Meldon's choirboys. But there were still a good many people round the cars.

'Do you think you could shift that car of yours a bit, J. J. ?' said the Major.

'Don't be fussy,' said Meldon. 'My car is perfectly safe where it is. Nobody will steal it. Nobody could. I don't believe there's a man in England who could make that car go except myself. It's a queer-tempered car—old age, I suppose. It ought to be a warning to you, Major, now that you're getting on a bit. Don't let your temper get the better of you. I couldn't help noticing the way you shook your fist at me when I passed you just now. If you're not careful you'll get to be as tricky to manage as my car is.'

The Major ignored this reproach. He felt that it was unjust, and he knew by experience that it was no use arguing with Meldon. Besides, he was really anxious to get away.

'But how am I to get out of this?' he said. 'I'm jammed.'

'You're not jammed in the least. All you've got to do is to back a bit up on the footpath and you'll get clear.'

The Major looked round anxiously.

'If I back on to that footpath,' he said, 'I shall run over five or six girls.'

'My dear Major, don't be captious; or, if you can't help that, at least be consistent in your captiousness. You've just said that you hope all my choirboys will be drowned. That's not a humane sentiment. Still you've a right to cherish it if you like. Only, if you are ready and willing to drown thirteen boys you can't consistently object to running over half a dozen girls. Girls aren't nearly as valuable as boys. All social philosophers admit that. And anyway it's a hundred to one against your killing them even if you do run over them. The worst you're likely to do is to break their legs, and most of their legs ought to be broken if they won't keep them covered up. I'm speaking now as an artist, not a moralist. The number of ugly legs on view is degrading to the public taste, and any one who breaks a few of them will benefit society. For goodness' sake, Major, start that engine of yours. I'm sick and tired of sitting here.'

The Major pressed the button of his self-starter and pushed his lever into reverse. He backed very cautiously on to the footpath, blowing his horn and shouting a warning. He need not have been careful. The sea-side girl is an active creature. Her legs would not, perhaps, have delighted Phidias, but she can use them when she chooses with great agility.

CHAPTER III

THE Major's house at Wyke was exactly what he said it was, a suburban villa.

A wooden gate, of aggressively simple design, separated its grounds from a high-road on which buses ran all day long, making horrid noises. Inside the gate was a narrow curved drive. There was no reason at all why it should have been curved and no good reason for its being narrow. Whoever made it was probably convinced that anything obvious, a straight drive, for instance, must be inartistic. Below the house was a trim lawn with flower-beds in it. It was the Major who had trimmed it. The original designer had aimed at a rock garden set in a wilderness.

The house itself was built at the period when our architects first became art-conscious. The outside was rich in steep gables and unnecessarily long stretches of roof with dormer windows in them. The Major had always been accustomed to straight walls and anything else worried him. The arrangements in the house inside were the result of early studies in the art of labour saving. The rooms were crushed together and opened into very narrow passages in unexpected ways. It was all that an Irish country house never is—compact, fussy and surprising. The Major, used to the dignity and calm of Coolarrigan, hated High Pines with bitterness. It was called High Pines because it was on top of a hill and had a fir tree just inside its gate. The Major hated the name almost as much as he hated the house.

To such refuges have the victims of the Irish revolution been driven, and, having been gentlemen in their own land, they feel degraded as well as uncomfortable. But High Pines, though the Major would not admit this, had its good points.

The bay-window in the drawing-room gave a broad view of Portland harbour, and, having three sides, kept the sun from midday until evening. It was in this window that the Major and Meldon settled down after a good luncheon. They had coffee before them and a bottle of brandy. The Major had a good cigar. Meldon had taken from his pocket a pipe of obvious maturity and was filling it with shreds of dark tobacco, cut from a solid lump and rubbed between the palms of his hands.

' Now, Major,' he said, ' out with your trouble, whatever it is. I am perfectly ready to help you in any way in my power. And there are very few troubles that I can't get the better of. You know that.'

Several times, during a long friendship, the Major had been helped out of troubles by the Rev. J. J. Meldon. Each time he felt that he greatly preferred the trouble to the help. He did not intend to be helped again if he could avoid it.

' I haven't any particular trouble, J. J.,' he said.

But he spoke despondingly and the denial was unconvincing.

' You have,' said Meldon, ' and it's far better to be frank about it. In fact, if you aren't frank I don't see how I can help you, though I shall try. The way you shook your fist at me to-day when I passed you in your car shows me that you are suffering from what the doctors call nervous breakdown. And that's a disease which only attacks men who are the victims of serious trouble. You wouldn't have behaved as you did if you hadn't been driven nearly desperate by some worry or other.'

' I shook my fist at you,' said the Major, ' because you were driving like a criminal lunatic in a crowded thoroughfare and very nearly killed me.'

' I passed you in the usual way, after sounding my horn. I had a boy on that horn who never stopped sounding it. If there'd been an accident, which there never is when I'm driving, it would have been your fault. I'll make the position perfectly clear to you by means of a diagram if you really want to argue.'

' I don't,' said the Major hurriedly.

' Then why begin ? I always regard arguing as waste of time and I only do it to please you.'

Meldon's pipe, at which he had to suck hard, was making a thick gurgling sound. The Major pressed a cigar on him and then offered to lend him a new pipe. Meldon ignored both offers.

' All these south of England watering places,' said Meldon, ' are full of unattached females, widows, spinsters, and so on.'

He waved his hand in a wide circle, as if to include Bournemouth, Eastbourne, Hastings and Folkestone as well as Weymouth.

' Has one of them been trying to marry you ? If that's your trouble——'

' It isn't,' said the Major.

' Well, if it isn't that it must be something else. Has any one let you in for running a company of Boy Scouts ? '

' No.   Certainly not.'

' Or Girl Guides ? '

' No.'

' Or a Woman's Institute ?   If not I don't really see that you can have any trouble serious enough to justify you in shaking your fist at me.   Here you are, comfortably settled down in a house which is perfectly easy to keep tidy——'

' Not with you in it,' said the Major.

Meldon had already upset several of the Major's favourite arrangements of chairs, tables and ash-trays. He was sitting with his heels on the window-sill in a way likely to damage the paint.

' You always professed to like tidiness and now you've got it, so you ought to be happy instead of miserable. You are living among people who in-variably speak the truth.   That's one of the most annoying characteristics of the English, but you profess to like it.   I prefer people with a little imagina-tion, so there'd be some excuse for me if I was unhappy in England.   But there's no excuse for you.   You've got plenty of money. The compensation which the Government paid you for the burning of Coolarrigan is enough to make you a rich man if you hadn't another penny.'

' The only compensation I've got,' said the Major, ' is a demand for payment of income-tax.'

' Major,' said Meldon gravely and severely, ' if you're trying to diddle the Irish Free State out of income-tax you've come to the wrong man to help you. I never condone fraud and I'm simply amazed at your suggesting such a thing to me.'

' I never suggested anything of the sort,' said the Major.   ' In fact, I never suggested anything at all.'

'You came to me,' said Meldon, 'whining—I might almost say blubbering—for help, and when I ask you what the trouble is you have the nerve to tell me that you're trying to cheat the income-tax people—and failing. If you weren't failing you wouldn't be in the sort of temper you were in when I saw you this morning.'

The Major rose from his chair and went to a bureau which stood in a corner of the room. From one of the pigeon-holes he took a bundle of papers, all neatly folded and held together by an elastic band. He handed them to Meldon.

Meldon unfolded the top one. It was headed Saorstát D' Éireann and had a good deal more Irish scattered about it in unimportant places. The main purport of the document was made clear in English. It was a demand for income-tax payable on the occupation value of Coolarrigan Castle. The next paper—Meldon went through them all—was very like the first. The third alluded politely to the existence of the first two. The fourth was a little peremptory. The fifth made a half-hearted appeal to the Major's honour, and set out in plain figures the rateable value of Coolarrigan on which the claim was based. The sixth was threatening. The seventh was very threatening indeed. In the eighth and ninth the writer's command of language seemed to have failed him. They merely repeated the threats of the seventh. Meldon scattered the whole series broadcast over the floor.

'Major,' he said, 'was Coolarrigan burnt or was it not?'

'It was burnt to the ground,' said the Major, 'and I never got a penny of compensation and never will.'

'Then the house has no occupation value. It can't have if it isn't there.'

'That's what I've told them,' said the Major. 'But they don't seem able to see it.'

'From what I know of you, Major, I should say that if you told them at all you've told them in such a muddled way that they couldn't possibly understand. You're the very worst man I know at explaining anything lucidly. Take this conversation as an example. You begin by asking me for help, and then——'

'I didn't.'

'You did. And when I inquire what the trouble is you give me distinctly to understand that you've been trying to swindle the income-tax people and got caught.'

'I never said anything of the sort.'

'Whereas,' Meldon went on, 'the fact appears to be that the income-tax people are trying to swindle you. That's quite a usual thing ; but it's not what you told me. I'm not accusing you of deliberate lying, Major. I know that you're a truthful man. All I say is that you put things in such a confused and muddled way that nobody can possibly make out what you mean. If I can't understand you, how can you possibly expect an income-tax collector, a fellow who simply delights in muddles himself, to make head or tail of any statement of yours ? However, now that I've at last got at what's the matter with you I can give you the advice you want in two words. Don't pay.'

'Thanks, J. J.' said the Major. 'But I never meant to pay. My mind's quite made up about that.'

'If your mind's made up, and as I gather, has been made up all along, why come to me for advice and help ?

Are you quite sure that you've given me all the facts, Major ? Did you rescue anything out of the house, anything of real value ? They might be charging you income-tax on that if you stored it in Ireland. I don't say they ought to or could legally, but they're quite capable of trying it on when they know that they have a simple-minded man like you to deal with.'

' I didn't save a single thing. I wasn't given time. At least——'

The Major hesitated.

' Now do be careful,' said Meldon. ' I know that you want to tell the truth, but you seem to find it uncommonly hard to do it. Either you rescued something or you didn't. Which is it ? '

' I put some candlesticks into a fishing-basket, the candlesticks that were on the dining-room sideboard.'

' I remember them,' said Meldon. ' The Paul Lamerie candlesticks. My dear Major, if you saved them I don't wonder they're trying to get at you with income-tax. They're worth one hundred and fifty pounds each, at least—and there are eight of them.'

' I'm afraid I only took seven. The basket wouldn't hold the other. Besides, they rushed me rather, and I wanted to see about the ponies.'

' Even seven,' said Meldon. ' Seven at one hundred and fifty pounds— They may be worth a lot more. I'll inquire about that. But seven at one hundred and fifty pounds each would be upwards of a thousand. The tax on the occupation value of property worth a thousand pounds is about—let me see. It's unearned, of course——'

' They couldn't possibly be worth all that. They're just silver candlesticks.'

' They were Paul Lamerie's, and you ought to know perfectly well what they're worth. Your aunt told you. I've told you. But you're such a sceptic that you didn't believe us. Or rather you didn't take any interest in what we said to you. However, you've got the candlesticks and that's the main thing.'

' But I haven't. I——'

' Major, you'd break the patience of the patriarch Job. First you tell me that you saved candlesticks and then you tell me that you didn't. Which do you mean ? '

' If you'd only let me speak——'

' You speak far too much. If you spoke less you wouldn't mislead people in the way you do. If you got those candlesticks out of the house before it was burnt——'

' I did, in a fishing-basket. I've just said so.'

' Well, then, unless you went back and threw them into the blaze—and even you, Major would hardly do that—you have them still. Where are they ? '

' At the bottom of the Shannon,' said the Major. ' Just inside the boat-house, in about three feet of water.'

He was often interrupted as he told his story. He was cross-questioned and upbraided, but he managed at last to get out the history of his own escape in the boat and the loss of the candlesticks.

' Well,' said Meldon, ' we've got to the point at last. I thought we would if I kept you at it. What you really wanted all the time was to get me to go over to Ireland with you and fish those candlesticks out of the Shannon. It would have saved a lot of time if you'd said so at once plainly, instead of leading me to suppose, first that you were swindling the income-tax people,

B

and then that they were swindling you. You might have known that if you wanted my help all that you had to do was to ask for it.'

'But I don't want it. I mean to say I haven't the slightest intention of going back to Ireland to get those candlesticks.'

'Fortunately,' said Meldon, 'I can take a holiday when I like. Let me see now. This is Wednesday. I'll take those boys home this evening. To-morrow and next day I'll hustle round and find a locum-tenens, just in case we have to stay over a Sunday. But I don't expect we shall. It'll be a perfectly simple business. All we have to do is to roll up our sleeves and pull that basket of yours out of the water. We'll take your car. You can make all the necessary arrangements about that. If you buck up and get a move on you'll get all the beastly Custom House papers signed before Saturday. On Monday I'll drive over here. It's only about forty miles. I'll leave my car here. We'll go on together in yours to Fishguard and cross that night.'

'But——'

'I can't stop to argue now,' said Meldon. 'If you really want to argue there'll be plenty of time while we drive to Fishguard and all across Ireland. But at present I'm in a hurry. Those boys of mine will be expecting some tea, and I must go and give it to them. Good-bye, Major. Thanks for the lunch, and remember whenever you're in any little difficulty come straight to me. You can't always calculate on meeting me by accident just when you need me most as you did to-day. And for goodness' sake try to cultivate the habit of saying straight out and plainly what it is you want.'

CHAPTER IV

IT was shortly after ten o'clock on Monday morning when Meldon turned his shabby grey car through the gate of High Pines and drove with immense clanking and banging up to the door. The Major had just finished breakfast and was sitting quietly with a newspaper in his hands.

'Major,' said Meldon, 'do you mean to say that you're not ready to start? I expected to see your car standing at the door with your suitcase strapped on. Don't you realize that we've got pretty nearly two hundred miles to drive and must be at Fishguard in good time if we're to get the car taken on to-night's boat? I don't know how you expect to get anything done in life at all if you dawdle in this way whenever a call for prompt action comes. I was preaching about that yesterday, a good, rousing, vigorous sermon on bucking up generally. If I'd known the way you were going to behave to-day I'd have put it even stronger than I did.'

'Didn't you get my telegram on Saturday?' said the Major.

'I got it all right.'

'Then you know that I'm not going on this insane expedition at all, either to-day or any other day.'

Meldon sat down, crossed his legs, pulled out his pipe, a plug of tobacco and a bone-handled knife.

While he sliced the tobacco he spoke to his friend. He spoke kindly and patiently, as an aunt might speak to a tiresome and rather stupid child, a child bent on doing something foolish, but hardly intelligent enough to understand the consequences of his own action. Like most aunts, like all really good aunts, Meldon began with an appeal to his victim's higher and better nature.

' I'm not asking you,' he said, ' to consider the way you're treating me. I'm afraid that you're too self-centred and indifferent to the feelings of others to be influenced by any appeal along those lines. At the same time I think I ought to mention the facts of the case. I find you in the depths of depression. After the greatest difficulty I discover what is the matter with you. It took me hours to do it, hours that I might have spent much more agreeably and usefully. More agreeably, because instead of sitting here in a stuffy room, I should have been sporting on the sandy shore of the sea—always a pleasant occupation. More usefully because I should have been teaching my choirboys to swim, thereby putting them in a position to save their own lives hereafter and perhaps the lives of thousands of others. Instead of occupying myself in this pleasant and useful way I spent my time in trying to find out what you were making yourself miserable about. I was met by a series of evasions and misrepresentations. I don't use a harsher word about the things you said to me, though I might. In the end it turned out that you'd thrown some valuable candlesticks into the Shannon, I don't say maliciously, simply through carelessness. I at once offered to help you to get them out of the river again, promising at the same time to adjust a little difference of opinion which had

arisen between you and the income-tax authorities.
Those are the facts so far.'

' They're not,' said the Major. ' They're not in the
least like any facts I ever came across, but I suppose
it's no use my saying so.'

' None,' said Meldon. ' It never is any use trying to
bluff facts out of being facts. Far better face them like
a man even if they happen to be unpleasant. Having
promised to help you I at once took the necessary steps
to make it possible to keep my promise. I spent
Thursday and Friday careering round Bournemouth
and Chichester and Salisbury, and even Bath, looking
for a parson to take my duty for me while I'm in Ireland
helping you. You may not know it, Major, but with
the present shortage of clergy it's almost impossible to
get a man of any sort, even a cripple. But I did it in
the end at a cost of five guineas. I don't grudge the
money in the least. I'd spend more than that any day
to help you out of a difficulty.'

' I'll pay you that with pleasure,' said the Major ;
' and now that you've got a man you can spend a week
with me. The holiday will do you good.'

' Holidays don't do me good. They bore me stiff.
What I like is a change of activity. If I'm not to
recover those candlesticks for you I'd rather be back
in my parish. As soon as I got home, after finding a
locum-tenens, your telegram arrived saying that you'd
given up the idea of going to Ireland. I at once wrote
a reply——'

' I never got it, J. J.'

' You did not,' said Meldon, ' because it was never
sent off. Being Saturday afternoon our post office was
shut. Half-holiday for the staff. There you are, you
see. The whole business of the country is held up for

the sake of holidays, things you approve of, Major, things that you and others like you practically force on people who don't want them. Now don't contradict me. You've just been urging me to spend a perfectly idle week with you kicking my heels round this miserable watering-place. That's what you mean by a holiday, and what the post office means, and what every member of the Civil Service means. And after that you complain that the country is going to the dogs. Don't say you don't, for you do. All retired Majors complain that the country is going to the dogs. I don't blame them for I know they can't help it. But I'm not appealing to you along those lines at all. I don't expect you to consider me or the officials of the post office, or any one else except yourself. What I want to put to you, Major, is simply this : If you won't take the trouble to go to Ireland and fish those candlesticks of yours out of the Shannon you'll lose about two thousand pounds. I said one thousand pounds the other day, but I've made inquiries since, and I find that candlesticks of that particular make are worth three hundred pounds each. Now, what have you got to say to that ? '

' I don't believe they're worth a tenth of it.'

' They're Paul Lamerie's work.'

' I don't know whose work they are,' said the Major. ' And I don't care. If they were Michael Angelo's——'

' Michael Angelo didn't make candlesticks. He built cathedrals.'

' Well, Raphael's then, or anybody else's. I'm not going to Ireland to get them, whoever made them. Just look at that.' He pulled a long buff envelope from his breast-pocket and handed it to Meldon. ' That came on Saturday morning.'

Across the top of the envelope, in letters which were threateningly underlined, were the words ' Saorstát Éireann.' In the right-hand corner was a picture of a harp. Round the top of the harp ran the words ' Diolta Ofigiuil,' which were translated underneath by the English ' Official.' In the bottom left-hand of the envelope was a request that, if not delivered, it might be returned to the Inspector of Taxes in Dublin. It was addressed to Major Kent. Meldon studied it carefully.

' I see no necessity,' he said, ' for mixing up the income-tax people with the candles at this stage of the proceedings. We shall, of course, go into their claim afterwards. They may claim something from you for the occupation value of those candlesticks, but as long as the things are at the bottom of the river they have no occupation value, and so the question can't arise. Besides, they may know nothing about the candlesticks. You weren't surely such a fool as to tell them that you had a mass of Paul Lamerie silver stored at the bottom of the Shannon ? '

' Of course not.'

' Then I don't see what the income-tax people have to do with the matter.'

' Open that envelope and you will see,' said the Major.

Meldon opened the envelope. It contained a letter which might have frightened a bolder man than Major Kent.

' A chara,' it began.

' A chara ' means ' O friend,' but it was perfectly plain that the writer did not regard the Major as a friend or even a respectable acquaintance.

' Having received no reply to our repeated demands for the payment of the income tax due by you it has become necessary to take immediately such steps as are open to the Commissioners of Inland Revenue. Le meas mór. . . .'

' Le meas mór ' means ' with great respect,' but it was certain that the writer felt no respect at all for Major Kent.

' That,' said Meldon, ' practically amounts to a confession that they can't do anything at all, and know it.'

' They can't as long as I stay here,' said the Major, ' but the moment I set foot in Ireland they'll arrest me. And I simply won't pay—ever. Not if they imprison me for life.'

' I see your difficulty now, Major, and I don't deny that there's something in it. Income-tax people are extraordinarily vindictive. They probably would arrest you if they found out that you were in the country. But they won't find out. I know you go in for what I should call an exaggerated kind of honesty, but I don't suppose that even you will feel it your duty to go round by Dublin and leave a card on that fellow just to tell him you've arrived. If you don't do that how are they to know that you're in Ireland at all ? '

' They'll find out.'

' No, they won't. How can they ? Unless—now this is a real difficulty, and it's a jolly good thing for you that you have a man with you who grasps these points. Did you give your own name as the owner of the car when you applied for the customs permit, triptique, or whatever it's called, to take it into Ireland ? But of course you did. It would never occur to you to give mine or anybody else's name. Well, we can't take the car. That's all. However, it doesn't matter much. We shall only be at Lisnamoe for one

night and we shall easily be able to hire a Ford or
something there to take us to Coolarrigan. If the worst
comes to the worst we can borrow a couple of bicycles.
The thing for you to do now, Major, is to telegraph to
the A.A. people, or the R.A.C., or whoever was working
the triptique for you, and cancel your application
before they communicate with Ireland. Tell them
that you're going to travel by train.'

' I'm not going to travel at all, by train or any other
way. I don't want to be arrested.'

' You'll be perfectly safe,' said Meldon. ' Nobody
will recognize you. However, if you're nervous——'

' I don't want to spend the rest of my life in an Irish
gaol.'

' Very well, then. Travel under some other name.
We'll label your suitcase " Colonel York." '

' J. J.,' said the Major, ' you can bully me and
hustle me into doing a lot of silly things. But there's
a limit. I'm hanged if I go about Ireland calling
myself Colonel York to please you or anybody else.'

' Well, say Cumberland, if you don't like York.
"General Cumberland." Come now, Major, I'm pro-
moting you every time. And Cumberland is quite a
nice county, full of mountains and lakes. Besides,
there once was a General Cumberland. He was a Duke
as well as a General, and by all accounts a most blood-
thirsty man. You ought to be rather proud of being a
descendant of his, even if it's only for a short time.'

' I won't call myself General Cumberland. I won't
call myself Field-Marshal Middlesex, or Rear-Admiral
Dorset, or anything else except my own name. I hate
telling lies.'

' Very well,' said Meldon. ' Then you'll have to
come over to Ireland without a name at all. I'll

introduce you simply as my uncle, if there's any introducing to be done. Then all you have to do is to keep your mouth shut. Nobody will ever dream of pursuing an uncle of mine for unpaid income-tax.'

' I'm not going to Ireland,' said the Major. ' And certainly not as your uncle.'

Meldon took no notice of this final protest. He got up from his chair. He ransacked the bookshelves. He entirely disorganized a neatly arranged newspaper-table. He opened, and left open, several drawers. He began a systematic search of the Major's bureau. He explained that he was looking for a Bradshaw in order to work out the journey to Fishguard and to discover at what hour it would be necessary to start in order to catch the steamer.

Major Kent sat still, a rigidly determined man, until he saw his papers pulled out of their pigeon-holes, and an ink bottle upset over his blotting paper. That was more than he could stand. He got up, found the Bradshaw and handed it to Meldon. It was in a book slide on a side table, along with Whitaker's Almanack, Who's Who, and an English dictionary. That is to say, exactly where Bradshaw ought to be in a well-ordered house. It was the only place which Meldon had not searched.

' If you must go to Ireland,' said the Major, ' you may as well find out when your train starts without pulling my house to pieces.'

' You're coming, too.'

' I'll be sent to gaol if I do.'

' No, you won't. You can't be. We won't be in the country more than two days altogether. One going, one coming back, and half an hour there for picking up the candlesticks. It would be utterly impossible for the income-tax people to hear of you in that time.'

' Why can't you go by yourself, J. J. ? '

' Because,' said Meldon, ' they very well might arrest me.'

' What for ? You don't owe them any income-tax.'

' No, I don't. But—— Just consider the position, Major. I, a total stranger, with no claim to anything in or about Coolarrigan, with no real right to go wading about in the Shannon—I turn up and try to walk off with hundreds of pounds' worth of silver. What could they possibly do except arrest me ? Not that I should mind. I could explain the situation. As a matter of fact I can explain almost any situation. But it takes time, and I might very well be kept there for three weeks or a month. I'd do a good deal for your sake, Major. I'll do that if you insist. But it's asking a good deal of me. Those choirboys of mine always break out if I'm away from them for a week, and I should say there'd be an open rebellion if I was kept in Ireland for a month.'

' Oh, very well,' said the Major wearily. ' I'll go. But it's all folly, you know, the whole expedition. We'll never get the candlesticks, and I don't believe they'd be worth five pounds if we did. They wouldn't even pay our expenses.'

CHAPTER V

RAILWAY companies in England grumble almost daily about loss of revenue. Irish companies complain even more bitterly. They attribute their poverty to various causes, the rise in the rate of wages, the shortening of the working day, the competition of motor-cars, and various other things. None of them mention as a contributory cause that they have been bullying the travelling public for three whole generations and that the meekest worm will turn at last.

So long as the traveller is content to go to places which the railway company thinks proper, no way of travelling is swifter, safer or more comfortable than a train. But the companies are of opinion that they and not the traveller ought to decide the points of departure and destination. If a man wants to go from London to Liverpool—or, in Ireland, from Dublin to Cork—his way is made easy for him and his journey pleasant. He is, from the point of view of the railway companies, a good citizen, and therefore ought to be encouraged. But if he wants to go from Lincoln to Worcester—being, perhaps, interested in cathedrals—the railway companies regard him as eccentric if not criminal, and do their best to prevent him carrying out his plan. They so arrange things that the journey is intolerably tedious, exhausting to the body because of the number of iron bridges which have to be crossed when changing trains, and destructive to the temper, because, with diabolical cunning, the trains to be changed into always start five minutes before the arrival of the train which the passenger has to get out of.

In Ireland the policy of controlling the journeys of the passengers is carried out even more thoroughly than in England.   But the Irish people are not patient. The Englishman, a submissive and well-disciplined creature, when he finds that it is almost impossible to go from Lincoln to Worcester, grumbles a little and then gives up the idea.   In time he comes to think that the railway companies are right and that it is better for him to go from London to Liverpool.   But the Irish, who were the original inventors of the point-to-point race, insist that they know better than the railways do and often try to have their own way.   Severe measures are therefore necessary to maintain discipline, severer than are necessary elsewhere.   In England a passenger has rarely to wait more than two hours at a junction. In Ireland a delay of five hours is common, and a journey of an unauthorized kind may very well take a whole day, even if the distance covered is no more than a hundred miles.

Meldon and Major Kent might quite easily have gone from Rosslare to Dublin or Cork.   The journey to Lisnamoe was a different matter.   They began it at 4 a.m. and did not complete it till 2 in the afternoon. They made five changes, each time into a train less comfortable than the one they got out of.   The Major was depressed in the steamer and despondent after landing.   He became acutely unhappy as the day went on.   At each stopping-place he wanted to turn round and go home again.

When the last of the trains dragged itself wearily into Lisnamoe, the Major was in a condition of drooping despair, incapable of an effort of any kind. Meldon's spirit was unbroken, but his appearance was more than usually disreputable. He had shirked the duty of shaving on the steamer. He had forgotten to bring a clothes-brush with him. He had torn a hole in the left knee of his trousers on a projecting nail, while dragging the Major's suitcase off the steamer. His hands were exceedingly dirty.

Jimmy Costello, who drove the car sent from the hotel to the station, looked doubtfully at Major Kent and suspiciously at Meldon. They were not the sort of guests he was accustomed to.

The hotel at Lisnamoe exists for the benefit of fishermen. They come at the proper season, clad in thick tweeds, laden with rods and landing-nets, unmistakably sportsmen, every one of them. The lady manager of the hotel, Miss Eileen Costello, whose brother drives the car, is ready to welcome any fisherman. She knows exactly how to treat him and what to provide for his comfort. She is unaccustomed to any other sort of guest, and indeed does not want any other sort. She regards the hotel which she manages as her own, and it very nearly is, for the actual proprietor is her aunt, a lady too old and too fat to take much interest in her property or any part in the management of it.

Eileen Costello, being an heiress, and occupying the position she does, is even more genteel than the convent-educated young ladies of her class in Ireland usually are. And her ideas of gentility extend to the hotel. It is for ' fishing gentlemen,' not for stray wayfarers who present themselves without proper credentials, that is to say without rods, gaffs or landing-nets. The moment Meldon appeared at the window of her little reception office she made up her mind that he was not the sort of man who ought to stay in the hotel. There was a good deal of excuse for her, for Meldon's appearance was against him. The Major's military carriage and his incurable habit of neatness might have conveyed the idea of respectability to her, if she had seen him. But the Major was standing morosely near the door of the hotel out of her range of sight. It was only Meldon whom she saw—Meldon with a bristly chin, ruffled red hair, crumpled clothes and a collar which was little more than a wisp of dirty linen round his neck.

She promptly assured him that the hotel was quite full and that no food could possibly be obtained.

Meldon, who knew that the Shannon salmon-fishing season was over, did not believe a word she said.

'All we want,' he said, 'is a couple of rooms for one night.'

' Rooms, is it ? ' said Eileen. ' Don't I tell you there's no rooms in it for you? Do you expect me to be wasting my time building rooms for the likes of you ? '

She tossed her head, and then, as if to put a complete end to the conversation, took a small puff from a box which stood on a corner of her desk and gave a dab of powder to her nose.

Meldon, who never lost his temper with any one, not even with the girls in post offices, showed no sign of irritation. Nor did he attempt to argue. Reason, as he knew, is wasted on damsels as haughty as Eileen was. Instead of getting angry he grinned, his lips stretching so far that Eileen could not help looking at him though she had intended to turn her back and look the other way. When Meldon felt sure of her attention he winked, slowly, his left eye remaining closed for a long time. It was a solemn, not a merry, wink. It suggested the confidences of a fellow-conspirator.

' Are you a Free-Stater or a Republican ? ' he asked her at last.

Eileen was surprised, though not so much surprised as an English girl in her position would be if she were suddenly asked whether she was a Socialist or a Conservative. In Ireland every one is interested in politics, which are almost as much a part of daily life as religion used to be—so our Neo-Catholics assure us— in the Middle Ages.

' There's a cousin of mine,' she said courteously, ' that draws a middling good salary out of the Government in an office up in Dublin. Jameson is his name, Peter Jameson.'

' I expect he's a Free-Stater,' said Meldon, ' if he draws a salary from the Government, and small blame to him.'

' He is,' said Eileen. ' But I wouldn't say but what I might be a Republican myself.'

' Ah ! ' said Meldon.

He said nothing more, but he looked Eileen full in the face, fixing his eyes on hers with a gaze which was as nearly solemn as he could make it. Having fascinated her in this way he slowly drew the first finger of his right hand across the back of his left wrist. This is a simple action ; but done as Meldon did it, very slowly and with a suggestion of intensity, it looks like the intimate sign of a secret society. Eileen had never seen anything like it in her life before and was greatly impressed. Meldon stretched out his right hand, knuckles upwards, and with a very rapid motion drew the first finger of his left hand across that wrist. Eileen was thrilled. She felt a delicious little shudder run down her spine. It is not every day, even in Ireland, that conspirators, complete with secret signs, are to be met in the early part of the afternoon.

' If that 's the way of it—' she said.

' It is,' said Meldon, ' and I'm glad to see that you're one, too.'

He looked round at the Major, and Eileen pushed her head through her little window and looked, too. Meldon nodded gravely, but not to the Major. Then he prodded his chin three times with the top of his right thumb. Eileen gasped with delighted amazement. She looked at the Major again, this time with a kind of awe.

' If that 's who he is—' she said.

' It is,' said Meldon, ' but the less said about it the better.'

Eileen Costello's vesture of gentility dropped from her. She became all at once an excited Irish girl. It was scarcely possible to believe that five minutes earlier she had been tossing her head and powdering her nose.

' Thomas ! ' she shouted.

Nothing happened, so she shouted, ' Thomas John ! '

Still nothing happened. Eileen's voice rose to a higher note, and she shouted, 'Thomas John MacMahon!'

An elderly and decrepit man, in a greasy dress suit, opened a door across which the words ' Coffee Room ' were written ; and tottered out.

' Take the gentlemen's luggage upstairs,' she said, ' and be quick about it. Take it up to number one and number two.'

Number one and number two are the best rooms in the hotel. They are reserved for highly-honoured guests, salmon fishers with particularly ample tweed suits. Thus Meldon's two fingers and his thumb triumphed over Eileen's gentility. And his success did not depend on his knowing what her political opinions were. He would have done the same thing, and with exactly the same result, had she declared herself to be a Free-Stater.

Thomas John MacMahon tottered upstairs with the two suitcases.

' You'll be wanting some lunch,' said Eileen hospitably. 'There's a cold ham you might fancy, and I could have a couple of eggs fried in three minutes. But if you're not in a hurry there's nothing to hinder me having some chickens boiled. There's plenty of them, and it won't take Jimmy more than a minute to kill a couple, or more, if you think you can eat more.'

' What we want now,' said Meldon, ' is a motor-car. Is there one belonging to the hotel ? '

' There is. There's the one that brought you from the station. My brother Jimmy, the same that does be killing the chickens when they're wanted—for the matter of that it's him that kills any pigs that has to be killed—he's the owner of the car, so you can hardly say whether it belongs to the hotel or not. But sure that's all one. You can have it if you want it. Will I call Jimmy in to speak to you ? '

' You will not,' said Meldon. ' You'll go out to him, wherever he is, and tell him to start the car up and bring it round to the door. But let him kill a couple of chickens first. We'll be back for lunch in—in about— let me see now, how far is it from this to Coolarrigan ? '

' I was just thinking,' said Eileen, ' that it must be there you'd be wanting to go.'

She looked at Meldon as if she were completely in his confidence and in full sympathy with his plans. This puzzled him a little, for he knew no reason why a militant Republican—that was what she thought the

Major was—should want to go to the scene of a long-extinct fire.

' If you'll take my advice,' he said sternly, ' you'll not think more than you can help. And when you can't help it you'll keep your mouth shut afterwards.'

Eileen flushed deeply at the rebuke, but she felt that it was just. In the best political circles in Ireland it is considered very rude to assume a knowledge of other people's affairs.

' How far is it to Coolarrigan ? ' he asked, still sternly.

Eileen answered with great meekness.

' It's not more than six miles from where you're standing this minute,' she said. ' And you'll do it in ten minutes easily with Jimmy driving you. He's a grand driver, so he is.'

' Say a quarter of an hour there,' said Meldon, ' and another quarter of an hour back. You can have lunch ready for us in an hour.'

Eileen slipped from her office through a small door at the back of it and went into the yard to search for Jimmy, chicken-killer, pork-butcher and chauffeur. Meldon turned to the Major.

' That'll give you time for a wash before eating,' he said. ' I'm considering your feelings, you see, Major. I know that unnecessary washing is a fad of yours.'

' But why shouldn't we lunch before we go ? ' said the Major plaintively. ' I'd much rather lunch at once. I've had nothing to eat to-day except a cup of tea and a plate of bread and butter on the steamer.'

' Of all the unreasonable men I ever met, you're the worst,' said Meldon. ' There's no satisfying you. Since we landed this morning you've done nothing but wish you hadn't come, and beg to be allowed to go back again at once. In order to pacify you, if such a thing were possible, I arrange to rush through your business—yours, remember, not mine—as quickly as possible. I don't want to dart off without a bite to eat. I don't want to plunge into the Shannon and catch a chill through bathing on an empty stomach. I don't want to risk my neck being driven at sixty miles an hour over vile roads by a man who spends most of his time killing chickens and pigs, and therefore, in all probability, sets no value on human life. I'm doing all this simply to please you, because of your insane fear of being caught by an income-tax collector.'

' I expect I shall be,' said the Major. ' But I'd rather have something to eat before I am.'

' As a matter of fact, you'll never be troubled about income-tax at all, no matter how long you stay here. I've arranged that.'

' What have you done ? '

The Major spoke anxiously. His experience of Meldon's way of arranging things made him acutely uncomfortable.

' Oh, it was quite simple,' said Meldon. ' I gave that young woman to understand—I didn't actually tell her anything. I never lie unnecessarily. There's no greater mistake than that. I simply gave her to understand by stroking my wrist——'

' By doing what, J. J. ? '

' Stroking my wrist. Don't say " What ? " Major, when you've heard perfectly well. It's a most irritating habit.'

' But I don't see how she could understand anything because you stroked your wrist.'

' Fortunately she's more intelligent than you are, Major. She understood at once that you are a senior officer in the Irish Republican Army—the out-and-out whole-hoggers, not the more or less tame lot who are paid by the Government.'

'If I believed for an instant that you'd really told that young woman——'

'I didn't tell her,' said Meldon. 'I let her tell herself, and it's a jolly good thing for you that she did. It'll be all over the village in the course of the next half-hour that you're come here to assassinate somebody, and I needn't tell you that no income-tax collector will venture within a mile of you. With your reputation—and I rather fancy that young woman will pile it on a bit—she looks as if she would—nobody will even ask you to pay rates, much less a tax.'

'I'm going home at once,' said the Major. 'Where's my suit case?'

'You'll go home to-morrow,' said Meldon. 'Not a minute sooner, for there's no train out of this to-day. If there was, I'd catch it, too. We'll have got your candlesticks and had our lunch—boiled chickens and cold ham—by three o'clock at the latest. I assure you I don't want to stay a minute longer than I need.'

'J. J.,' said the Major, 'I wish you hadn't said I was that. I hate being that more than anything. I'd rather pay the income-tax. I'd far rather lose those wretched candlesticks altogether than be a Republican General. Did you say General, J. J.?'

'I *said* nothing,' said Meldon, 'but I rather fancy from the admiring way she looked at you that she regarded you as a Field-Marshal.'

Jimmy Costello, warned by his sister of the high position of her newly-arrived guests, bestirred himself. He cut the throats of two chickens, and flung them, still bleeding, through the kitchen window. He swung

the starting handle of his Ford car round and round
with a rapidity which startled the sulky engine into
activity. He backed out of the cowshed in which the
car was kept and circled swiftly round the dusty yard.
He almost saved himself the trouble of cutting the
throat of a fat pig, destined to die in a few days. The
creature lay sound asleep in the yard, and the wheel of
the car missed its head by less than an inch. Having
displayed his mastery of the machine by these evolu-
tions, Jimmy drove round to the door of the hotel.
There he pounded on his Klaxon horn until Meldon and
the Major came out.

' It 's Coolarrigan your honour's wanting to go to,' he
said.

' I suppose your sister told you that,' said Meldon.

' She did not,' said Jimmy. ' But she told me who
he was.'

He nodded over his shoulder towards the Major, who
sat in the back of the car. Meldon had taken his seat
in the front.

' And sure as soon as I knew who he was,' said
Jimmy, ' I knew it would be Coolarrigan he'd be
wanting to go to. Where else would he go ? '

Only once or twice in his whole life had Meldon
failed to grasp the full meaning and implication of
what was said to him. But the Costellos, sister and
brother, baffled him twice in a few minutes. He
could not understand why both of them should take it
for granted that he wanted to go to Coolarrigan. The
Major was regarded as a Republican leader, but that
seemed no reason why he should want to go there.
Yet not only Eileen, but Jimmy seemed to think that
the place was sure to attract an ardent patriot.

Meldon, silent for once, sat thinking deeply.

CHAPTER VI

THE car swung round from the main road into the lane which led down to the gates of Coolarrigan Castle, in the days when there was a castle with gates at the end of its drive. The Major, though his father and grandfather had regarded themselves as Irish, had enough of the original English blood of the Kents in him to make him capable of sentimentalizing. He sighed deeply and a slight film of extra moisture dimmed his eyes. He was on very familiar ground, a lane along which he had ridden, driven and walked a thousand times, always with the certainty of seeing at the end of it the tall iron gates, the grey gabled lodge, and in the distance, among the trees, the long, straight front of his house.

Now—he braced himself for the shock—the house would be gone. The iron gates would be lying flat in the rank grass. The once trim avenue would be weed-grown. The lodge—the Major remembered that the lodge was Michael Gannon's home. It would not be burnt. But he could scarcely bear to think of the condition in which he would find it. There would be broken windows, paintless doors hanging loose on their hinges, walls half stripped of their rough-cast covering, and a swarm of dirty Gannon children playing in the mud among hens and perhaps pigs.

The Major was a sound churchman who rarely

missed mattins on a Sunday. He recalled the words of Nehemiah, which once a year are read aloud to inattentive congregations: ' Why should not my countenance be sad when the place of my fathers' sepulchres lieth waste and the gates thereof are burnt with fire ? ' It was only an aunt who had been buried in the neighbourhood and the gates could not actually be burnt because they were made of iron, but the destruction was quite as complete as that of Jerusalem during the captivity. Of all that the Major remembered and loved only the lane would remain.

A moment later he began to doubt whether the lane had not disappeared, too. Once it had been fairly smooth and tolerably well-kept. Now—the car gave a heavy lurch, and yellow water from a deep pool splashed high behind the wheels. The Major rubbed the dimness from his eyes and looked round him. The lane had been widened. It had encroached on each side on the strips of grass which once lay between it and the fences. There were deep ruts which could only have been made by the wheels of very heavy vehicles, and the fences, beautiful wire fences of recent pattern which had shut the polo ponies into their pasture, had been broken down. Great vehicles, lorries, perhaps, or even heavier things with caterpillar chains to go on, had cut deep tracks into the fields.

Jimmy, as daring a driver as Meldon himself, kept up a good pace and proved, unnecessarily, for it was a thing that every one knew before, that the older Ford cars had invincible springs. But even Jimmy was forced to slow down at last.

A steam engine, dragging three heavy trucks after it, came lurching through the slough of mud and ruts which had once been the Major's beloved lane. Jimmy swerved sharply to the left. One of the front wheels plunged into a deep hole. The other embedded itself in a soft bank of glutinous slime. It seemed for a moment as if even a Ford car could do no more. But Jimmy, with undaunted confidence, pressed down the pedal which brought the lower gear into operation. The car gave a responsive leap and went forward a few feet. Then one of the back wheels dropped into the hole and the Major was thrown violently against the door.

Jimmy looked round at the steam engine.

' Them things,' he said, ' is the curse of this country. There isn't a road but they have it destroyed on us, worse than what it was destroyed before, and the Lord knows that was bad enough.'

The car struggled out of the hole and the Major got back into his seat.

' What—what—what's that infernal train doing here ? ' he asked.

He stammered, because the words were forced from him explosively by a series of heavy bumps, and the last part of his sentence came out with a rush. Jimmy made no attempt to answer the question. His wrestle with the steering wheel and his determination to get up speed again kept him too busy for talking. But an explanation of the presence of the engine and of the condition of the road surface of the lane made itself obvious almost at once.

Where Coolarrigan Castle had once stood there was a long row of hideous huts, buildings of the kind called temporary, roofed with grey galvanized iron, many of them with galvanized iron sides. In the stable-yard, where the polo ponies had paraded for admiring inspection, half a dozen great lorries were parked.

From the huts to the river, over what had been a lawn, through the ruin of a shrubbery, ran a roughly laid, very narrow line of rails. Along them men pushed small iron tanks, slightly glorified wheel-barrows, laden when they left the lorries, empty when they came up the hill again.

Jimmy, unable to go further, stopped the car. Meldon jumped out briskly. The Major followed him slowly, a bewildered man. His worst imaginings about the state of his property were not to be compared to this horrible reality. He had thought of desolation and loneliness. The activities of a horde of navvies were—the Major did not read Shakespeare. If he had he might have found words to express his feelings about the condition of the Coolarrigan grounds.

' Worse than the worst
That lawless and uncertain thought imagines howling.'

' Back in half an hour or so,' said Meldon to Jimmy. ' You wait for us.'

Then he took the Major by the arm and led him down towards the river, keeping close to the rails in order to avoid the worst of the mud.

' This complicates things,' he said. ' Not much, of course, and not seriously. Still, it is a complication, and I think you ought to have told me what was happening before we came.'

' But I didn't know. I assure you, J. J., this is a complete surprise to me. If I'd known——'

' You must have known,' said Meldon. ' You may have forgotten now. But at one time you must have known. And I'm bound to say that this puts an entirely different complexion on the demand of the income-tax people. If you're drawing a couple of hundred a year for the use of your land you ought to pay the tax on it.'

'But I'm not,' said the Major. 'I didn't know the land was being used at all. I don't know what it's being used for now and what all these lorries and things are doing here.'

'As I said, Major, you may have forgotten. But you must at one time or other have given your consent and agreed to some rent or compensation.'

'Never,' said the Major. 'I couldn't have forgotten a thing like that. What do you suppose is going on, J. J. ? '

'What's going on,' said Meldon, 'is perfectly obvious to anyone who keeps abreast of modern industrial progress and takes an intelligent interest in public affairs. There's been enough talk and newspaper articles about it to have impressed even you. At least so I should have thought. Have you, or have you not, ever heard of the Shannon Scheme ? '

'Some dodge for getting electricity, isn't it ? I've heard of it, of course, but I didn't know they were actually doing it.'

'Well, they are,' said Meldon. 'That seems to me pretty obvious, and what's more they're doing it here.'

'Doing what ? '

'From the look of things,' said Meldon, ' I should say they were damming the river. I don't profess to be an expert electrical engineer, but I have the sort of general knowledge of most subjects that an educated man ought to have, though you, I'm afraid, have not. Rivers are dammed in order to make them disgorge whatever electricity or anything else of value they happen to have in them. Take the case of the Nile, for instance. It wasn't electricity they wanted out of it, but old temples. And they got them, at Luxor and other places, simply by damming the river. Now they want to dam it higher up so as to get cotton. You may take my word for it, Major, the only way to get anything out of a river is to dam it. That's been understood since the very earliest times. Cyrus, the Persian king, understood it practically when he dammed the river in order to capture Babylon. The theory was worked out by Archimedes, who said " Eureka ! " when he found a gold crown in the bottom of his bath.'

' Are they damming the Shannon ? '

' Of course they are. But if they weren't it wouldn't matter to us. The question is how their operations, whatever they are, are going to affect our business. Fortunately they haven't got very far in their work yet. If they'd built a thick concrete dam right on top of your candlesticks it might have been difficult enough to get them out. I don't say impossible. " All things are possible to well-directed labour." I forget who said that, but he was perfectly right, whoever he was, and we'd have got the candlesticks even if there had been a hundred tons of concrete dumped down on top of them. Luckily there isn't. There are only a few blocks laid down, and they're quite near the shore, not so far out in the river as your candlesticks.'

' They've probably dug out my candlesticks long ago,' said the Major.

' No, they haven't. If they had we'd have heard of it. Do you suppose the newspapers would have missed a stunt like that ? " Wonderful find in the Shannon Bed." " Pile Driver Discovers Valuable Old Silver." "Mysterious Artistic Treasure Trove. How Did it Get There ? " Why, England would have blazed with headlines and posters if a find like that had been made. Look at the fuss there was over the things they dug up at Ur of the Chaldees, and it was perfectly natural to find things there, whereas Paul Lamerie candlesticks at the bottom of the Shannon would be a wild surprise to the most imaginative archæologist. No. You may take my word for it, Major. If the things had been found we'd have heard of it, and if they haven't been found they're there still.'

' If they are,' said the Major, ' they're sure to be buried under tons of mud. Those fellows '—he pointed at the workmen who were toiling, some on a narrow wooden pier, others knee-deep in water—' those fellows have knocked the whole place about to such an extent that nothing could possibly be found. Besides, I don't suppose they'd let us search. They'd think we were interfering with their work.'

' The first thing to do,' said Meldon, ' is to establish the exact position of your boat-house. It's gone, and there's nothing left to show exactly where it stood. But you ought to know.'

Major Kent, protesting all the time against the uselessness of what he was doing, went back to what once was his lawn and traced the course of the path which had led to the boat-house, through the trampled shrubbery. The trees had all been cut down to be turned into piles and props, but their stumps remained. The Major, goaded on by Meldon, picked his way among them, trying to guess, by the size of the stumps, where the trees he remembered had stood. He fixed on the site of his boat-house at last. It was decided with fine assurance by Meldon, with great doubt by the Major, exactly where the boat slip had run. Meldon made some calculations on the back of an envelope. Then he picked up a small stone and threw it gently into the river. It fell with a splash a few yards upstream from the narrow wooden pier on which the labourers were at work.

' That,' he said, ' is where your fishing-basket lies, with the candlesticks in it.'

' You're quite sure about that, I suppose, J. J. ? But I needn't ask. You're always quite sure about everything.'

' No one,' said Meldon, ' can be positively certain about any conclusion which depends on information supplied by you. All I can say is that if you've fixed the site of your boat-house correctly, and if you've given me an accurate account of what happened on the night of your escape, the fishing-basket with the candlesticks in it is lying on the bottom of the river where that stone fell or within a couple of feet of it. All we have to do now is to wade in and fetch it out. Then we can go back to the hotel and have lunch.'

' I'd much rather go back to lunch at once,' said the Major. ' We could come again to-morrow and wade about in the river, if we must wade at all.'

' Nonsense, Major. We are here now and we may as well go through with the job at once.'

He sat down and began to pull off his shoes and socks.

' But perhaps,' he said, ' you'd rather fish out that basket yourself, Major. If so, I'll stay on shore and let you go. After all, they're your candlesticks, though you don't seem particularly keen to get them back.'

' I'd much rather not wade about in that mud.'

' It'll be a thrilling moment,' said Meldon, ' when you put your fingers on the top of that basket. It seems a pity for you to miss it.'

He was stuffing a sock into one of his shoes as he spoke and he paused before untying the next lace.

' I'll make you a present of any thrill there is,' said the Major generously.

Meldon took off his other shoe and sock.   He pulled his trousers up as far as he could.   He slipped off his coat and rolled up his shirt-sleeves.   Then he stepped into the water and waded out.

A man who was wheeling a barrowful of mud along the wooden pier, stopped and watched.   A second man, knee-deep in the water, who was filling another barrow, laid his shovel on the pier, turned round and stared at Meldon.   Two men, who were driving a pile, striking the head of it alternately with heavy mallets, let their tools hang down while they looked to see what Meldon was going to do.   Men on shore stopped pushing trucks on the rails, stopped mixing lime with sand, stopped piling timber in stacks.

' The water,' said Meldon, ' is rather deeper than you gave me to understand.'

He waded ashore again and began to take off his trousers.   The Major protested helplessly.

' I haven't a second pair with me,' said Meldon, ' and I'm not going to walk about all day soaked to the waist merely to satisfy your feelings of delicacy. Though delicacy is quite a wrong word to use.   If you'd studied the new science of sex psychology, as you very well might, for you've nothing much else to do in life, you'd know that the fellow who protests against another fellow taking off his trousers is a jolly sight more indecent than the fellow who takes them off. Just you read Freud or any of the real masters of the subject and you'll find out that what I say is true. What you're suffering from, Major, is what's called an

Œdipus complex, aggravated by an acute inhibition. You ought to struggle against it.'

He laid his trousers beside his boots and stepped into the water again, his shirt-tails fluttering in the summer breeze. The few men who had gone on working when he first went into the water stopped immediately. The whole Shannon Scheme, the greatest electrical enterprise in the British Isles, was hung up for the time.

But Meldon did not get very far. He was stopped by a man who came hurrying down towards him through the tree stumps.

'Hullo!' the man shouted. 'There's no bathing allowed here, so if it's bathing you want you'll have to go somewhere else to look for it. Come along out of that, now, when I tell you.'

CHAPTER VII

THE Major recognized the voice, as he had recognized it once before in the middle of the night when the speaker wore a mask on his face. He turned round and saw Michael Gannon, once his head groom, a man specially skilful in the management of polo ponies; afterwards an active incendiary, a firm believer in arson as a means of national regeneration; now foreman of the works at Coolarrigan, part, though not a very important part, of the great scheme of electrifying Ireland from the Shannon.

' Michael Gannon ! ' said the Major.

Michael took his eyes off Meldon for a moment and recognized the Major at once.

' Gosh ! ' he said ' if it isn't the Major himself ! '

He ran down the muddy slope, his mouth stretched in a wide smile, his eyes shining with affectionate welcome.

' Well now,' he said, ' if it isn't a sight for sore eyes to see you here again, Major. It's like old times, so it is. Many and many's the time I've said that the country will never be the same till we get the Major back again. And I'm not the only one that says that. There's plenty more as sorry as I am for the day that you went away.'

He seized the Major's hand and shook it with the utmost heartiness. The Major, a prejudiced man with

c

old-fashioned ideas, did not want to shake hands with
the ruffian who had burnt down his house, who might
very well be, and probably was, a murderer. But it
was impossible to escape the warmth of Michael
Gannon's demonstration of welcome.

' It was a bad day for the country when you and the
likes of you left it,' Michael went on. ' Why did you
do it, Major ? You may wander the width of the
world and you'll never find them that will like you
better than what we did.'

His voice had a note of pathos in it, a suggestion of
enduring loyalty. Just so the voice of a Scottish
Highlander, or of some one who wants to pretend that
he is a Scottish Highlander, vibrates with emotion
when he sings : ' Better lo'ed ye canna be. Will ye
no' come back again ? '

To the Major the reason why he left Ireland seemed
plain enough, while the affection which Michael Gannon
and the others bore him was by no means obvious. He
was, besides, owing to his English descent, a man who
often spoke out, saying exactly what he thought, even
if he hurt somebody's feelings by doing so.

' You took a curious way of showing your liking for
me,' he said, ' when you burnt down my house.'

Meldon, an odd figure, but entirely unembarrassed,
waded ashore, when he heard himself hailed by Michael
Gannon.

' What on earth do you mean by shouting at me in
that way ? ' he said. ' I've a perfect right to paddle
about in the Shannon if I like. Anybody has if he
isn't trying to net the salmon. I expect that's what
you thought I was at. You'd be sure to think that.
From the look of you I'd say that the only time that
you ever wetted your skin with fresh water for the last

ten years was when you went poaching with other blackguards like yourself.'

Meldon had no trousers on. His legs were streaked with Shannon mud. His hair was tangled through long want of combing. His face was bristly. His shirt was torn in two places. But, in spite of appearances, Michael Gannon at once recognized him as a man of a superior caste. He explained afterwards to his friends that he knew 'the kind of talk that's proper to a real gentleman.' Instead of resenting Meldon's attack on his morals and his personal habits, he turned to the Major with a gentle smile.

'Sure, if I'd known the gentleman was a friend of yours,' he said, 'I wouldn't have said a word about what he was doing, whatever it might be. Who has a better right than yourself or your friends to be in the water, or on the water, or throwing flies over the water, or dragging a net under the water? And there's nothing I'd like better than to see you do it, only,' here his voice sank to a whisper and he looked round cautiously, 'only the boss is a terrible hard man.'

'The boss?' said the Major. 'What boss?'

'You may well be asking what boss,' said Michael, 'seeing there ought to be no boss in the place only yourself. Nor there wouldn't be if you hadn't gone away out of it and left us. But the way things is since you left, there's a fellow come here who thinks he's the boss of the world and more. Some kind of foreigner he is. A German, they tell me, and all I can say is if the rest of the Germans is like him I'm sorry for them that had to be fighting against them in the war. He's a terrible hard man on them that works for him. There's no getting round him, nor past him, nor out on the far side of him no matter what you do. There was

one time that the childer did be playing here—the
creatures, where else had they to play?—and the way
he hunted them out of it was terrible to listen to.'

'He was probably quite right there,' said Meldon.
'Your children—how many are there? Six?'

'Nine, thanks be to God, and the youngest is no
more than walking.'

'I don't see what they wanted here,' said Meldon.
'A great engineering work is no place for babies.'

'Wherever there's mud there'll be childer,' said
Gannon. 'Sure you couldn't keep them out of it,
though that fellow did with the language he used.
The creatures are afraid to set foot out of the house
since he spoke to them. He's a terrible man entirely.
I declare to God, if a man was to stop working for as
long as it would take to spit on his hands so as to get a
better grip of the shovel, that fellow would dismiss him
the day after. It's tearing mad he'd be if he saw you
taking the fish out of the river, though it's very little
use salmon is to him, for he's no fisherman, and wouldn't
know which end of a rod to hold in his hand if you were
to give him one. But he's took the notion that he owns
the river and all that's in it, which is why I shouted at
you just now. Though I wouldn't have done it, not
to please every German in Germany, if I'd known you
were a friend of the Major's.'

The contract for the great Shannon electrical works
had gone, as Meldon knew, as the Major dimly remembered having heard, to a German firm. The boss
of whom Michael Gannon spoke so bitterly was no
doubt some engineer or manager who had undertaken
the task of imposing Teutonic thoroughness in work
on the Munster peasants. According to Michael
Gannon he was succeeding marvellously. An Irishman

likes to spit on his hands, often, and in a leisurely manner, while he works. If these slight pauses in his labour are denied him—but were they? Meldon looked round. Every man in sight had ceased to work and was staring at the group on the bank with a broad grin on his face. The German boss was not, apparently, so terrible as Michael Gannon described him.

Then suddenly, while Meldon looked at them, all the men began to work again with remarkable vigour. Wheelbarrows were pushed along at a brisk trot. Men with shovels dug deep and flung the mud up to the waiting barrows. The trucks raced along the rails at perilous speeds. Those who drove piles swung their great mallets high in the air and brought them down with the rapidity and regularity of good machines. Michael Gannon stiffened himself, cupped his hands round his mouth and shouted :

' Will you get on with your work, the whole of yes ! ' His voice rose to a yell, ' Or do you want to get the sack at the end of the day ? What do you think you're being paid for ? Is it to be standing there grinning every time a man happens to take off his trousers ? It's no business of yours whether he does or not. So get on now with whatever you're doing, and if you stop working again you'll hear more about it. And what you'll hear will be what you won't like.'

The access of energy among the workers was sudden. Michael Gannon's realization of his duties as foreman was abrupt. The reason was plain enough for a man of Meldon's intelligence. A tall man, with an un-mistakable air of authority, came along the path through the ruined shrubbery. He was, without doubt, the boss of whom Michael Gannon had spoken. He was—this was perfectly plain when he drew nearer—a

German. He had no back to his head. His hair was short and stood up like stiff bristles. He had heavy eyebrows and large cheek-bones. But he spoke excellent English, though he spoke slowly and formed his sentences with a careful regard for grammar.

' There is a notice,' he said, ' which announces " No admittance except on business." Have you seen it ? Perhaps not. I will show it to you.'

' One moment,' said Meldon genially. ' Just let me slip on my trousers and then I'll go and inspect your notice. So will the Major. There's nothing in the world he'd rather do. I'm sure it's an excellent notice, but of course it doesn't apply to the Major and me.'

This second allusion to the Major's rank produced a certain effect on Herr Deissmann. All Germans respect military titles.

' If you have business,' he said, ' it is with me that you ought to discuss it.'

' The gentleman,' said Michael Gannon, still quite loyal to the Major, ' took the notion of trying could he catch a salmon.'

He knew perfectly well that the boldest salmon would not venture within five hundred yards of the work that was going on. He knew that the most skilful poacher must have something, a gaff, a net, or at the very least a wire noose, if he hopes to catch a fish. He could see that Meldon's hands were as empty as his legs were bare, but Deissmann, so Michael Gannon believed, knew nothing about fishing. It was quite possible that he would believe that Meldon was wading into the disturbed and muddy water near the piles in the hope of catching a salmon with his hands. Michael went on to elaborate his apology in a soothing tone.

' Knowing well that your honour doesn't care about

fishing yourself, I thought it would be no harm to let the gentleman have a try at what he could do.'

Granted that Deissmann knew nothing about fishing this was quite a good explanation of Meldon's performance. But Deissmann did not believe a word of it Some months' experience had taught him that Michael Gannon never spoke the truth and that the only safe course was to take it for granted that what he said was entirely unconnected with the actual facts. After listening to Michael Gannon's statement he felt certain that whatever Meldon's object in wading into the river was, it was certainly not to fish.

' Go at once,' he said to Gannon, ' to the yard and see that the men who are stacking timber are doing their work properly.'

' I will, your honour,' said Michael, with every appearance of alacrity, ' and if I find so much as one of them that's not, I'll give him a talking-to that he'll remember for however long he lives.'

Can a foreman of works do better than that ?

' Horrid liar that fellow is,' said Meldon after Gannon had gone. ' They all are, every one of them. I'm so glad you've grasped that. It'll make things so much easier for you. If you'd believed that story about my poaching salmon it might have taken me hours to get it out of your head. Whereas now, thanks to your intelligent scepticism——'

Meldon's words were flattering and his tone friendly. But Deissmann interrupted him, almost rudely.

' Please,' he said, ' we will now discuss your business.'

His manner was that adopted by official people all over the world when dealing with civilians. The Germans excel in it. Deissmann was ahead of most

Germans. Major Kent was irritated ; but he had too much self-respect to attempt any kind of reply.

' Come along, J. J.,' he said. ' Let's get out of this as quick as we can.'

But Meldon, though he had put on his trousers, was not inclined to stir. He enjoyed talking to official people. When he could not get into direct touch with them he enjoyed writing them letters. There are in England to-day several educational authorities, in County offices and at Whitehall, who from time to time squirm at the letters they have received from the Rev. J. J. Meldon. There are church officials who wriggle uncomfortably when they remember the things he has written to them. Deissmann offered him an opportunity for what had become a favourite sport.

' You've heard, I daresay,' he said, ' in fact, you must have heard, of the Washington and Arkansas Auriferous Deposits Company Inc.'

Deissmann frowned. He had never heard of the company, and though he knew English well he did not know American. The word ' Inc.' puzzled him.

' Inc.,' he said.

' Yes,' said Meldon, ' I.N.C.—not I.N.K. Nothing whatever to do with fountain pens. Short for incorporated.'

Now incorporated is a longish word and the three broad vowels in the middle of it give it a solemn sound. Deissmann was impressed. He was not at all sure that he had not come up against officials of a dignity at least equal to his own. He bowed, but stiffly.

' Acting under the terms of the Commission granted by the Irish Free State,' said Meldon, ' the Company has sent me over here as their representative to report on the Irish river-beds. In order to do that properly

I must of course obtain specimens of what's there, under water, I mean, and even, as far as possible, underneath what we may perhaps call the primary deposits, gravel and so forth. Now I needn't tell you —by the way, Michael Gannon didn't introduce us. Would you mind telling me your name? It's so much more convenient to know what to call you.'

'Deissmann,' said the German, 'Dr. Deissmann.'

His knowledge of English was very good and he was quickly learning to understand Michael Gannon's way of speaking that language. But Meldon's very rapid flow of words and the unfamiliar thoughts they expressed left him a little puzzled.

'Thanks,' said Meldon. 'I needn't tell you, Herr Doctor Deissmann, that the secondary and tertiary deposits of our greater rivers aren't the easiest things in the world to get at. The quartary and quintary, of course, are more difficult still. One has to excavate. Now between you and me there's nothing I dislike so much as excavating. Of course it's my job, more or less, but I don't do it if I can get any one else to do it for me. That's why we came here—lighted off the cars and stopped in—' Meldon's knowledge of the American language was small, but he felt sure that Deissmann's was smaller still, so he ventured on 'lighted off' and 'stopped in,' hoping for the best. 'Stopped in,' he went on, 'the moment we heard that you were digging down into the bed of the Shannon. We knew you'd do it thoroughly if you did it at all. And you have. Now you understand the position. I wasn't poaching salmon. That was just a lie, invented by Michael Gannon. I was simply scraping up a specimen or two of what I hope will prove to be at least a tertiary, quite possibly a quartary, deposit. The Major will analyse it afterwards. Did I mention that he's an analytical chemist?'

'I'm not,' said the Major.

'Now, now, Major,' said Meldon. 'Don't be captious. I may not have got it quite right. Perhaps I ought to have said chemical analyst. But it comes to the same thing in the end, and Dr. Deissmann quite understands. These scientific men,' he said to Deissmann, 'are always fractious when hungry, and the Major hasn't had his lunch yet.'

He sat down as he spoke and slipped on his socks and shoes. He talked rapidly as he did so, being very unwilling to allow the Major a chance of speaking again.

'Now that you understand the situation, Dr. Deissmann,' he said, 'I'm sure you'll have no objection to my scooping up a few handfuls of mud. Quite a small quantity will do. *Ex pede herculem*, you know, and the Major can reconstruct an auriferous deposit from a mere handful of sand, if there is an auriferous deposit there. He can't if there isn't, of course. Wonderful thing analytical chemistry! Some men prefer the organic kind, and they may be right; but I put my money on the analytic every time, especially when dealing with tertiary deposits.'

He stood up, both shoes on his feet, and took the Major firmly by the arm.

'Good-bye, for to-day, Dr. Deissmann,' he said. 'We'll see you to-morrow if it's moderately fine. Shall we say about 9 o'clock? It won't take us more than half an hour to get what we want out of the river. Come along, Major.' He gave a tug at the arm he held, for the Major showed signs of trying to speak. 'If you happen to have a good landing-net, Dr. Deissmann,' he looked back over his shoulder as he spoke, ' it will come in useful, but if you haven't it doesn't matter. I can manage quite well with my hands.'

The last words were scarcely audible to Deissmann, for Meldon was hurrying the Major off and was already half-way through the tree stumps when he stopped speaking.

CHAPTER VIII

'J. J.!' said the Major, as he was towed along. 'I'm not going to stand any more of this.'

'Any more of what?'

'Of the lies you're telling. If I could contradict you it wouldn't matter so much; but every time I open my mouth you interrupt me or drag me away or something. However, thank heaven, I can write and I will. I'll write a letter to that German to-night and tell him I'm not a chemist. Suppose he asks me to make up a prescription for him, or to bandage his leg or something—I can't, you know. And anyhow I hate being taken for a chemist. I'd almost as soon be a murderer, which is what you told that girl in the hotel.'

'You shouldn't exaggerate,' said Meldon. 'Exaggeration is really worse than direct lying. It's a meaner form of deceit and far more insidious. I never told the girl in the hotel that you were a murderer. I never actually told her anything at all about you. I allowed her to infer that you were a strong patriot—Irish; which is a very different thing. All patriots aren't murderers, and no one who wasn't absolutely blinded by political prejudice could say they were. That's what I complain of, Major. You've no sense of fairness towards your political opponents, and you distort the simplest thing that anybody says by grotesque exaggeration. Not that I mind your doing it. I don't in the least. All I say is that if you play fast and loose in that sort of way with the truth yourself, you've no right to call other people liars. Take that statement you complain of. I never said you kept the sort of shop in which tooth brushes and pills are sold or that you made up prescriptions. That's simply another example of the way you exaggerate. What I did say—Hullo! Here's Michael Gannon again. I thought he was doing slave driver over some men who are stacking timber. That's what Deissmann told him to do.'

Michael Gannon was engaged in what seemed to be an interesting and strictly private conversation with Jimmy Costello. The two men were seated together in the car, their heads close, absorbed in their talk. While Meldon and the Major were crossing the lawn—while Meldon was explaining the nature of exaggeration—Michael caught sight of them. He at once got out of the car and went to meet them.

'Begging your pardon, Mr. Meldon,' he said. 'But I'd be glad if I could speak a word to you.'

'You can,' said Meldon. 'But not many words. I'm in a hurry to get back to Lisnamoe, and the Major's temper is completely broken through sheer hunger, so get to the point as quickly as you can. Major, trot on and hop into the car. Tell Jimmy to start up the engine. I'll be with you in a minute. What Michael Gannon has to say may be private, and anyhow, it's almost sure to be something which will upset you worse than you're upset already. Almost anything would do that at the present moment, though you'll be all right again when you've had something to eat.'

The Major, dumbly obedient through utter despair, went on and flung himself into the car.

' Now, Gannon,' said Meldon, ' out with it whatever
it is. But if you want to borrow money it's no earthly
use coming to me. I haven't got a penny. Since
Queen Anne's Bounty took to collecting my tithe for
me I've been up to my ears in debt. You may be under
the impression that Queen Anne is dead. But she's
not, as you'd very soon find out if you owned any tithe.
I'll explain the whole business to you if you like, but
not now. It's very complicated and it would take you
an hour to grasp it ; still, if you really want to know
about it——'

Queen Anne, while alive, did something very complicated to the finances of the English Church, and
called what she did a Bounty. No one has ever understood what it was, but a body of men, all passionately
fond of complications, has gone on ever since, continuing Queen Anne's work, and even improving on her
method. Their activities are a sheer delight to Meldon.
He is a spiritually-minded man and counts the loss of
twenty per cent. of his income a small price to pay in
return for an inexhaustible source of argument. Like
the Athanasian Creed, another bulwark of the Church of
England, Queen Anne's activities can be discussed,
either good-naturedly or acrimoniously, for years,
without ever getting any nearer finding out what they
are.

' In fact,' Meldon went on, ' I think I'll give you a
short sketch of the situation. Even if you don't quite
understand it it'll do you good. Queen Anne——'

' Queen Anne's nothing to me,' said Michael. ' I'm
not much of a one for queens, or kings for the matter of
that. How could I when I'm a Republican and always
was ? '

' You ought not to allow yourself to be cut off from

historical research,' said Meldon, ' by political prejudice. Lots of good Republicans have taken the
greatest delight in studying the lives of kings.'

' What I want to know,' said Gannon firmly, ' is the
meaning of what Jimmy Costello is after telling me
about the Major.'

' That,' said Meldon, ' I shall very likely be able to
tell you in a few words as soon as I know what it is that
Jimmy said to you.'

' He said,' said Gannon, ' that his sister, who 's what
they call the manageress of the hotel, is after telling
him, that you're after telling her——'

' That 's enough,' said Meldon. ' You want to tell
me what Jimmy told you that his sister told him that I
told her. That 's it, isn't it ? Very well. Whatever
it is that you tell me will be utterly different from the
original fact which I am supposed to have told Jimmy's
sister. I mean what the original fact was before I told
it. That being so, I strongly advise you to dismiss the
whole subject from your mind. You simply can't get
at whatever that fact was—which is what you profess
to want—by tracking it back in that sort of way
through four distinct and independent conversations.'

Michael Gannon thought this over for some time. He
had a great respect for Meldon's ability and was willing
to give due weight to anything he said. Perhaps
he did not quite understand him. Perhaps, though
understanding, he was unconvinced. He went back
obstinately to his original demand.

' What Jimmy told me,' he said, ' was that the Major
was a high-up man in the Irish Republican Army,
which is a thing I wouldn't find it too easy to
believe.'

' Listen to me now, Michael,' said Meldon. ' Jimmy

talks too much and so does his sister. It'd be a great deal better for themselves and for everybody else if they'd learn to keep their mouths shut. But since they have talked, I'll just say this much to you : If what that Costello girl said was true—mind you, I'm only saying " if." If it was true, is it a thing the Major would like to have talked about? Don't you know that there's nothing the Free Staters would like better than to lay their hands on a man like the Major, supposing he is what Jimmy's sister says I told her he was. Would that be a thing that ought to be talked about ? '

' It would not,' said Michael with conviction, ' and I'd be the last to say a word to anyone on the subject, only to be asking you was it true. For if it is it's the queerest thing ever I heard, and the Major's the last man in Ireland I'd have thought it of.'

' I don't say it's literally true, exactly as it reached you through all the people who repeated it,' said Meldon, ' but I'll just say this much. Did the Major get a penny of compensation for the house that you burnt down ? He did not. Who ought to have paid him ? The Free State Government. What are they doing instead of paying him ? Bothering the life out of him for income-tax, reducing him to a nervous wreck because he won't pay them what they ought to be paying him. Is that the kind of treatment that makes a man fond of any Government ? And if he doesn't like the Government what is he likely to do ? What did you do yourself, Michael, when you didn't like the English Government ? Did you sit down and smile or did you buy a gun ? '

' I'd never have thought it of the Major,' said Gannon. ' Of him above all men. But of course if you say so, Mr. Meldon——'

There he stopped abruptly. Instead of finishing his sentence he hurried away and Meldon saw him running at high speed towards six men who were seated, smoking comfortably, on a log of wood. Deissmann was walking up from the river.

The six men stuffed their pipes into their pockets, sprang to their feet and tugged hard at the log on which they had been sitting. Gannon, with shouts and a good deal of gesticulation, urged them on. Deissmann, though he must have seen all that happened, did not approach the men. He made straight for the car in which Jimmy Costello sat at the steering wheel, in which the Major was stretched, with his eyes shut and an expression of despair on his face. Meldon stopped him with a shout of greeting and a wave of the hand. If Deissmann had anything to say Meldon did not want it said to the Major.

' Excuse me,' said Deissmann, ' I am sorry to delay you. But I wish to ask if you would be so kind as to tell me again the name of the company you represent. I have forgotten it, and it is desirable that I should know it. This time,' he took out a pencil and a note-book, ' I shall write it down and then I shall not have to trouble you again.'

His manner was as polite as his words, but there was no doubt that he meant to get the information he asked for. Meldon hesitated for a moment, not because he was unwilling to answer Deissmann, but because he could not at first recollect what the name of the company was, nor, when he did remember, did he get it quite right.

' The Washington and Arkansas Tertiary Deposit Company Inc. ' he said.

Deissmann began to write and then stopped.

'I thought you said something about gold,' he said, 'a gold-mining company?'

'I can't possibly have said that,' said Meldon, 'because it wouldn't have been true. What I said down at the river is exactly what I am saying now.' The mention of gold showed him his mistake. 'The Washington and Arkansas Auriferous Deposit Company Inc.'

'But that is not what you have just said,' said Deissmann. 'You said "Tertiary Deposit."'

'My dear Deissmann,' said Meldon a little petulantly, 'you really must believe that I know the name of my own company better than you do. I'm on the Board of Directors. I drew up the original prospectus, and when I say "auriferous" it's no use your correcting me and saying "tertiary." Try to be reasonable. Nobody would start a company to buy up tertiary deposits. You couldn't raise the capital for an enterprise of the kind. Tertiary deposits may be anything. Lots of them are perfectly worthless. Ordovician sediment, for instance, has no commercial value whatever. You may have as low an opinion as you like of the United States, but you can't suppose that Wall Street is going to put up money to dig out a lot of ordovician sediment, or jurassic fossils or anything of that sort. What we're after is something that pays. I don't say gold precisely —that's another of your mistakes—but I do say auriferous. The Washington and Arkansas Auriferous Deposit Company Inc.'

'But,' said Deissmann, 'you certainly said "tertiary."'

'If I did, though I don't see how I possibly could, it was a slip of the tongue, and I've given you the name right now. Head office—If you're thinking of applying for shares you'd better write direct to the head office. I don't believe they're quoted on the English Stock Exchange, though they will be soon. Head office, 39 West 98th Street, Philadelphia, Pa. Got that ? ' Deissmann wrote down the address carefully. ' Do be careful. I don't want your coming to me afterwards and complaining that I said New Orleans Fa, a thing I couldn't say, any more than I could say " tertiary deposits " because New Orleans isn't in Fa.'

He left Deissmann writing in his note-book and hurried away to the car. This time he took his seat beside the Major instead of getting in with Jimmy in front.

' Nasty, self-sufficient, pragmatic swine, that German,' he said. ' Just the sort of fellow I particularly dislike.'

' I suppose,' said the Major, ' that you're down on him because he didn't believe that I was a dentist.'

' Chemist, not dentist,' said Meldon. ' He believed that all right.   At least he didn't say he had any doubts about it. What he was fussing about was the name of the company. I detest people who fuss about details.'

' Evidently he's not quite a fool,' said the Major. ' Where you go wrong, J. J., is in assuming that nobody except yourself has the smallest intelligence.'

' Anyone who hadn't a disgustingly suspicious mind,' said Meldon, ' would have believed in that company at once. Anyhow, he believes in it now, for he's written the name down in a note-book, so as to buy shares. He didn't actually say that, but I fancy it was in his mind and I encouraged him.'

' In all probability,' said the Major, ' he wrote down the name so as to make inquiries whether there is such a company. You'll be in a nice hole when he finds out that there isn't, and I shan't be a bit sorry for you.'

' I don't care what inquiries he makes,' said Meldon. ' We shall be back at Weymouth long before he finds out anything. We've arranged to fish up the candlesticks to-morrow. We'll have them safe back in the hotel before eleven and catch the twelve train which will get us to Rosslare in time for the boat. After that Deissmann can find out anything he likes, and if he chooses to scrape the bottom of the Shannon for ordovician sediment I don't mind a bit.'

' What sort of sediment did you say, J. J. ? '

' Ordovician. That's what Deissmann thinks we're after. He said so distinctly. At least he said tertiary deposits and they are ordovician sediment, or anyhow they may be. I don't know what good he thinks the stuff will be when he gets it, but he's convinced it's of some value because he knows we wouldn't be after it if it wasn't. That's the sort of mistake these men with hyper-suspicious minds are always making. He wouldn't believe me when I told him that we weren't after it. He simply thought I was trying to put him off the scent. I only hope there is a scent. I hope ordovician sediment stinks. If it does Deissmann will be sorry for himself when he has his house full of it and can't get any one to cart it away.'

The Major was perfectly right in his opinion that the German was not a fool. While Jimmy Costello's car was racing towards the hotel Deissmann was writing out a long telegram to the head office of his firm in Hamburg. He asked whether anything was known of the Washington and Arkansas Auriferous Deposit Company Inc.: which might—Deissmann was very thorough—be known as The Washington and Arkansas

Tertiary Deposits Co. Inc. : with an office at 39 West
98th Street, Philadelphia, Pa., or perhaps—this was
thoroughness again—in New Orleans, Fa. or La.

The message was sent in German and the telegraph
clerk in Lisnamoe post office only knew English and a
few words of Irish, just enough to qualify for a place in
the Free State Civil Service, therefore no news spread
through the village that inquiries were being made
about Meldon's company.

CHAPTER IX

MISS EILEEN COSTELLO was willing to do her best for Major Kent once she understood that he held a high position in the Republican fighting forces. She provided an excellent and abundant luncheon. She opened four bottles of porter, the very least her guests were likely to drink. The Major, who was very hungry, ate heartily and emptied both the bottles allotted to him. The consequence of that was that he went sound asleep in an arm-chair afterwards, and did not wake again until Miss Costello roused him for another meal.

Meldon ate more than the Major did and drank quite as much ; but the food had its proper effect on him, the effect which food and drink, especially strong drink, are meant by nature to have. He renewed his vigour of body and mind. As soon as he had finished his meal and lit his pipe he went out into the yard at the back of the hotel. He had a long conversation with Jimmy Costello, whom he found there as he expected.

Jimmy was quite willing to talk. So, later on, was Miss Costello, when Meldon joined her in her little office. Irish people of their class are always willing to talk, but the stranger who supposes that he is learning anything from them is generally mistaken. They tell him what they think he would like to hear, without giving him the smallest scrap of information about what they themselves think or what the facts are. But Meldon was an Irishman himself and understood this way of talking. He would not have been deceived for a single moment if the Costellos had told him that there was nothing they wanted more than to see the English Government functioning again. He would merely have grinned if they had said that they always detested and now deeply regretted the murders which led to the independence of Ireland.

But the Costellos had no wish to treat Meldon as an inquiring stranger. He came to them with the most excellent credentials. They were prepared to talk freely and fairly truthfully to the secretary, possibly the A.D.C., of a great Republican leader. There was nothing that Meldon particularly needed to know. The local politics of Lisnamoe were of no importance to him, for he expected to be out of the place the next day and meant never to return there again. But he was a man of the broadest sympathies and a real lover of humanity. He took an interest in all affairs, particularly political affairs.

He learned from the Costellos—Eileen confirmed what her brother said—that Deissmann was not popular with his workmen. Like the Dutch merchants in the well-known poem ' he gave too little and asked too much.' The wages paid by the German firm were far from satisfactory to a people who supposed that once the English disappeared from the country all wages would be trebled or quadrupled. The hours of work— and Deissmann tried to insist that they really were hours of work—were an outrage. Every one had always understood that once Irish independence was secured the necessity for work would cease. It was a bitter disappointment to find that work, as distinguished from a specious appearance of work, was still required before wages, even unsatisfactory wages, were paid.

The Costellos themselves were unaffected by the German firm's rate of pay or the German's insistence on work. Eileen had a comfortable post as manageress of her aunt's hotel. Jimmy had a still more comfortable post, for he had nothing to do except kill a few chickens or a pig occasionally, and drive people about in his motor car when he felt inclined to do so. When he preferred to stay at home, he made cryptic statements about his carburettor. Then even eager people had to forgo their drives.

But the Costellos, though not personally interested in the Shannon Scheme, were like Tennyson's hero, the man who wanted to marry Maud, in being 'one with their kind.' They thoroughly understood the feelings of their neighbours and were able to tell Meldon exactly what people thought of Deissmann. They spoke at length and with great vigour. Before dinner-time Meldon understood how Labour regarded Capital in Lisnamoe.

'There's some of the boys,' said Eileen, 'that would as soon see Deissmann dead as alive.'

'Sooner,' said Jimmy, with spirit.

'And if the word was to be given,' said Eileen, 'given by a man who had the right to give it, it mightn't be long before Deissmann was dead.'

'Only somebody would have to speak the word,' said Jimmy.

'That's what I'm after saying, isn't it?'

'And who's to do it?' said Jimmy.

'There's them that might,' said Eileen.

Through the window of her office the Major could be

seen—and heard—sleeping profoundly. Eileen nodded slightly in his direction.

' Don't get it into your heads,' said Meldon, ' that the Major has come here in order to set on Michael Gannon to murder that German.'

' The Lord save us ! ' said Eileen. ' Who's talking of murder ? '

' You were,' said Meldon. ' You distinctly said that if the Major gave the word Gannon and a lot of other fellows would murder Deissmann. I'm not at all sure that you didn't say you'd do it yourself.'

' What I said,' said Eileen, ' was that if the Major gave the word Deissmann might find out afterwards that he was dead. I wouldn't call that murder, nor no more would any one else who had any sense.'

After that the time passed pleasantly and swiftly, for Meldon found that Eileen was well able to defend her own views of what was murder and what was not. He took the greatest pleasure in explaining his.

The information he gathered during the afternoon was of no immediate value and had so little interest that the Major yawned pitifully when Meldon repeated to him what the Costellos had said.

' You're an extraordinary man, J. J.,' he said. ' I can't even imagine what pleasure you find in listening to a lot of local gossip. It doesn't matter to us whether Deissmann pays decent wages or not.'

' What you forget, Major,' said Meldon, ' is that all knowledge is useful. Take for example what I know about tertiary deposits, ordovician sediment and jurassic fossils. If you'd seen me reading that subject up—and I may say that it took some reading—you'd have said I was a fool. That sort of knowledge—this is the line you would certainly have taken, Major——'

' I would not,' said the Major, who was still very sleepy. ' I'd have taken the line, as you call it, that reading about sediment or anything else was an excellent thing if it stopped you talking when other people want to go to bed.'

' The line you would have taken at the time—though you may not think so now—would have been that it was mere waste of time for me to master the science of ordovician sediment, and that I should have been better occupied in reading up the law dealing with Parochial Church Councils. That's what you'd have thought, and no doubt said : but as it turns out you'd have been quite wrong. It hasn't mattered in the least, so far, whether I knew the law about Parochial Church Councils or not. Mine never meets. But if I hadn't understood primitive geology pretty thoroughly I couldn't have made Deissmann believe that we ought to be allowed to scoop up your candlesticks, whereas now I shall be a bit surprised if he doesn't provide us with a landing-net. Very likely he'll offer to help us himself. That's where the usefulness of knowledge comes in, almost every kind of knowledge, even the most recondite.'

' That's all right, J. J.,' said the Major. ' I quite give in. Now what about toddling off to bed ? '

' Not yet,' said Meldon. ' You asked why I spent the afternoon gossiping, as you call it, with Jimmy Costello and that fuzzy-headed sister of his. You asked that question in a way that I can only describe as offensive, and when I, without the smallest show of temper, answer you quietly in the fewest possible words, you interrupt me and want to go to bed. But that won't do, Major. You must be told what you asked to be told. I put it to you in the form of a simple syllogism. Knowledge is useful. You admit that, I suppose. You can't help admitting that, for I've proved it to you by citing the instance of the jurassic fossils. Very well. What I learned from the Costellos this afternoon was knowledge. You admit that, too, don't you ? '

' No, I don't,' said the Major, goaded into protest. ' All you have learnt from them so far is that the men here think they ought to work less and be paid more. You can't call that knowledge. Any fool would have known it without being told.'

' The mere fact that a fool knows it,' said Meldon, ' even if that's true, which it probably isn't, doesn't prevent its being knowledge, which, as you'd know if you'd listened to me, was all I ever said about it. Now. All knowledge is useful. What the Costellos told me this afternoon is knowledge. Therefore—the syllogism is in the mode known to logicians as A.I.I., and therefore quite valid. '' *Barbara celarent darii ferioque prioris.*'' That's the way the mnemonic rhyme goes, and you'll scarcely deny that the fellows who made it up knew a sound conclusion when they met one.'

' I haven't the remotest idea what you're talking about now, J. J.'

' I'm talking about logic,' said Meldon, ' what's called formal logic, and I'm doing so in order to convince you that my syllogism is perfectly sound, a thing which you would otherwise probably deny. All knowledge is useful. What the Costellos told me this afternoon is knowledge. Therefore—mark the inevitability of the conclusion once the major and minor premises are properly stated. Therefore what I heard this afternoon from the Costellos was useful. From which it follows that I wasn't wasting my time, though you were. You went to sleep in a chair, like what Shakespeare calls a " lazy, yawning drone," whereas I was like Dr. Watts' busy bee, collecting useful knowledge. That's the situation as I see it, and I don't think that any reasonable man can see it in any other way.'

After that the Major went to bed. Meldon, though not in the least sleepy, was forced to go to bed, too. Jimmy Costello had disappeared for the night. So had his sister. There was no way of collecting further useful knowledge, except, perhaps, by reading the poems of Alexander Pope. A volume of his works, bound in calf, was, by some curious chance, in the hotel and was the only book to be found except a spiritual manual called ' The Key of Heaven.' Meldon preferred poetry to theology and took the works of Pope to bed with him. But he did not read much. The first hundred lines of the Dunciad did what travel, fresh air, hard work and abundant food failed to do, induced drowsiness which ended in sound sleep.

He was wakened, much earlier than he wanted to be, by Jimmy Costello, who himself looked as if he had been roused at an untimely hour. It was obvious that he had neither shaved nor washed and such clothes as he had on were incompletely buttoned. There was some excuse for Meldon's sleepiness, for it was only a few minutes after seven and he had no sleep the night before. There was no excuse for Jimmy's. As a member of the hotel staff he ought to have been out of bed at a much earlier hour.

' It's Michael Gannon,' said Jimmy, ' and he's wanting to see you in a hurry.'

' He'll have to wait till I get my clothes on, whatever hurry he's in,' said Meldon. ' I didn't bring a dressing-gown with me and I'm not going to wander about your hotel in my pyjamas. Not that I object to being seen in pyjamas. Lots of men wear less—in the Solomon Islands and places like that—but as it happens mine are torn nearly to ribbons.'

'Michael Gannon,' said Jimmy, 'has to be at his work by eight o'clock, so he can't wait. That's what he says himself and he ought to know; though I'd have thought that he could wait well enough if he wanted to, work or no work.'

'If you tell him about my pyjamas,' said Meldon, 'he'll see that he must wait. Unless you can lend me a dressing-gown. But I don't suppose you have one.'

'I have not,' said Jimmy. 'My sister Eileen has, and if you like I'll get it for you.'

'Certainly not. Nothing would induce me to enter into business negotiations with Michael Gannon—— It must be business or he wouldn't have come here at this hour. Nobody would. I simply won't do business, very likely important business, with Michael Gannon or any one else, wearing a pink silk *négligée*. I suppose that's what she calls it.'

'What she does be calling it is her morning robe,' said Jimmy.

'Whatever she calls it,' said Meldon, 'it's sure to have frills sewed on to it all over, and a costume of that sort would put me at a distinct disadvantage in dealing with a man like Gannon. I'd rather do the business, whatever it is, in bed, than put on a ridiculous garment of your sister's!'

And this was what Meldon did. Michael Gannon, who really was in a hurry, made his way up to Meldon's bedroom. He knew his way about the hotel very well, and the only wrong room he entered was the Major's.

That mistake did not matter for the Major slept profoundly through the opening and shutting of his door.

' If you'll excuse me, Mr. Meldon,' he began.

' I'll excuse you,' said Meldon, ' if you've got anything really important to say, but if you've merely dropped in to tell me that your youngest child has got the chicken-pox or that your aunt didn't like the last bottle of medicine she got from the doctor—and that's the sort of thing I expect you've come to say—then I certainly won't excuse you. Nobody would. Now what is it ? '

' It's a private matter,' said Gannon, looking round at Jimmy. ' Not that I object to your hearing it, Jimmy, for you will hear it some day, if so be that Mr. Meldon will do what I want him.'

' Clear out, Jimmy,' said Meldon. ' But open the window before you go. I want to be able to hear you whistling outside in the yard. " Kathleen Mavourneen " is the tune you're to whistle, and when I hear that I'll know you're not listening at the keyhole.'

' Listening at keyholes,' said Jimmy, ' is what I never did, nor wouldn't.'

' If you don't know " Kathleen Mavourneen," ' said Meldon, ' you may whistle " God save Ireland." I don't care what tune you choose as long as I know it's you that's whistling it.'

Jimmy was inclined to be sulky ; but he did what he was told. First ' Kathleen Mavourneen,' then ' God save Ireland,' and then ' Danny Boy ' came shrilly through the open window.

' Now then, Gannon,' said Meldon, ' what do you want ? '

' What I'm wanting,' said Gannon, ' is for you to

use your influence with the Major, for well I know that
what you ask of him is what he'll do.'

'I'm not so sure about that,' said Meldon, 'the
Major can be pretty obstinate sometimes.'

'What we're wanting him to do is to help us.'

'There's not the slightest use asking the Major to do
that. He never helps any one. He'd like to, being a
thoroughly kind-hearted man, but he can't. The plain
fact is, Gannon, that so far from being in a position to
help other people, the Major has to be helped himself.
I'm helping him at the present moment. I enjoy doing
it and it's a thing I'm particularly good at, so if you
want help you'd far better ask me for it and let the
Major alone. He, poor man, is worried enough already
over his own affairs, and if you tangle him up in yours
he'll probably collapse altogether.'

'All I want of him,' said Gannon, 'won't take him
long. It's no more than just to sign his name to a little
paper that a few of the fellows down at the works drew
up last night along with myself. I have it here with
me, if you'd care to see it.'

He took a dirty piece of paper from his pocket and
handed it to Meldon. It began as if it was a letter to
Deissmann, but after a few lines the form changed and
it became something like a state proclamation. It
announced that every man employed on the works
managed by Deissmann intended to go on strike next
day, unless wages were doubled and hours of work
halved. It ended : 'Signed on behalf of the Irish
Republic,' and then a blank space intended for Major
Kent's name.

'If you think,' said Meldon, 'that the Major will sign
that document, you're making the biggest mistake of
your life. He detests all strikes, and anyhow I don't

see what good his signature would be to you. If you're going to strike you will, whether he signs it or not.'

' The way of it is this,' said Michael Gannon thoughtfully, 'if there's to be a strike, and there should be one, for the way that fellow Deissmann's going on is worse than the Black and Tans was——'

' Making you work a bit, I suppose,' said Meldon. ' Jolly good for you.'

'It's what we're not going to put up with,' said Gannon, 'only if there is to be a strike, there's some of us would like it to be done respectable. I'm that way of thinking myself. " If we are to strike," that's what I said, " let it be done in the name of the Irish Republic." For it's a poor thing to be striking, or for the matter of that doing anything else, without we have some patriotism in it.'

It is certainly true that an Irishman prefers to have a noble motive for action. An Englishman is not ashamed to strike for the sake of more wages, and he says so plainly. An Irishman wants more wages just as much as an Englishman does, but he prefers to keep up an appearance of indifference to such material things and to strike for the sake of Faith and Fatherland, in the sacred name of patriotism, and if possible of religion. Meldon understood this thoroughly and felt that he was beginning to get at the meaning of the desire for the Major's signature.

' I see,' he said, ' you want to put a political complexion on what otherwise would be a sordid labour scrimmage.'

' You've got the notion now,' said Gannon, ' and the Major being a high-up officer in the Republican Army, which is what you told Miss Costello he was, and she told Jimmy, and he told me——'

' I distinctly told you,' said Meldon, ' that the Major is down here on private business and it won't do to have his name publicly associated with a strike like yours.'

' I was thinking all along,' said Michael Gannon a little sulkily, ' that the Major wasn't as keen on the Irish Republic as what you said. It'd be a queer thing if he was, and that's a pity, too, for without we can get somebody to sign that paper I don't see how there's to be any strike at all. There's fellows that's so mean that they'd put up with what Deissmann does to them and says to them for the sake of the wages he pays them, fellows that'll never go on strike at all unless they see that the Republic is at the bottom of it, for then they'll know that it'll be the worse for them if they don't strike.'

' You may put that paper into your pocket again,' said Meldon. ' If you wait till the Major signs it there'll never be a strike at all. I won't advise him to, and even if I did he wouldn't do it.'

CHAPTER X

THE directors of Deissmann's company in Hamburg were alert and vigorous men. The very moment they received the telegram which asked for information about the Washington and Arkansas Auriferous Deposit Company Inc. they met in consultation. Not one of them had ever heard of the company ; but that was no proof that it did not exist. Telephone connections were made with London, Paris, and, as an afterthought, with Vienna, which no longer holds the place it did in the financial world. Cables were sent to New York, Philadelphia and, to prevent all possibility of error, New Orleans. The answers were all the same. The Washington and Arkansas Auriferous Deposit Company, Inc. or not Inc., was unknown. The New York correspondent went so far as to say definitely that it had no existence.

Shortly after midnight Herr Deissmann, at Coolarrigan, was wakened from his first sleep by the ringing of the telephone bell. He was informed by the London agent of his firm that the company he asked about had never been heard of in any part of the world, and that it had no offices, either in Philadelphia or in New Orleans. Deissmann, very naturally and properly, made up his mind that Meldon and Major Kent were engaged in working some kind of swindle.

It was not very clear to Deissmann how Meldon

proposed to get money for himself, or to take money from other people. There was no prospect of making a profit out of mud scooped up from the bed of the Shannon, and it was not clear how anybody could be robbed in such a way. But Deissmann did not trouble himself with these considerations. His own duty seemed to him perfectly plain. Meldon wanted to wade into the river with a landing-net in his hand. He said that he represented a company, but that company had no existence, therefore—so Deissmann argued—Meldon must not be allowed to wade into the river, at all events not into that part of it where Deissmann's works were going on.

At nine o'clock Deissmann went to the yard in which the lorries gathered with their loads. There he waited. At a quarter past nine Meldon and the Major arrived, driven by Jimmy Costello in his car. Meldon was cheerful and very friendly. He began by trying to shake hands with Deissmann. But Deissmann stepped back and put his hands behind him. He was an upright man, and, unlike some archbishops and many statesmen, disliked shaking hands with criminals, even if they were nothing worse than directors of bogus companies. Meldon became effusively apologetic.

' I don't wonder you're a little annoyed,' he said. ' I promised to be here at nine and I don't arrive till a quarter past. We've kept you waiting, and there's nothing so trying as that for a busy man. I quite understand your feelings. I'm invariably savage myself when I have to stand about doing nothing because other people aren't punctual at their appointments. But it isn't my fault. Major, apologize at once.'

Major Kent, who did not realize that he had a definite

appointment with Deissmann, murmured that he was sorry.

' The Major,' said Meldon, ' has never in his life hurried over his meals. Always reads *The Times* through before stirring after breakfast. He potters round a flower-bed or two before lunch. He dodders down to the club about three, if the day is fine, and gets home again in good time to dress for dinner. Afterwards he dozes in a chair till bed-time. That's the life he's led for the last two years. Naturally he found it hard to realize this morning that he'd got to get through his breakfast in something less than an hour, which is the time he usually allows himself. I did my best but—well, as you point out, we're a quarter of an hour late and we've kept you waiting. However, we're here now, so we need not keep you waiting any longer. We'll trot straight down to the river. By the way, did you find the landing-net ? No ? Well, it doesn't matter in the least. I'll scoop up all I want with my hands.'

' I regret,' said Deissmann, coldly, ' that I cannot permit you to go to the river.'

' What ? ' said Meldon.

' I must request you,' said Deissmann, ' to leave these premises at once.'

' But, my dear Deissmann, said Meldon, ' surely you can't mean that ? Or if you do, there must be some curious mistake, a misapprehension, quite natural, no doubt, and quite excusable. You have to be careful of the interests of your company and all that sort of thing, but a word of explanation from me——'

' I desire no explanations,' said Deissmann, with increased stiffness of manner. ' I merely request that you go away at once.'

He may not have desired explanations, but if he had been better acquainted with Meldon he would have known that he was sure to get them.

' I hope you don't think,' said Meldon, ' that the Major and I have any idea of interfering with your work, diverting the course of the Shannon, or anything like that. I could quite understand your attitude if you've got that into your head. But— Come now, my dear Deissmann, do be reasonable. The Shannon is a large river, the largest in the British Isles. It's more like the Rhine than the Thames. Could one man—the Major isn't going into the water. I'm the only one who means to do that. Could one man with nothing but his hands do anything serious to the Rhine ? You know he couldn't. Well, he couldn't to the Shannon either. You see that, don't you ? Surely you must see that.'

Deissmann may have seen that. He probably did. But his determination remained unchanged. He stood up stiffly with a fixed and glassy look in his eyes.

' Come along, J. J.,' said the Major. ' What's the use of standing here arguing ? '

' I'm not arguing,' said Meldon. ' I'm trying to clear away a misapprehension. Dr. Deissmann may perhaps think that we're spying into his business, trying to learn the carefully guarded secrets of his firm. I quite understand his objecting to that. It isn't everybody who knows how to get electricity out of a river, and naturally the man who does know doesn't like outsiders prying round discovering how the thing's done. That's your idea, I expect, Deissmann ? But it's quite mistaken. Neither the Major nor I know the first thing about electricity. We shouldn't be a bit the wiser about how it's got if we saw you getting it, and you're not as far as that yet. The Major's an analytical chemist, which shows that he's a scientific man, and that makes you suspicious of him. But what you forget is that all first-rate men of science nowadays— and the Major is that if he's anything—must be specialists. A specialist may or may not know his own subject. The only thing quite certain about him is that he doesn't know any other. Take an astronomer, for instance. He specializes in comets. Does he know anything about aniline dyes ? Of course not. You don't expect him to. He'd simply gape at you if you talked to him about synthetic indigo. Well, that's the Major's position exactly. So long as he's analysing chemicals he's all right. But electricity is entirely out of his line. You might hand him a volt or an ampère and give him a magnifying glass to study it with. He wouldn't have the remotest idea what it was. And you needn't be the least nervous about me. I'm a man of wide general education. There's no use my denying that for you can see it for yourself. But oddly enough I know nothing about electricity. I've always intended to take the subject up ; but somehow I never have. Besides—I hope I need not add that if we did light on a secret process or a formula or a new insulation and understood it, which as I say we shouldn't, nothing would induce us to talk about it. Major, tell Deissman that you don't know what an erg is.'

' A what, J. J. ? '

' Did you ever hear of an erg, outside of a cross-word puzzle ? '

' Do come away, J. J.,' said the Major. ' I hate standing here. If he won't let you grub about in the river, he won't. And I'm rather glad. I thought this was a silly expedition before I started, and since I've been over here I hate the whole thing.'

' Now then, Deissmann,' said Meldon. ' I've explained to you that I don't want to do any harm to the
river, and couldn't if I did want to. I've assured you,
and the Major 's assured you, that we don't either of us
know anything about electricity and so can't discover
your trade secrets. What possible objection can you
have to allowing me to wade a few yards into the river ?
I'm not contemplating suicide. If you think that,
you're quite right to stop me. I can understand your
not wanting to have a damp corpse left on your hands,
especially as you're a foreigner and don't understand
the law about Coroners and inquests and that sort
of thing. But I haven't the slightest intention of
drowning myself. If you think I have, I don't mind
your tying a rope round my waist before I go in. Then
if I show the slightest sign of putting my head under
water you can haul me ashore at once.'

' I repeat my request,' said Deissmann, ' that you
leave these premises at once.'

' For goodness sake, come on, J. J.,' said the Major.

' Very well,' said Meldon. ' Deissmann's attitude
appears to me slightly unreasonable, but—I expect
you'll see that yourself, Deissmann, later on, after
lunch, perhaps. Have a bottle of beer at lunch and then
try. If you do see it and change your mind, all you
have to do is to send word to me at the hotel in
Lisnamoe. They're on the 'phone and I shall stay at
home all afternoon. I can't believe—I really cannot
believe that a man like you with a reputation for
business ability and all your immense knowledge of
ergs and volts and monads—that you can possibly
allow yourself to remain permanently the victim of
what I must call an obsession. You needn't feel any
awkwardness about ringing me up. I shan't be the

least angry or make myself unpleasant in any way. All the uncomfortable recollections of this interview will be forgotten, wiped out.'

With the Major tugging at his arm, Meldon went back to where the car was waiting.

' Jimmy,' he said, ' that silly ass of a pragmatical German won't let me set foot inside what he calls his premises. Do you think you could manage to slip round by some back way, out of sight, and tell Michael Gannon I want to see him as soon as possible.'

Jimmy saw no difficulty about doing this. He did not even make any attempt at secrecy. He walked through the yard, through the shrubbery and towards the river until he found Michael Gannon.

' J. J.,' said the Major suspiciously, ' what do you want Michael Gannon for ? '

' Gannon,' said Meldon, ' asked my help this morning, my help and advice. I never refuse a request like that. I regard it as my duty to do what I can for other people, always. But I do not regard it as my duty to tell everybody else the private affairs of those I am helping. I haven't mentioned your candlesticks to Gannon, and I'm not going to mention Gannon's little troubles to you.'

' I don't want you to, J. J. It wouldn't interest me in the least if you did. All I want you to do is to drop this ridiculous business and come home.'

' If you mean to suggest that I should abandon the search for the candlesticks, I may tell you at once that I won't. I never abandon any enterprise. Once I've taken a thing on I invariably see it through. That's the right spirit, and if you had more of it you'd be a better man than you are. History is full of examples of what I mean. Would that fellow who sprinted from

Marathon to Sparta ever have got there if he'd lain down and gasped directly he got out of breath ? He would not. What he did—and it was quite the right thing—was to keep going till he got his second wind. After that he trotted on without any particular difficulty. Think of him, Major. Or if you don't know any Greek history, think of Henry VIII. Would he ever have succeeded in getting a really satisfactory wife if he had been daunted by the difficulty of getting rid of the first two or three ? And there were difficulties. Cardinal Wolsey and the Pope, men, I imagine, very like Deissmann. But did King Henry give up ? He did not. He kept pegging away. A great example to you, Major. Think of that spider of Robert Bruce's. Would that insect be in every history book, as it is, if it had crept back into its hole and sulked the first time its web was broken ? No, it wouldn't. It's the most famous insect in history or literature, far more famous than Dr. Watts' bee, or the ant in the Book of Proverbs, simply because it refused to give in. Difficulties, Major, exist in order that we may overcome them. That's a great moral principle which has been stated, generally in those exact words, by hundreds and hundreds of bishops, when they were trying to raise funds to pay for more curates. It's too much, perhaps, to expect you to read history. But you ought to listen to bishops more attentively than you do.'

' I don't believe any bishop would approve of the way you go on J. J. No bishop could. You told that German that I'm an analytical chemist, whatever that is. You told the girl in the hotel——'

' If it's any comfort to you, Major, we shall now be able to drop the analytical chemist story. I only told it to please Deissmann, but he's showing such a thoroughly nasty, cantankerous, and captious spirit that I don't feel the least inclined to go out of my way in order to gratify him any more.   Of course I quite admit that we ought to go on being kind to people after they've ill-treated us.   That's a Christian principle, and I'd be the very last man to go back on it.   All the same—   Well, you may talk of bishops disapproving of me, but I don't believe that any bishop—I don't believe that an archbishop, would object to my dropping that analytical chemist story after the way Deissmann behaved just now.'

' A bishop wouldn't in the least object to your dropping it,' said the Major.   ' He'd be glad, I should think.   What he would object to is your telling it in the first instance.   Any bishop I ever met would say it is wrong to tell deliberate falsehoods in the way you do.'

' Why drag in the poor bishops ? ' said Meldon. ' Surely they've troubles enough of their own without being bothered with your petty affairs.   Think of the fellows who will stick up pyxes where they oughtn't to be.   Think of the fellows who can't say a simple thing like the Apostles' Creed without telling every one they don't believe it.   Horse flies every one of them, settling on bishops and exasperating them.   And then, as if that wasn't enough, you expect—   It's utterly unreasonable and selfish of you, Major, to expect a bishop to come to a place like this just to look after your wretched conscience.   Suppose you were a Presbyterian.   Then you wouldn't have a bishop at your beck and call, and you wouldn't be able to complain that there wasn't one waiting on you in Lisnamoe.'

' The last thing in the world I want,' said the Major ' is to have a bishop mixed up with this business.'

' Very well.   If you don't want a bishop don't go or

whining because you haven't got one. I wonder what
Jimmy is doing ? He could have given that message
of mine to Gannon and been back here hours ago if
he'd really tried. But people will dawdle. That's the
cause of half the trouble in the world. Deissmann
wouldn't have been half as bad-tempered as he was if
you'd hurried up over your breakfast and kept your
appointment punctually. And now Jimmy is behaving
in exactly the same way.'

But Jimmy did not deserve this censure. He had
delivered the message promptly and Gannon was quite
willing to go to Meldon at once. Unfortunately he had
to wait until Deissmann, who was making a round of
that part of the works, had gone elsewhere. As soon
as the way was clear he followed Jimmy to the car.

CHAPTER XI

'I THINK, Major,' said Meldon, 'that you'd better drive straight back to the hotel. I must have a talk with Michael Gannon, and that may take some time. Like all these fellows Gannon is garrulous. Now, don't say you're not, Gannon, when you know you are. You never will be content with saying anything in five words if you can spread it out over fifty. A tiresome habit, but there's no reason why the Major should suffer. Send the car back for me in about an hour.'

'I'd rather stay here,' said the Major. 'I'm afraid to leave you, J. J.'

'You needn't be. Gannon burnt down your house, I know, and more or less threatened to shoot you; but that's all over and done with now. He won't do me any harm.'

'I will not,' said Gannon stoutly.

'I wasn't thinking of you, J. J., I was thinking of myself.'

'That's what you're always doing,' said Meldon, 'though you know it's wrong.'

'If I leave you with Gannon,' said the Major, 'you'll plot some fresh complication and involve me in it. I can't help that, I know, but I'd rather like to know what it is before it happens. I hate being dragged blindfold into the sort of things you do.'

Meldon took him by the shoulders and pushed him into the car, in the kindliest way but with decision.

' I give you my word of honour, Major, not to involve you in any plan of Gannon's.   But you can't stay here and listen to what he's going to say to me.   I don't see how you can expect that.   Gannon's private affairs are just as private as yours are.   Try and remember that.'

He nodded to Jimmy, who started the car.   The Major, still protesting, was driven away.

' Now, Gannon,' said Meldon, ' I've been thinking over that strike plan of yours, and I'm inclined to regard it as sound.   How many strikes have you had since these works began ? '

' Ne'er a one,' said Gannon.   ' There hasn't been a thing of the kind in the locality since the Lord knows when.   Though there's been talk.   Nobody would deny that there's been plenty of talk.'

' Then it's quite time you did something more than talk,' said Meldon.   ' I'm surprised you haven't done it before.'

' There was talk of getting up some sort of a strike last May,' said Gannon.   ' But there was some who were opposed to it.   And I needn't tell you, Mr. Meldon, that unless everybody's unanimous——'

' Quite so,' said Meldon.   ' But do you think they'd be any more unanimous now ? '

' They would, for they'd be afraid of their lives not to be if it was done in the name of the Irish Republic. I'm speaking plain and straight to you now, Mr Meldon.   That's what we want the Major's name for. Him being a General or the like, there isn't one but would strike if the Major was to sign the notice.'

' I told you this morning that the Major won't

You heard what he said to me just now. "Don't you go trying to mix me up in any of that blackguard Michael Gannon's beastly plots." That's what he said, or words to that effect. You heard him.'

' I did,' said Gannon sadly, ' but I thought you'd be able to persuade him.'

' Nobody,' said Meldon, ' could possibly persuade the Major to sign a strike notice ?'

' It's a pity, so it is,' said Gannon, ' for without the Major's name——'

' I was saying to the Major just now that difficulties exist in order to be overcome, and it's always a pleasure to me to overcome them, especially in a good cause. And this cause of yours is thoroughly good. If ever a man deserved a strike it's that fellow Deissmann. He was positively insolent to me this morning, and treated the poor inoffensive Major like mud meant to be trampled on. That's why I say that your strike is an excellent thing. And I'm prepared to help you in any way I can.'

' If you can persuade the Major——

' No. I can't do that. I'm ready to overcome difficulties because I happen to be a man of unusual courage and resource ; but I'm also a man of common sense and I never fly in the face of impossibilities.'

' Maybe,' said Gannon hopefully, ' you wouldn't mind signing the Major's name for him, unbeknown to him, of course. It would do him no harm, for he wouldn't know a thing about it, and it would be just as good to us as if he'd signed it himself.'

' What you're suggesting now,' said Meldon, ' is forgery, and that's a thing I never do. I'm a clergyman and bound to be more particular about my morals than other people are ; but even if I wasn't a clergyman I should draw the line at deliberately forging a friend's name to an important document. I'd just as soon pick his pocket or burn down his house. So you may put that idea out of your head at once.'

' If the Major won't sign his own name and you won't sign for him, I don't see how it's going to be signed at all, so if that's all the help you're going to give us——'

' How many people in this neighbourhood know Irish really well ? '

'There's ne'er a one knows it at all, without it might be the schoolmaster, who has to be teaching it to the children every day. And I wouldn't say he knew too much. He didn't know a word of it six months ago before the law was made that he had to be teaching it.'

' He can't have learnt a great deal in six months.'

' If he's learnt to spell his own name in it,' said Gannon, ' it's as much as he has learned. And it wouldn't surprise me if any one was to tell me that he wasn't too sure about that.'

' Spelling names,' said Meldon, ' is one of the most difficult things about that language. I'm told that the very best scholars are bothered a bit where they come across their own names spelled in Irish where they're not expecting them.'

Gannon was uninterested in the Irish spelling of proper names. He went on to justify his attitude towards the Gaelic Revival, a thing which no one who takes part in public life in Ireland can afford to ignore or belittle.

' Mind now,' he said. ' I'm in favour of the Irish language myself, and always was. It's a thing that anybody who calls himself an Irishman ought to be in favour of, and if any one was to say to me——'

' Quite so,' said Meldon. ' I thoroughly understand

your position. You'll do anything for Irish except learn it. But to get back to what I was saying about the language just now, spelling proper names is pretty nearly the hardest thing about it. Take Kingstown, for instance : would anybody guess by looking at it that Dunlaoghaire spelled Kingstown ? Nobody would ; unless he'd a really good knowledge of the language. Or take a perfectly simple name like James. How is James spelt in Irish ? You don't know. Well, I'll tell you. It's spelled Seumas—not a single letter the same except the m in the middle and the s at the end. You see what I'm getting at, don't you, Gannon ? '

' I do not.'

' Well, suppose you saw a document headed Baile ata Cliath, would you know that it was Dublin, spelled in Irish ? You would not. Unless you knew the language really well, you'd never even guess. If you saw a paper signed Bealtain could you swear that that wasn't the way President Cosgrave spells his name in Irish ? You could not, and if any one you really trusted told you it was the Irish for Cosgrave you'd believe him. You follow me so far. Don't you ? '

' I do not,' said Gannon, ' nor I don't see what good it would be to me if I did.'

' It'll be this much good to you,' said Meldon. ' And even if you are so abnormally stupid that you can't appreciate the line of argument, you'll surely be able to grasp the practical importance of the conclusion it leads to. If I sign that strike document of yours Seoirse Caghaenghet would you be ready to deny that that was Major Kent's signature in Irish ? Of course not. Nor would anybody else in this neighbourhood, except perhaps the schoolmaster, and all he'll know, at most, is that Seoirse is the Irish for George, and it won't

matter his knowing that because he can't possibly know
that the Major's Christian name is John.   The rest of
it, the surname part, will strike him as being as likely to
be Kent in Irish as anything else.'

' I see what you're at now,' said Gannon, ' and I
wouldn't say but what it would be a good enough plan.
Only what's to hinder you signing the Major's name in
plain English, so as every one can read it, if so be that
you're willing to sign it at all ? '

' I've told you already,' said Meldon, ' that I'm not
going to commit forgery, and if I was I'd look out for
something better to forge than a silly old strike notice
of yours.   But apart from my moral principles, which
I don't expect you to share or even to understand, you
ought to realize that it's a great deal better for you to
have that document signed in Irish than in English.
What you want is to give a thoroughly patriotic tone to
your strike.   That's so, isn't it ? '

' It might,' said Gannon.

He was a quick-witted man, but he was finding it a
little difficult to follow Meldon's line of reasoning.   ' It
might ' committed him to nothing in particular, but
he hoped it might induce Meldon to go on with the
development of his plan, whatever it was.

' Very well,' said Meldon, ' which is the more patriotic
language, Irish or English ?   Irish, of course, in this
country, though English is when you're in England.
What you're aiming at in this strike is more wages.
What you want to pretend you're aiming at is the
substitution of a Gaelic civilization for the materialistic
capitalist systems prevalent in England and Germany.
Therefore—observe the force of this reasoning—the
Major's name signed in Irish would be much more
valuable to you than if it was signed in English.'

' If so be it was the Major's name,' said Gannon,
' either in Irish or English.'

' I don't see that it makes the least difference whose
name it is or whether it's anybody's name, or a name at
all. So long as everybody thinks it's the Major's name
that's all you want. And if you tell them it's his they're
sure to believe you—unless they know Irish, which you
say they don't. Now then, Gannon, stop arguing, and
trot out that proclamation of yours, the one you showed
me this morning. You've got it in your pocket, I
suppose.'

' I have,' said Gannon.

He produced it. It was dirtier and a good deal more
crumpled than when Meldon saw it in the morning, and
it had not been spotlessly clean even then.

' I don't think much of this effort of yours,' said
Meldon. ' It ought to be on a larger sheet of paper for
one thing, and there ought to be something in it somewhere about having nothing to lose except your chains.
If I'd drawn it up for you I'd have put in a lot more
capital letters. In documents of this sort every word of
any importance ought to begin with a capital. Wages,
for instance, and Work. However, we haven't time to
write it all out again now. The great thing in these
cases is speed. That's why lightning strikes are so
much more impressive than any other kind. We'll just
scratch out the word " To-morrow " and say this afternoon instead. You can start it this afternoon, I suppose.'

' To tell you the truth, Mr. Meldon, I cannot. I'd
only be deceiving you if I was to say I could. The men
wouldn't do it for me, not if the Major's name was
signed ten times over.'

' If they're willing to strike to-morrow,' said Meldon,
' they may just as well strike to-day.'

' The truth is, Mr. Meldon, ' that the wages are paid this evening, and if we was to be out on strike then, I wouldn't put it past that fellow Deissmann not to pay them at all.'

' I'm sorry,' said Meldon, ' that you allow these sordid considerations to interfere with what ought to be a purely patriotic action based on the loftiest considerations. However, to-morrow will do if to-day can't be managed. But don't let there be any mistake about it. There mustn't be a single man about the works when the strike starts.'

' There won't be,' said Gannon. ' If the Major's name is at the bottom of that notice there isn't a man in the place that would dare to go back to work.'

Meldon spread the paper out on a flat stone by the roadside, and wrote his Irish version of Major Kent's name. He used Irish letters as far as he knew them and gave an air of authority to the signature by writing ' Mise, le meas mór ' in front of it. He remembered that the words occurred in just that place in all the demands for income-tax that the Major had received.

' Now, one thing more, Gannon,' he said. ' The men aren't to go lounging about the works to-morrow. It'll spoil the whole effect of the strike if they do. It's most important that the place should be left absolutely solitary. There's nothing so impressive as complete silence following the busy hum of industry. Every paper in England noticed that during the General Strike.'

An hour later Meldon sat at luncheon with the Major in the hotel. Eileen Costello was still in a mood of awed admiration of the Major's high rank. She made a great effort over the luncheon, and she was a young woman who could cook if she chose, though she generally preferred to leave the work to another young woman who could not.

'I don't think,' said Meldon, 'that we need start quite so early to-morrow morning. Eleven o'clock would be quite time enough.'

'The train doesn't go till a quarter to one,' said the Major.

'We're not going by train,' said Meldon. 'For one thing there isn't a train to go by, and even if there was a train Jimmy's motor would be far more convenient.'

'There is a train,' said the Major, 'and we can't go all the way to Rosslare in that car. We'd never get there.'

'We're not going to Rosslare to-morrow. We may go the next day. In fact, I'm pretty confident that we shall. But to-morrow we're going to Coolarrigan.'

'What on earth for?'

'To fish those candlesticks of yours out of the river. You appear to forget that that's what we came to Ireland to do.'

'What's the use of trying again?' said the Major. 'If that German fellow wouldn't let you go near the river to-day he won't to-morrow.'

'To-morrow,' said Meldon, 'he won't be there. He'll be in his house a mile away, smoking his pipe and writing letters to the office of his firm in Germany. We shall have the place entirely to ourselves. The fact is, Major, there's going to be a strike.'

'J. J., for heaven's sake tell me the truth. I'd rather know it whatever it is. Did you promise the men that I'd make good their wages in strike pay?'

'Certainly not. You ought to know me better than to suppose that I'd let you in for a heavy financial responsibility like that without telling you about it beforehand.'

' You've let me in for worse things than financial responsibility before now.   You haven't—J. J., you can't have told them that I'm a Bolshevist agent from Russia ? '

' If you weren't so full of yourself, Major, you might be able to realize that other people aren't always thinking of you, especially when they're engaged in a serious job like striking.   You've nothing to do with this strike—nothing at all—except to reap the benefits of it.'

' There are no benefits to be reaped out of strikes,' said the Major.

' Well, to take advantage of the opportunity offered, if you prefer to put it that way.'

' What opportunity ?   The only opportunity I see is the opportunity I'm giving the income-tax people of arresting me.   If I stay here they're bound to get me. I told you that all along, and you promised we'd only be here for a day.   I should never have come—I shouldn't have come even for the sake of a hundred candlesticks if I'd known that we were going to stay for weeks.'

' Weeks !   Don't exaggerate, Major.   We've been here two days so far.   And we'll not be here more than three, unless something very unexpected happens.'

' Something very unexpected will.'

' And anyhow it'll be quite time enough to run away from the income-tax people when they show some sign of knowing that you're here.'

CHAPTER XII

MICHAEL GANNON managed his lightning strike efficiently. Not a single man appeared at the works in the morning. The lorries lay motionless and silent. Deserted wheelbarrows gave the place an air of utter desolation. The river flowed untroubled among half-driven piles and through the supports of the wooden pier. Dr. Deissmann viewed the scene with puzzled disgust. He waited for an hour in the hope of the arrival of some representatives of the men with whom he might discuss the situation. No one appeared: but just as he was getting weary of complete solitude Gannon's nine children arrived. They began an interesting game in a particularly muddy spot where the barrows had tipped their contents the day before. Deissmann at once ordered them off the premises. It was a relief to his feelings to be able to give orders to somebody. But the children were quite well aware that Deissmann's authority was in abeyance for the time. They moved from their mud-heap because Deissmann had a stick in his hand, but they did not leave the premises. They moved on to another mud-heap and began their game again. Deissmann chased them away several times with threats, but in the end he gave up a business which was plainly unprofitable, and the children played undisturbed.

Except for Gannon's strike notice, with its totally

unintelligible Irish signature, Deissmann had no information at all, or any way of accounting for what had happened. He had, like all leaders of industry, some experience of strikes, and he felt sure that a deputation of the men would wait on him. No deputation appeared, nor any sign of one. At last Deissmann—as Meldon had foreseen that he would—went back to his house. There he sat down to write and he wrote diligently.

He sent off no fewer than four reports, two telegrams, which were long, but not long enough to satisfy him, and two letters, which were very full of detail. One telegram and one letter went to Germany and were written in German. The other telegram and letter went to Dublin to an important Free State Cabinet Minister. It was cautiously worded, for Deissmann had small faith in the discretion of the post office officials who handle messages. The letter which followed this telegram was carefully sealed. It laid the whole blame of the strike on two agents of the Communist party—in Dr. Deissmann's opinion Russian spies—who had appeared suddenly in Lisnamoe, giving an account of themselves which had already been proved to be false.

If Deissmann had stayed at the works until eleven o'clock instead of going home at nine, his opinion of Major Kent and Meldon would have been confirmed, but he might have been a good deal puzzled by what they did. It is generally held that Communists, and especially Russian Communists, seldom wash, having a strong dislike for water, which they regard as a bourgeois invention. Yet the first thing that Meldon did was to wade into the river. This time there was no one to watch him except Major Kent, Jimmy Costello, and the nine Gannon children at a distance. He took off all his clothes as if he intended to swim. But he did not swim. He waded out until the water reached his waist. Then he began a thorough search of the river bed. He plunged his arms in shoulder deep, and sometimes put his head under water. He worked systematically in parallel lines, each a little nearer the bank than the last. He stirred up a good deal of mud. He picked up, from time to time, a largish stone which he immediately flung far out into the river. He did not find anything more interesting or valuable than mud and stones.

At last he came ashore, put on his shirt and trousers, sat down and lit a pipe.

' I have now,' he said, ' searched the river bed over a space of fifteen yards long, or thereabouts. It's difficult to step yards exactly when you're constantly treading on sharp stones—and five yards broad. That is to say, from a depth of water about four feet down to a depth of eighteen inches.'

' It's awfully good of you to have taken all that trouble, J. J.,' said the Major.

Meldon waved this gratitude aside.

' I have not,' he said, ' found the candlesticks. From that, it seems to me to follow that they're not there.'

' They can't be,' said the Major. ' You couldn't have missed them if they'd been there. I expect the stream has washed them down. They're probably somewhere below Limerick now, or out in the Atlantic. Anyhow it's quite impossible to find them.'

' Don't leap to conclusions in that way, Major, especially wrong conclusions. The current here isn't nearly strong enough to carry down a fishing-basket

with seven large silver candlesticks in it. Nothing
short of a mountain torrent would do that, and the
Shannon here is quite sluggish.'

' Whatever has happened to them,' said the Major,
' they're not there, so we may as well go home. Put on
the rest of your clothes, J. J.'

' What we've got to do,' said Meldon, ' is to reason
the whole thing out. You're not much good at
reasoning, Major, but I am. We start at the fact that
you dropped those candlesticks into the river.'

' Perhaps some one else found them and took them
away.'

' That theory,' said Meldon, 'we may at once dismiss
as so improbable that it may be considered impossible.
If any one had found those candlesticks it would have
been somebody like Michael Gannon. Now what
would Michael Gannon do with them if he found them ?
Sell them at once. He might not know their full value,
but he'd tumble to the idea that they were worth
something. But Paul Lamerie candlesticks, of the
second and greater period, are very rare things. There
aren't many of them in the world, and if seven of them
had been thrown on the market suddenly something
would have been heard about them. I keep a pretty
close eye on current events in the world of art, and I can
assure you, Major, that there's been no really important
sale of Paul Lamerie candlesticks for the last five years.
That, I think, disposes of your second theory.'

' That's all very well, J. J., but if they haven't been
washed away and haven't been found by any one, where
are they ? '

' That,' said Meldon, ' is precisely what I propose to
find out in the only way in which anything ever is found
out, by the exercise of reason. We start again at the

fact that you dropped or kicked them into the river. Where were you when you did that ? '

' In the boat-house,' said the Major.   ' I've told you that before.   I laid the basket down at the end of the slip and while I was launching the boat I kicked it into the water.   I should say the water was about three feet deep there.'

' Good.   Now where exactly was the boat-house ? '

' Just about where we're sitting now.'

' That's what you believe, Major.   But you're evidently mistaken.'

' I can't possibly be mistaken.   Hang it all ! it was my boat-house and I know where it was.'

' Unfortunately,' said Meldon, ' the facts are against you.   If the boat-house stood here, as you say it did, the candlesticks would have been somewhere in that area, fifteen yards by four, which I have just searched. Therefore, observe the irresistible logic of the inference —therefore, the boat-house was somewhere else.'

' I daresay the inference, as you call it, is all right. But all the same the boat-house was just where I say it was.'

' Don't be obstinate, Major.   When it's proved to you that you've made a mistake, you ought to admit it. That's the frank and manly course.   It's the course I expect you to take.   In the meanwhile let's go on with our reasoning.   The boat-house wasn't where you say it was.   Therefore it was somewhere else.   There's no getting away from that unless we believe that there never was a boat-house, and we can't believe that, for we've both seen it.   If, then, it was somewhere else, where was it ? '

' It wasn't anywhere else,' said the Major.   ' It was here.'

'You're not what I should call a careful observer, Major. Nor are you always accurate in the statements you make. Still, if you're positive that the boat-house was just here it's not likely to have been very far off. What scientific men call the margin of error is in this case fortunately small. It's unlikely, for instance, that the boat-house was as much as a hundred yards away from this spot.'

'The way you reason, as you call it, I should have expected you to end by fixing the thing somewhere on the Liffey or the Bann.'

'We may take it, therefore,' Meldon went on, 'that the actual site was a few yards from this, either upstream or downstream. The question is, which ? Fortunately, at this point nature comes to our aid. Above where we are sitting now a reef of singularly jagged rocks runs far out into the river. No one would have built a boat-house there, or if he did build it he wouldn't have used it for keeping a boat in. But you did keep a boat in your boat-house. Therefore it follows that the site is below, not above, that which you originally pointed out. If that is so, then the slip on which your boat lay was in all probability almost exactly where Deissmann's wooden pier now is, and the basket with the candlesticks in it lies among the piles which he has been driving. I claim no more than a high degree of probability for this conclusion. It's not an absolute certainty, because you may have been more wrong than I think you were in your identification of the site. The real position of the boat-house may have been fifty yards down the stream, but I do not believe, Major, that you can be as far wrong as that.'

'If the boat-house was there,' said the Major. 'It wasn't, but if it was, then the candlesticks would be sunk under that pier. If so, you may just as well give up trying to get at them.'

' I don't see why.'

' Because you can't grub about under the foundations of a pier. Why, hang it all, J. J., Deissmann has been laying down blocks of concrete. If the candlesticks are there they'll have to stay there.'

' What I propose to do,' said Meldon, ' is to remove Deissmann's pier.'

' Blow it up with gunpowder ? '

' I don't anticipate having to blow up anything,' said Meldon, ' but if it turns out that explosives are required we shall use gelignite, not gunpowder. Gelignite is the proper stuff for work of this kind. The next thing is to get hold of Michael Gannon.'

The Major gasped. His face grew very red. He gasped again, and then choked a little.

' Don't, Major,' said Meldon. ' Don't try to say what you're thinking. You'll probably get apoplexy if you do, and it's not in the least necessary for you to explain your views. I know exactly what you want to say. You think that I'm going to persuade Michael Gannon to steal some gelignite and blow up that pier. But I'm not. He'll only borrow the gelignite. And when we've got the candlesticks you shall pay Deissmann the full value of it. There's nothing the least wrong or criminal about that. In fact, I expect Deissmann would agree to let us have the gelignite for nothing if he knew that there were Paul Lamerie candlesticks under his pier. The Germans are an educated race. They appreciate the value of artistic treasures.'

The Major, while Meldon spoke, regained control of his voice.

' I don't care whether the gelignite is stolen or
borrowed—or at least I do care, of course. But that's
nothing compared to—J. J., you can't really mean to
blow up that pier, to be a dynamiter.'

' Geligniter, if anything. Be accurate if you can.
But as a matter of fact I don't think we need use any
explosive. The concrete blocks are all nearer the shore
than the candlesticks are. We shall only have to pull
down the wooden part of the pier and root up the piles.'

' The use of explosives,' said the Major, ' for wrecking
public buildings is a foul crime. Only anarchists do it.'

' Do try to think a little occasionally. If you only
would, instead of flying into a violent rage at the mere
sound of the words blow up, you'd save yourself a lot of
nervous wear and tear. Even supposing we do blow up
a concrete block or two, that's not necessarily a criminal
act. It's sometimes wrong to blow things up. I quite
admit that. Guy Fawkes, for instance, was undoubt-
edly wrong in trying to blow up the House of Commons.
But it's sometimes quite right. Take the case of a
quarry out of which people are trying to get stone. Is
it right or wrong to blast ? Right, of course, if proper
precautions are taken. And yet what is blasting
except blowing up a cliff, or a seam of coal, or whatever
it is that it happens to be. Very well. Blowing things
up with gelignite or otherwise is what's called by
moralists an action indifferent in itself. If you'd ever
studied even the elements of moral philosophy you'd
know that. Whether it's right or wrong depends partly
on what the thing is which is blown, but mainly on the
motives and intentions of the blower. Having established that principle we now proceed to apply it in this
particular case.'

' You may talk yourself hoarse, J. J., but you'll never

be able to persuade me that it's anything but wrong to hire a fellow like Michael Gannon to commit a crime.'

' What,' said Meldon, ' are we going to blow up, if we blow up anything, which I don't expect we shall ? A paltry pier. A thing which could be built again without the slightest difficulty. What are we going to get by blowing it up ? Seven Paul Lamerie candlesticks, a precious possession, things which, if lost to the world as they are at present, can never be replaced. Now I'll put it to you, Major : If it's right, as you admit it is, to blow up a small cliff for the sake of a ton or two of stone to make roads with, mustn't it be far more right——'

' What you're suggesting is plain *sabotage*, one of the worst results of the worst kind of strike, and— Oh, I do wish you'd stop arguing and come home.'

' I've not the smallest desire to argue with you, Major. I don't know any less profitable way of spending my time. But if you will accuse me of stealing gelignite and hiring desperadoes to commit a crime so bad that there's no recognized name for it, I must explain what it is that I'm really doing. Your charge against me is that I'm going to commit, or encourage Michael Gannon to commit, what our latest thinkers call an anti-social act, by which they mean an act likely to injure the people of this country ; whereas the smallest consideration ought to show you that even if I intended to blow up the whole place, concrete blocks and all, I should be doing an act which ought to be described as pro- and not anti-social. What are these works of Deissmann's for ? Why are they being carried on ? '

' I don't know and I don't care. *You* said they were to get electricity out of the Shannon.'

' That is the ostensible object, Major, which is quite

a different thing from the real object. These works are being carried out, as, according to the latest theories of economists, all works are carried out, in order to provide employment for fellows who would otherwise be unemployed. Very well. When the works are finished, what happens to those poor fellows ? They are unemployed again. Even a callous capitalist like you, Major, can hardly contemplate that with satisfaction.'

' The works never will be finished if you keep blowing them up,' said the Major.

' Exactly. You've grasped my point with most unusual quickness, Major. But if the works are never finished, then the men will always be employed, and the whole problem which is baffling our statesmen will be solved at once. There will be no more unemployment, and I, if I blow up Deissmann's concrete blocks, which I don't intend to do—will have performed an act of the very highest social usefulness. That, I think, ought to be plain to you ; so we can now go back to the point at which we started.'

' Don't,' said the Major. ' Do anything but that. I can't—I really can't bear it all again.'

' The point at which I started,' said Meldon firmly. ' What is the quickest and easiest way of getting at Michael Gannon ? '

The nine Gannon children had watched Meldon's performance in the river with deep interest. The way he plunged his arms and shoulders into the water, the great handfuls of mud which he brought up and the vigorous manner in which he flung stones about, convinced them that, though plainly a grown-up man, he must have the heart of a child. They thought that he would be an agreeable man to know. They left their

own game and came cautiously over to where Meldon
and the Major were. They hoped to be invited to join
in what was evidently a very superior kind of mud and
water game.

The appearance of the Major made them hesitate a
little. With the unfailing instinct of children they
knew that he was not the sort of man who would enjoy
a really good game. But the attraction of Meldon was
stronger than their fear of the Major. They arrived
and gathered in a little group just as Meldon inquired
the second time how best to get at Michael Gannon.

' I shouldn't wonder,' said the Major, ' if those were
his children. Nobody else's would be so dirty.'

Meldon turned to them.

' Where 's your da ? ' he asked.

It was the eldest girl who answered him.

' He 's beyond.'

Her brother, a year younger, frankly contradicted
her.

' He is not,' he said, ' but within.'

' It was down west along the road he was going,'
said a third child.

' Beyond, within, or down west,' said Meldon, ' I
suppose you know where to find him ? '

' We do, of course,' said the children, all nine of
them speaking at once.

' Major,' said Meldon, ' give those children a penny
each, or a sixpence and a threepenny bit will do if
you haven't got coppers enough.'

' Now,' he went on, when the Major had given the
money, ' go and find your da and tell him I want to
speak to him at once.'

CHAPTER XIII

PETER JAMESON sat by the smoking-room fire of his club in Dublin. His friends—as in the case of the Patriarch Job there were three of them—gathered round him sympathetically, because they saw that he was in trouble. They meant to comfort him as soon as they knew what his trouble was. That was not easy to guess, for Peter Jameson was an unusually fortunate young man. He had a comfortable post in a Government office, a post of some distinction with a good salary attached to it. That ought to have placed him beyond the range of the slings and arrows of fortune, however outrageous. He was widely popular, possessing many friends, as well as the three who gathered round him in the smoking-room. It was generally believed that he was engaged to be married to an heiress who owned an hotel somewhere in the south, an attractive girl whom any one might have been pleased to marry even if she had not been an heiress. Peter Jameson denied that he was actually engaged, saying that Eileen Costello was no more to him than just a cousin. That made every one certain that the date of the marriage was fixed. He also said that her fortune was nothing very great, which led to the belief that the hotel was immensely valuable. Nobody doubted for a moment that Eileen owned it.

E

With so many gifts of fortune and so little to
complain about it was hard to see why Peter Jameson
should have been depressed. Yet he certainly was.
His three friends, acting precisely as Job's did, sat
round in silence, waiting for Peter to open his grief
to them.

' Did you hear about the strike down in Lisnamoe ? '
he said at last.

' I did not,' said Miller.

He took the place of Eliphaz, the leader of Job's
three comforters.

Thompson and Jacobs had not heard of it either,
and said so. They might have been called Bildad
and Zophar.

' Well, there is one,' said Peter.

' I wouldn't wonder,' said Miller. ' Strikes is
plenty, eveywhere.'

' That's where the Shannon works is going on,'
said Thompson.

' Well,' said Jacobs philosophically, ' let them strike
if it pleases them.   What harm ? '

' There'd be no harm, none in the earthly world,'
said Peter, ' only that they're sending me down to
see what's up.'

To such desperate actions even staid Government
Departments are driven when harassed by letters
and telegrams. Deissmann had telegraphed and
written, enclosing a copy of Michael Gannon's strike
notice with the Irish signature at the bottom. The
directors of the firm in Hamburg had telegraphed,
at great length, and they too had sent the signature,
slightly mangled in transmission. The London representative of the German firm had telegraphed, urging
the immediate arrest of Caghaenghet. His version of

the name differed from the other two, but there was
no doubt that the same name was meant by all.

The responsible head of affairs in Dublin, in order
to ward off a further shower of telegrams, ordered
Peter Jameson, a young man of whom he thought
highly, to go down to Lisnamoe and find out what
was happening. All expenses were, of course, to
be paid on a lavish scale and Peter was given the
title of ' Special Commissioner.'

Miller, Thompson and Jacobs looked at each other
in some surprise. They did not yet see why Peter
was in need of comfort. Any one of them would
gladly have accepted the Special Commissionership.

' Isn't it in Lisnamoe that Miss Costello does be
living ? ' said Miller who knew all about Peter's affairs.

' It could be,' said Thompson, ' that there's been
a falling-out between them.'

The suggestion was a plausible explanation of Peter's
depression. If he and Miss Costello had quarrelled he
would feel an awkwardness about going to Lisnamoe,
especially as he would have to stay in her hotel when
there.

' There's been no falling out,' said Peter.

' Then,' said Thompson, a little annoyed because his
guess was wrong, ' what's at you that you don't want
to be going there ? '

By way of reply Peter drew from his pocket a copy
of Michael Gannon's strike proclamation. It had been
made for him by one of the typists in the office and
she had printed the signature in red. It seemed to
her the most important, as it was certainly the most
striking, part of the document. The colour attracted
Thompson's attention at once. He stared at the
name before reading the proclamation itself.

'It looks as if it might be Irish,' he said.

'It is Irish,' said Peter. 'What else could it be?'

With its two aspirated g's and its superabundance of vowels it could not very well belong to any other language.

'It's some fellow's name,' said Thompson in a hopeful tone.

'Any fool could see that,' said Peter. 'But whose name is it?'

'I don't know that I could say whose name it is,' said Thompson. 'Let you have a try at it, Miller.'

Miller took the paper and scrutinized it. Jacobs, deeply interested, peered at it over Miller's shoulder.

'Well,' said Jacobs at last, 'I thought I knew all of them ones, the names of them anyhow, but I'm bothered if I ever heard of that one. Who is he?'

'He's a stranger to me,' said Miller.

'Maybe now,' said Jacobs, 'we'd be able to guess who he is if you'd read the name out loud the way it would be pronounced if any one was fool enough to be wanting to say it.'

Miller began boldly enough:

'Seoirse,' he said.

Then his confidence vanished. After several attempts he was obliged to confess that he could not pronounce Caghaenghet.

'I can't do it,' he said feebly.

'Can't you now?' said Peter. 'Well now, that's queer, for you've always had the name of being good at the Irish.'

Miller, who had passed six examinations in Irish, deserved his reputation, but Meldon's version of Major Kent's name defeated him. If it had been possible to suspect an earnest Republican of making a joke, he might have thought that the tangle of gh's was a trick of some light-hearted humorist. But, as Miller knew very well, a joke is now as rare as divorce in southern Ireland and just as liable to public denunciation.

It was impossible to suppose that the signature of the proclamation was anything but what it seemed to be, the Gaelicized form of the name of a Republican leader.

' Anyhow, you're not the only one in the world that can't read it,' said Peter. 'It had everyone in the office beat. And mind you, there's some there that knows Irish, middling well. But they couldn't say for certain what that thing was—only one fellow, and he said it might be Murphy, but he wasn't what you'd call sure.'

' Murphy ! ' said Miller.

' It might be Murphy,' said Jacobs, ' though it doesn't look like it.'

' If it's Con Murphy—if it's Red Con Murphy—' said Thompson and then stopped abruptly.

His pause and the tone in which the other two spoke were full of deep meaning. Caghaenghet was strange to them. Murphy was a name which they knew well and regarded with a feeling which was perhaps respect, more probably fear. Abject terror —and no one was reduced to that—would have been excusable when the name of Red Con Murphy was mentioned.

The Irish, alone among European nations, understand the art of being governed. All peoples want the same thing, to be allowed to live their lives quietly without being worried and harassed. Most peoples, the English especially, believe that they will attain peace by patiently and uncomplainingly obeying the laws imposed on them by their Governments. The Irish alone have grasped the fact that obedience to existing laws is simply an invitation to Governments to make more. A Government must do something. If it did not it would proclaim its worthlessness. Therefore, any Government which finds that its subjects obey laws quietly is forced to make more and still more laws, until at last—England is the most striking example of this—all hope of peace and quietness vanishes. The wise Irish realize that if a Government is kept occupied it will neither have time nor inclination for making tiresome and worrying laws. Therefore, the Irish always maintain a few men whose whole energies are directed to breaking the simplest and most fundamental laws, like that which forbids murder, for instance. The Government is kept busy in suppressing these desperadoes. It realizes that there is no use making new laws until the old ones are more or less observed. Thus the Irish people escape the fate which has overwhelmed everyone else in Europe.

It is, of course, inconvenient to have murderers and brigands at large. But it is on the whole less inconvenient than it is to be harried with vexatious laws which daily increase in number. That is why popular sympathy in Ireland always supports murderers. Their existence is the less of two evils.

In 1924, when Major Kent and Meldon came to Lisnamoe, Con Murphy was the best known and most influential of these outlaws. His reckless daring had become proverbial all over the country, and his way of dealing with those who threatened him was drastic.

He had—so it was generally understood—killed more of his political opponents than any man then alive in Ireland.

'If it's Red Con,' said Thompson again, 'well, if it's Red Con Murphy, all I can say is I'd sooner it was you than me that was going to Lisnamoe.'

'I wouldn't be going out of my way to interfere with that one,' said Jacobs. 'If he wants a strike, let him have a strike. That's what I say.'

'I'll not be interfering with him at all,' said Peter. 'You may bet your life on that. What I'm afraid of is that he might be interfering with me.'

It was Miller who spoke the first word of real comfort, and even it was not very cheering.

'I don't see how the name on that paper can be Murphy,' he said, 'considering it begins with C.A. You couldn't begin Murphy with a C, no matter what language you wrote it in.'

'You might in Irish,' said Peter, refusing to be comforted.

'The last I heard of Red Con,' said Thompson, 'he was up in Donegal, having rows with the Custom-house officers over a motor bike that he bought second hand in Derry and wanted to bring over the border into Dunfanaghy. If that's what he's at he can't be starting strikes down in Cork.'

'It's not in Cork the strike is,' said Peter. 'It's in Lisnamoe.'

'Well, he couldn't be there either. If he's in Dunfanaghy he couldn't be in Lisnamoe.'

This was well-meant encouragement but not convincing. Con Murphy, having defeated the Custom-house officers in the battle about the motor bicycle, might very well have used it to travel to Lisnamoe.

'Them ones,' said Peter, 'wouldn't go on strike the way they have, without it was Red Con that told them to. There's been letters and telegrams coming into the office all day about this damned strike. I tell you it's the real thing this time. Every man jack of them has cleared off the works without so much as asking whether they were to get more wages or not. And them fellows was well enough satisfied with what they had. The most of them was, anyhow. Though I'm not denying there might be one or another that would be willing to raise trouble if he could. But most of them wouldn't have gone on strike without it was Red Con that told them to.'

'It might have been some other one, not Red Con,' said Thompson.

'It could not,' said Peter, 'for there's no other one could put the fear of God into them that way, only Red Con.'

'You couldn't spell Murphy like that,' said Miller, 'C.A.G.H. . . .'

'You could if you tried,' said Peter. 'You could spell it or any other name that way in Irish if you was to give your mind to it.'

'Well, if you did,' said Miller, 'how would the men know it was meant for Murphy? I didn't know, and I'm as good as most men at the Irish. They didn't know down in your office.'

'There was one fellow did,' said Peter, 'though he wasn't overly sure about it.'

'Well, if I didn't know,' said Miller, 'and the rest of them in your office didn't know, how do you suppose that a lot of ignorant bosthoons down in Clare, or Limerick, or wherever the place is, would know what them letters stand for? And if they didn't know that it was Murphy's name that was there, would they strike ? '

It was a good point and well made. A signature is not of much value on a cheque or a warrant or a proclamation unless it is possible to be sure whose it is. But Peter, though a little reassured, was by no means confident.

' They'd have known right enough if they'd been told,' he said. ' And there's plenty would tell them. Murphy would tell them quick enough if he wanted them to know.'

' It's my belief,' said Jacobs, ' that if it was Murphy he'd have done more than call a strike. I'm not saying this to pacify you, Peter. I'm saying it because it's true. Nobody ever knew Red Con Murphy do anything that didn't have more to it than just a strike. Believe you me, it's not him at all, but some other one, and there's no need for you to be timorous.'

' He may do more yet,' said Peter. ' It could be that the strike is only the beginning and the next thing he does will be more. I wish to God they'd send anybody else down there in the place of me.'

' It'll suit you best to keep quiet when you get there,' said Thompson, ' supposing it's Red Con that's in it.'

' If it hadn't been for them Germans in Hamburg raising Cain the way they have,' said Peter petulantly, ' there'd have been nobody sent at all, neither me nor any other one.'

' Germans is the devil,' said Thompson, ' and that's a fact. But I wouldn't be inclined to be altogether too fretful, Peter. I knew Con Murphy one time and he was a decent sort of a lad enough, not one to be doing any harm to a man that wasn't thinking of trying to do some harm to him. The thing for you to do is to keep your mouth shut, and not to be writing letters about what's going on.'

'Sure, how can I help writing letters,' said Peter, 'when it's that I'm sent there to do? I'm a commissioner, so they tell me, and what's a commissioner for if it isn't to write letters?'

'If it turns out that it's not Con Murphy after all,' said Thompson.

'And it isn't,' said Miller, 'for you couldn't spell his name that way.'

'If it isn't,' said Jacobs, 'you can write what letters you like. But if it is, the best of your play will be to write one letter and no more, just to say that there isn't a strike and never was. That'll please Murphy, and if the Germans don't like it let them send some fellow of their own to conduct the negotiations. Con Murphy can do what he likes to him, and what harm? Them fellows has no friends.'

'It's to-morrow morning I have to go,' said Peter sadly.

'And it is the day after that you'll come home,' said Jacobs, 'if you do what I tell you and write the letter I'm after suggesting. Where'd be the use of your staying there, wasting the taxpayer's money on hotel bills, when there's no strike in it?'

The plan struck Peter as possible and even hopeful. He became mildly cheerful and went to bed in a good temper.

His train left Dublin next day at eleven o'clock. He was on the platform in good time and secured a comfortable corner in a first class compartment. He felt that the danger he dreaded might be avoided. It was just possible—so buoyant were his spirits that he felt this—that Con Murphy might not be in Lisnamoe at all.

Then, just before the train started, Miss Rooney, one of the typists in the office, came hurrying along the platform. She had a telegram in her hand, a telegram which had been opened, which no one had taken the trouble to put back into its envelope.

' It came to the office half an hour ago,' she said to Peter, rather breathlessly, ' and they bid me hurry the way you'd have it before you started.'

With a cold premonition of disaster Peter read the message.

' Report total destruction of works and plant during the night.   Dam blown up.   Pier and piles destroyed. Lorries burnt.   Light lines for trucks torn up.   Prompt action necessary.'

' The Lord save us,' said Peter.   ' I'm done now ! '

CHAPTER XIV

MICHAEL GANNON, with eight willing helpers, spent a laborious but delightful night. Deissmann's store of explosives was kept in a small building a little apart from the rest of the works. The door was locked, but there was not the slightest difficulty in breaking it down. The quantity of explosives found inside was entirely satisfactory to Michael. There were several hundred gallons of petrol in another shed. Coolarrigan is a long way from any regular supply station, and Deissmann had eight or ten lorries in constant use, so he kept a good supply of petrol. There were several large piles of wood, cut up ready for use in the construction of the dam. There were ten tons, or perhaps a little more, of excellent coal. Never in all his experience of works of arson had Michael Gannon been so well supplied with material. He was in a position to do his work thoroughly and he did not waste his opportunity.

Five huge bonfires were lit at about three a.m. They were lit in convenient places, so that everything movable, lorries, barrows and trucks, could be put into them. The explosions began half an hour later, and went off with most satisfactory bangs until after four o'clock. Gannon and his friends took refuge at some distance from the scene and lay safe in a ditch till nearly five o'clock. By that time there was not a single charge of explosive which had not gone off.   The fires had burned themselves out into piles of glowing ash.   There was nothing left unconsumed except some twisted scraps of iron.   Gannon sent his helpers home to bed.   He himself rode off on his bicycle to Lisnamoe. He felt it his duty to report his success to Meldon without delay.

He reached the hotel shortly after six o'clock, and succeeded, with some difficulty, in rousing Jimmy Costello.   He had less difficulty in waking Meldon, who slept lightly, and came into full possession of his faculties as soon as his eyes were open.

' I have it done,' said Gannon.

' Pier completely cleared away ? ' said Meldon. ' And the piles ? '

' Gone,' said Gannon.   ' And whatever else was in the place is gone along with them.'

He spoke with such obvious pride that Meldon felt a little uneasy.

' Do you mean to say,' he said, ' that you've destroyed the sheds and lorries and things ? '

' Damn the scrap of anything that 's left,' said Gannon proudly.

Meldon got out of bed and began to dress.

' That 's the worst of you, Michael.   You will run into extremes.   If you'd only read the works of the philosopher Solon, one of the wisest men who ever lived—in fact, for downright common sense, almost—I say almost, not quite—for I don't want to be accused of disparaging the Bible—almost equal to Solomon. If you'd read him—and it 's not necessary to know Greek. There are English translations of his two best-known remarks.   If you'd read him, or even listened to other people when they told you about him, you'd know that his great rule for the conduct of life is this : " Don't overdo things." What you think, what nearly everybody thinks who hasn't read Solon, is that if a little of a thing is good—which is true about almost everything —a lot of the same thing must be better, which isn't true at all. As a matter of fact, Solomon, whom you must have heard of even if you know nothing about Solon, says the same thing when speaking about eating honey.'

' It would fail you to eat honey here,' said Gannon, ' for all the bees died of the disease two years ago.'

' The principle of the thing,' said Meldon, ' as laid down by Solon and Solomon, is exactly the same whether bees get diseases or not. The fellow who gorges himself with honey, shovelling the stuff down his throat in tablespoonsful, is simply sick and gets no pleasure out of it at all, whereas—I am now telling you what Solomon says—Solon put it much shorter. In fact, he got it all boiled down into two words, Greek words, of course, which it's no use repeating to you, though I will if you like—whereas—I'm going back to Solomon now—whereas if he'd been content with a moderate helping and spread that on bread and butter, he'd have got a great deal of pleasure out of it without the slightest ill-results. If, as I began by saying, you had listened to what Solon and Solomon had to say——'

Meldon, who dressed rapidly and did not waste time in washing, was buttoning his waistcoat, and felt that he had not time to finish his lecture properly.

' If you'd imbibed the philosophy of Solon—or Solomon,' he said hurriedly, ' you wouldn't have gone burning lorries and huts when the only thing you were asked to do was to root up a pier. However, it's done now, so there's no use grumbling about it. Only in future, Gannon, do try to recollect that moderation is a virtue, one of the seven principal virtues as laid down by the Church, for that's the real meaning of Temperantia, or Temperance. Come on.'

' Come on where ? ' said Gannon.

He feared that if he stayed longer in Meldon's company he might find himself let in for another lecture —this time on temperance. He had distinctly heard Meldon use the word, and if there was anything that he really hated, it was the use of abusive language about whisky.

' To the works, of course,' said Meldon, ' but you needn't come if you don't want to. I'll get Jimmy to drive me, or if I can't get him I'll start up his car and drive myself.'

' I was thinking,' said Gannon, a little sulkily, ' that it might be as well if I was to go home to my bed. I was up the whole of the night, so I was, and sleep is what a man wants some of, now and again, sleep and a drop of drink. That fellow Solon, or whatever his name is, may say what he likes, but a man is the better of a drink after a night the like of what I've had.'

The word temperance was still rankling in his mind, lingering there like a bad taste in the mouth after swallowing a spoonful of medicine.

' If you can succeed in waking up Eileen,' said Meldon, ' you may tell her to give you whatever you like to drink and charge it to the Major's account. I suppose you'd rather do that than be driven by me in Jimmy's car.'

' I would.'

' Then you'll have to cycle home,' said Meldon, ' for I won't wait for you. Anyhow you can't be in any particular hurry about getting to sleep. In fact, I don't see what you want to sleep for at all at this time of day. And that reminds me that I must speak to the Major before I start. He's asleep. Sure to be. And he'll hate to be wakened. He always does. What a time you and he must have had when you lived together! I suppose you both slept day and night, summer and winter.'

' We did not.'

' It's all that either of you seem to care for now,' said Meldon. ' The wonder to me is that you ever woke up enough to burn his house, and that he managed to get his eyes open enough not to be burned in his bed.'

Meldon left his room, followed by Michael Gannon, who was grumbling gently. He knocked at Major Kent's door, and then, without waiting for an answer, walked in.

' Major,' he said, ' Wake up for one minute. I'm not asking you to get out of bed, for I know you wouldn't do that. But you must wake up enough to listen to what I'm going to say to you.'

The Major opened his eyes.

' I'm awake all right, J. J.,' he said.

' You're not,' said Meldon. ' You'll have to wake a great deal more than that. Excuse me one moment. I must just see if that ruffian Michael Gannon is listening outside the door. It doesn't really matter, of course, whether he's listening or not, for the matter is practically settled, and nothing he can do can stop us now. Still, there's no use letting him listen to what's no business of his—a thing he's far too fond of doing.'

Meldon wronged Michael Gannon. He was not

listening outside the door. He had gone upstairs to the top floor of the hotel and was trying to attract the attention of Eileen Costello.

' I'm quite awake now, J. J.,' said the Major, ' but I want to go to sleep again. I wish you'd say whatever you have to say and go away.'

' What I have to say,' said Meldon, ' is that in two hours or less those seven Paul Lamerie candlesticks will be in your hands again. Michael Gannon has removed that pier of Deissmann's during the night. So there's nothing to do but pick the things out of the river. I'd ask you to come and see me do it if I thought it was the slightest use. But I know it isn't. Rather than get up half an hour before your usual time you'd allow every great work of art in the world to rot to pieces at the bottom of the sea. Fortunately there are other people with a keener sense of duty. Michael Gannon, though an ignorant man who has never heard of Paul Lamerie, stayed up half the night ; and though they don't belong to me, I'm off to rescue your candlesticks.'

' All right, J. J. All right,' said the Major.

He had not the smallest expectation of ever seeing the candlesticks again and he was longing to finish his night's sleep.

Meldon banged the door of the room as he left. The Major groaned deeply, but almost immediately went to sleep again.

Jimmy Costello, once wakened by Michael Gannon, did not go to sleep again. He suspected that something exciting either had happened or was soon going to happen. He was unwilling to miss even a small sensation. He was ready to start when Meldon came downstairs. He fetched the car out of its shed, and, urged on by Meldon, made good time over the road to Coolarrigan.

'Gosh!' he said when they arrived. 'Michael's done it this time and no mistake.'

He had lived through the war between Ireland and England. He had lived through the later war between the more fervent and the less fervent Irish patriots. In both wars he had seen things destroyed. But he had never seen any destruction so devastatingly complete as that wrought by Michael Gannon on Deissmann's works.

Even Meldon was surprised, though after his talk with Gannon he should have known what to expect. But, though startled, he remained calmly intent on the business in hand.

'A few huts and lorries and things don't really matter,' he said. 'Though, mind you, Jimmy, I'm opposed to this kind of wanton destruction, and I told Gannon so. You never can tell about anything that it won't turn out to be useful in the end. Therefore we ought not to destroy it, except for a thoroughly good purpose. Any political economist will tell you the same thing if you ask him. Take, for instance, the case of Germany after the war. Lots of people wanted simply to smash it up, to wipe it out, as Michael Gannon has these huts and lorries and things. But then Keynes, who's a professor of political economy at Cambridge, came along and said— I don't believe you're listening to me, Jimmy.'

'I was not,' said Jimmy. 'I was wondering how Michael managed to make a big enough fire to burn them lorries.'

'You may go on wondering,' said Meldon. 'Stay here and wonder. Wonder till you feel a kind of gap coming in the pit of your stomach, which is what happens to people who wonder too much. By the time you've got that far I'll be back and finished what I was going to say about the professors of political economy and German reparations.'

Meldon stepped out of the car, ran past the ashes of the bonfire down to the river bank, where the pier had once stood. Jimmy, perhaps, went on wondering. But he had not time to reach the stage of discomfort in his stomach. Meldon was back with him in a couple of minutes, and when he returned he was in no mood to go on with the discussion of Mr. Keynes' theories.

'Drive me straight back to Lisnamoe,' he said, jumping into the car. 'I want to speak to Michael Gannon at once, and we're pretty sure to meet him on the road. Of all the besotted imbeciles that it has ever been my lot to come across, Michael Gannon is the worst. If I wasn't a clergyman and therefore a strong opponent of profane language, I'd say things of Michael Gannon which would make the last fifty verses of the eighth chapter of Deuteronomy taste like sugar and water.'

'He always was a bit of a lad, that one,' said Jimmy mildly.

'Bit of a lad! He's a blundering hippopotamus. He's worse. No hippopotamus would do what he's done. A herd of mad elephants wouldn't. If you were to let loose every lunatic in Europe there'd be more sense in the crowd than there is in Michael Gannon.'

'It might be,' said Jimmy, very mildly, for he was feeling a little frightened. 'It might be that he needn't have twisted up them roofs the way he did. There's many a one who might be glad of a bit of galvanized iron an odd time, if it was even as much as middling flat.'

" Roofs ! ' said Meldon.   ' He might have destroyed every roof in Munster and it would not have mattered nearly so much as what he has done.   He's blown up the entire bed of the River Shannon ! '

' The Lord save us ! ' said Jimmy, greatly startled. ' And what did he do that with ? '

' Gelignite, I suppose, or dynamite, or some infernal mixture of the two.   Anyhow, he's done it.   From the shore out to half way across, the whole bottom of the river is turned inside out.   There's rocks and stones and mud and gravel and the entire place is strewed with great chunks of concrete, nasty jagged things sticking up out of the water, and, what's worse, a few inches below the surface.'

' Them would be bits of the concrete dam they were making,' said Jimmy.

' Exactly ; and now the whole thing is blown to bits.'

' Well,' said Jimmy, ' what harm ? '

' What harm ?   You're as bad as Michael Gannon is. Don't you see that if you cover the whole bottom of the river with shattered debris it's utterly impossible to find anything that was there before ? '

' Sure there never was anything there, only stones,' said Jimmy.   ' And if anybody wants stones, aren't the ones that's in it now every bit as good as the ones that was there before ? '

Meldon realized suddenly that he had been on the verge of revealing the secret of the Major's candlesticks. He knew what the consequences of that would be. Every man in the neighbourhood would spend his leisure hours—that is to say during the strike all his hours—in dredging the river, and the Major's chances of getting back his property would be exceedingly small. He looked sharply at Jimmy to see whether his curiosity had been awakened. Jimmy was staring straight in front of him with an expressionless face. But Meldon thought it better to offer some sort of explanation of his anger at the disorganization of the river bed.

' You probably don't realize,' he said, ' the immense importance of geological strata.'

' What's them ? '

' Exactly. " What's them ? " That's your attitude towards one of the most fascinating lines of study offered to us by modern science. " What's them ? " That's just what I expected you to say. It's no doubt what Michael Gannon was thinking last night when he blew up Deissmann's concrete blocks and scattered bits of them all over the place. If he'd known what strata are— I don't say geological strata. That would perhaps be asking too much, but strata of any kind—he'd have realized that by covering the river bed all over with jagged bits and scraps of concrete he was destroying any possible chance of finding strata. River beds—I ought not to have to tell you this, and if you'd any sort of decent education I wouldn't have to. River beds are by far the best places for finding strata. They are what entomologists call the natural habitat of the best strata. Now you understand why I'm annoyed about what Michael Gannon has done.'

' I'd have thought,' said Jimmy, ' that if them things you're after, whatever you call them— —'

' Strata,' said Meldon.

' If they was chased out of this by Michael Gannon, and I don't deny but what they might be if they're any ways timorsome at all—but if they are, isn't there plenty more places for them to go to. Why wouldn't you be trying half a mile further up, if it's strata you want?'

'If you'd talk about things you understand,' said Meldon, 'and keep your mouth shut about things you don't, you wouldn't make a fool of yourself as often as you do. The strata I want, the strata I've come all this way to get, were in the particular bit of the river that Michael Gannon has blown up, and nowhere else.'

CHAPTER XV

MELDON had very nearly made a bad mistake in dwelling on the importance of the river bed when he was talking to Jimmy Costello. He had, he hoped, prevented any unfortunate consequences by his explanation of the scientific value of the strata. But he was unwilling to run any more risks. His attack on Michael Gannon, made a few minutes later, was much milder than it would have been if Gannon had been with him when he discovered the condition of the river bed. He dared not make a special point of the blowing up of the concrete blocks. All he could do was to include the explosions in a general denunciation of unnecessary destruction. Since he did not really care what had happened to the huts and lorries, he spoke without conviction and Gannon was unimpressed. He saw that Meldon was seriously annoyed about something but he could not find out exactly what. What he had heard earlier in the day about Solon's philosophy was still fresh in his mind. But he did not understand why Meldon or anybody else should be angry about that.

While Meldon talked, vaguely and without his usual incisiveness, Michael Gannon thought deeply. There came to him in the end an explanation of Meldon's urious anger. He at once became apologetic.

'Sure, I wouldn't have done it,' he said, 'if I had known you felt that way about it. I'm a Catholic. It's what I've always been and it's what I always will be, please God, but it never was said of me yet that I went out of my way to insult another man's religion. You're a Protestant, Mr. Meldon, and what I say and always did say, is that a Protestant has as good a right to his religion as what I have to mine.'

'For goodness sake, Gannon, don't drag religion into it. Things are bad enough without that.'

'It was owing to me not knowing about Solon and them ones,' said Gannon, 'that I did what I did. Why didn't you tell me before that they was Protestants? Sure, if I'd known that I wouldn't have gone against them. Only you never said a word to me about them till this morning. And it was too late then, for what was done was done the night before.'

Meldon, grasping at an elusive and fantastic idea, realized that Gannon had come to think of Solon and Solomon as saints in the calendar of the Protestant Church, to whose cult, perhaps, Meldon and the Major were specially devoted.

'Only—' Michael Gannon went on slowly— 'you'll excuse me saying it, Mr. Meldon, if it displeases you. But it's a mighty queer religion that would object to a man's blowing up a few lumps of concrete that never was any use to any one. But sure,' he added resignedly, 'I never did understand Protestants and it's not to be expected that I ever will.'

After that Meldon felt that if he gave any further expression to his feelings, he would incur the odium of attempting to undermine Michael Gannon's faith. The merest mention of Solon's 'Nothing in excess' might appear to Michael Gannon as an insidious attempt to turn him into a Protestant. Meldon was a courageous man, but he dared not risk being suspected of such an abominable act.

' Gannon,' he said sadly, ' if I mention Sir Isaac Newton to you, will you think that I'm proselytizing ? '

' Mention whoever you like,' said Gannon. ' I'm a broad-minded man and I don't care who you mention. There's some that might, but I'm not one of them.'

' Very well,' said Meldon, ' I'll repeat his words to you. ' " Diamond, Diamond," he said, " you little know what mischief you have done." Go down to the river now, Gannon, and look at the condition it's in where you blew up that dam. Then meditate on Sir Isaac's words. Don't let yourself be prejudiced by the idea that religion's mixed up in this in any way. He wasn't Saint Isaac. Get a firm grip of that. He was Sir Isaac—an extremely different thing as you'd know if you'd read what was said in the House of Lords a few years ago about these minor titles. If you meditate long enough, keeping your eye on the river all the time, you'll probably come to see in the end that although I'm not really angry, any more than Sir Isaac was, I've jolly good reason—better reason than he had —to be absolutely furious.'

He shook hands with Gannon as he spoke and then went away. Just as he was stepping into the car he turned back.

' Perhaps I ought to have mentioned,' he said, ' that Diamond was a little dog. You ought to know that, but perhaps you don't, and if you thought that Sir Isaac was addressing a tiepin or a ring, you'd miss the whole idea and never understand what he meant, which is exactly what I mean.'

Major Kent was at breakfast when Meldon reached

the hotel.   He looked up from his bacon and eggs with a friendly smile.

'Well, J. J.,' he said, 'you've got the candlesticks all right, I suppose.'

'No, I haven't,' said Meldon. 'Thanks to the amazing stupidity of Michael Gannon, I've failed. For the immediate present only. I need hardly remind you, Major, that when I undertake a thing I don't fail altogether.   The enterprise, whatever it is, may take a little longer than I expected, but in the end I invariably bring it to what is called a successful issue. That ass Gannon has acted precisely as if he was an earthquake and covered the candlesticks up with several tons of debris, concrete and stones and things of that sort.   By the way, Major, I suppose you're perfectly certain that it was just where Deissmann's pier once was that you dropped the candlesticks ? '

'I'm perfectly certain it wasn't.   I told you where the boat-house was, and it wasn't there.'

'My impression,' said Meldon, 'is that you first fixed on one place as the site of the boat-house and then, when it became clear that the candlesticks weren't there, you changed your mind and said that the boat-house was somewhere else.'

'It was you who said that.'

'There's nothing,' said Meldon, 'more unprofitable than a prolonged wrangle about what somebody says he said, when somebody else says he said something different.   As a practical man I dislike wasting time in that sort of discussion.   The thing to do now is to face the new situation, created by your latest change of mind.   You're inclined now, as I understand, to go back to your original opinion.   Very well.   You've wasted a good deal of time and you're responsible for a

good deal of unnecessary damage. Gannon, owing to
my misunderstanding of what you said—I'm putting
it that way in order to save your self-respect, though
in reality there was no misunderstanding. Couldn't
have been, for what you said was perfectly plain. But
Gannon—owing to what I agree to call a misunderstanding—has blown up the entire neighbourhood in
the most drastic manner.'

'Good heavens! J. J.! Hadn't we better bolt at
once?'

'Bolt? Certainly not. What we've got to do is:
calmly, collectedly and in the light of pure reason to
approach the problem created by the statement you
have just made. I may say at once that you have
relieved my mind a good deal. If you'd stuck to your
second opinion—the one on which Gannon acted—and
persisted in saying that the boat-house stood where
Deissmann built his pier, I should have been faced with
the task of clearing the river bed, a thing I could hardly
have done without hiring a dredger. But now that
you've gone back to your first opinion—and I give you
every credit for owning up that you were wrong. Lots
of men would have stuck obstinately to what they'd
said, but you've been honest enough not to do that.'

'Thanks, J. J. But I scarcely deserve the compli-
ment. I never changed my mind about the situation of
that boat-house.'

'As I said before, I'm not going into all that. I can
see that you want to argue; but I don't. What I
want is to get the candlesticks. And in order to do
that we must consider the facts with the utmost
accuracy and care. You have fixed the site of your
boat-house a few yards upstream from the spot where
Deissmann built his pier. Very well—a little way

from the shore—the length of the boat slip—you dropped the candlesticks—therefore——'

'Don't say they're there,' said the Major, 'for they're not. You searched the place yourself and couldn't find them.'

'Therefore,' said Meldon, 'either—I'm putting the thing as plainly as I can. Either (1) they're there still. That was the hypothesis we adopted at first, but it was proved, by actual experiment, to be untenable. We now turn to the second possible hypothesis : or (2) someone has found them and taken them away.'

'I said so all along,' said the Major. 'That's why I wanted to go away at once. In fact, that's why I didn't want to come.'

'You didn't want to come because you were afraid of being made pay your income-tax.'

'I shall have to,' said the Major, ' if you keep me here much longer.'

'Even if you do—though I don't see the smallest chance of such a thing happening. But even if you do you won't have to pay anything like the value of the candlesticks. They're worth at least a thousand pounds. Your income-tax comes to one pound, two shillings and eightpence, or some such sum.'

'Over fifty pounds.'

'Well, over fifty pounds if you like. The exact amount doesn't affect my reasoning. When you get the candlesticks you'll be, say, a thousand pounds richer than you are now. If you have to pay fifty pounds——'

'But I shan't get the candlesticks. You've just made up what you call an hypothesis to prove that somebody else has them. I don't generally think much of your hypotheses, J. J., but that one seems to be sound.'

'I'm glad to hear that,' said Meldon. 'We can now

go on with our line of reasoning, and I do hope, Major, that having admitted the soundness of the hypothesis you won't go back on it and pretend afterwards that you didn't. Assuming that somebody else found the candlesticks, we're at once forced to ask " Who ? " To that question there is only one answer, at least only one which can be regarded as at all likely to be right.'

' I should have thought,' said the Major, ' that there are as many answers as there are men, women and children in Ireland. Anybody might have found them.'

' It is of course *possible,*' said Meldon, ' that a waitress in a tea-shop in Dublin came down here on a cheap half-day excursion and happened to find the candlesticks while she was looking for the return half of her ticket, which she lost while playing Kiss-in-the-Ring with her young man. Is that the sort of thing you're trying to suggest ? '

' No, it isn't. I wouldn't suggest anything so idiotic.'

' In dealing with hypotheses the only sound rule— the rule adopted by men like Galileo in astronomy or Jenner in the discovery of smallpox—is never to accept an extremely unlikely hypothesis—I don't say idiotic, Major. That was your word—until every probable hypothesis has been exhausted. In this case we have an hypothesis so probable that it may be regarded as practically certainly true. It was Deissmann who found the candlesticks. Just consider the position calmly. Deissmann came here to fix on a site for his dam. What was the first thing he was sure to do when he arrived ? To examine the bed of the river thoroughly. Any practical engineer would be sure to do that. He rowed about, up and down, dredging as he went to find out what was at the bottom of the river, a most important thing for him to know. If there had been quicksands he'd have had to go somewhere else to build his dam. Being a conscientious and laborious man he dredged thoroughly. Therefore he found the candlesticks.'

' It's a pity you didn't think of all that before,' said the Major. ' If you had, there needn't have been that strike, or the earthquake or whatever it was you set on Gannon to do.'

' Approach the problem from a different angle,' said Meldon. ' If anyone else had found the candlesticks. If that tea-shop girl of yours had found them, what would she have done ? Posted them straight off to Christie's in a registered parcel to have them auctioned. We can scarcely doubt that. It's what any inhabitant of the British Isles would inevitably have done when he found seven Paul Lamerie candlesticks. But—note this—Deissmann is not a native of these islands. He's a German. He has never heard of Christie's and does not know how to dispose of the candlesticks. He therefore decides to keep them until he goes back to Germany and to have them auctioned there in whatever corresponds to Christie's in Berlin. Now the candlesticks have not been auctioned at Christie's. Therefore it seems to me to follow that it was Deissmann and not your tea-shop waitress who found them.'

' It doesn't seem to me to matter whether it was Deissmann or a girl. Whoever has them isn't likely to give them back.'

' We have now,' said Meldon, ' approached the problem in two entirely different ways and have reached the same conclusion by both. That is what scientific navigators call taking a cross-bearing. First they look at a lighthouse from one place and take a bearing with a prismatic compass. Then they move on a bit, look

at it from a new place and take another bearing with
the same compass. The place where the two lines
intersect is the place where the lighthouse is. That is
what's known as the science of cross-bearings.'

' I know all about cross-bearings,' said the Major.

He did. He had sailed his yacht the *Spindrift,* about
the Connaught coast for years, and, though not an
expert ocean navigator, understood how to find his
position on a chart.

' If you do,' said Meldon, ' you must appreciate the
force of the reasoning which has forced us to the
conclusion that Deissmann has the candlesticks.'

' You'd better go and get them from him, then.'

' That,' said Meldon, ' is precisely what I intend to do
next.'

' And when he denies that he has them,' said the
Major, ' I hope you'll be content to come home.'

' From what I've seen of Deissmann,' said Meldon,
I should say that he's a fairly truthful man. He
struck me as abrupt in manner, slightly wanting in
courtesy and inclined to be egotistical, that is to say, to
have too good an opinion of himself. But he did not
strike me as a liar. That kind of man seldom is. I
shall be very much surprised if he denies that he has the
candlesticks.'

' Anyhow, he'll refuse to give them up.'

' I hope,' said Meldon, ' that being a truthful man
he'll turn out to be an honest man too. I shall explain
the situation to him in detail, and——'

' If you do that,' said the Major, ' he may give them
up. In fact, I think it's likely he will. I'd give up
anything to escape one of your detailed explanations.
f he turns out to be obstinate try him with a hypothesis
or two.'

CHAPTER XVI

MELDON, whose appetite had been sharpened by his early expedition to the works, breakfasted heartily. Then he sat down and smoked a pipe in a leisurely manner. He seemed to be in no hurry about going to see Deissmann. The Major gradually became fidgety.

'Why don't you start J. J. ? ' he said. 'If you'd get your interview with that German over early we might catch the train to Rosslare. But if you hang about here all the morning we shall have to spend another night in Lisnamoe, and heaven knows I don't want that.'

'What am I going to Deissmann for? ' said Meldon. ' In other words, what is the object of my visit to him ? '

'To get the candlesticks,' said the Major. 'He hasn't got them and if he had he wouldn't give them up. But that is what you're going for, so you say, and I wish you'd start at once and get it over.'

'My task,' said Meldon, ' will obviously be easier if Deissmann is in a good temper when I call on him.'

'He won't be. He'll be in an infernally bad temper, if Michael Gannon has done half you say he has.'

'Exactly. He'll be seriously ruffled when he discovers that all his work has been destroyed and his plant burnt. But no man can remain in a furious rage for very long. The more frantic he is—and I expect

Deissmann was pretty bad at first—the sooner he will begin to calm down. Therefore the sensible thing is to wait patiently until Deissmann has had time to cool a little. That's why I'm not hurrying. Of course I could pacify Deissmann whatever sort of temper he was in, but it would take time and it might be very hard work. It's far simpler to wait till the worst of his rage blows over; in other words, to allow the laws of nature to operate of themselves instead of hurrying them up by putting in too soon. That, though doctors can seldom be got to see it, is the true basis of all medical science. It may be briefly expressed in aphoristic form by saying ' Don't operate till you've tried change of air." The principle is exactly the same in all other sciences and applies equally well to the practical affairs of life. That's why I'm waiting a bit before tackling Deissmann.'

' If you wait till Deissmann is in a good temper again,' said the Major, ' you'll probably wait months.'

' You're wrong,' said Meldon. ' Just as wrong as you always are. Four or five hours of solitude will in all probability restore Deissmann's temper to its normal condition. But rather than see you suffer from nervous agitation brought on by the kind of impatience which I can only describe as childish, I'll go at once. If you were a calmer man than you are, Major, and had more self-control, things would be easier for me. But ' A friend must bear a friend's infirmities." That's in Shakespeare, so there's no use hunting it up in Eileen's copy of Pope's poems. You'll just have to take my word for it that it's a perfectly genuine quotation and that I've got it right, or pretty nearly right.'

He knocked the ashes out of his pipe and rose.

' All the same I expect it would do you good to read

F

the Moral Essays.   Try them while I'm away.   You'll
find the Pope in my bedroom.'

He left the room and went to Eileen Costello's little
office.

' If Jimmy's anywhere about,' he said, ' tell him to
get the car round at once.'

' Jimmy was saying this minute,' said Eileen, ' that
it might be a good day for killing the pig.   I expect it's
that he's at.'

' He'll have to give up the idea of killing the pig
now,' said Meldon, ' for I want him to drive me.'

' I'll tell him ; but sure if he's half-way through with
the job——'

' I don't expect he is.   We'd have heard the pig
squealing if he'd begun.   But even if he has started
he'll have to stop.   I don't expect the pig will mind.
It's better to be half killed than not to be alive at
all.'

Eileen put her head out of the window and shouted
for Jimmy.

' I'm sorry to upset your plans in this way,' said
Meldon, ' and I'd be perfectly willing to wait till the
pig was dead if I'd only myself to consider.   But the
Major insists on my starting at once.   The fact
is——'

Jimmy's voice sounded from a distant corner of the
premises.

' What are you wanting with me now ? '

' You're to get the car round as quick as you can.
It's for Mr. Meldon it's wanted.'

' The fact is,' said Meldon, continuing his apology,
' that the Major is suffering this morning from a slight
nerve strain.   Temperament, you know.   All these
great men suffer from it.   It's what the French call the

defect of their qualities, and the Major has it this morning. I don't say badly ; but it might be as well if you looked in on him a couple of times while I'm out. Take him that copy of Pope's poems, bound in calf. It's in my bedroom somewhere. If that doesn't soothe him, try him with a little cheerful conversation. You know the kind of thing I mean. Nothing in the way of flirtation. He wouldn't like that. Just mild badinage or little anecdotes about Michael Gannon when drunk. Almost anything will do so long as you keep clear of politics and religion. But you know the sort of thing that's wanted.'

Thus Meldon, always thoughtful for others, arranged that the Major should be entertained during the morning.

Jimmy, no doubt greatly to the relief of the pig, brought the car to the door.

Deissmann was sitting at his typewriter when Meldon found him. He had already sent off six long telegrams. He was at that moment composing a detailed report of the outrage of the night before. The laws of nature may have been working on his temper, but they were working very slowly. When he looked up and saw Meldon it was quite plain that his anger had by no means evaporated. The scowl on his face was terrifying.

'Good morning,' said Meldon cheerfully. 'Nasty state your works are in to-day. However, things are not quite as bad as they might be. Every cloud has a silver lining. You ought to bear that in mind.'

Either Deissmann could not discover the silver lining or else he was unwilling to look at it. His scowl grew more threatening. He appeared to be about to speak. He was a good linguist, but in moments of tense emotion no man finds it easy to express himself in a foreign language. Deissmann hesitated.

Meldon gave him no chance of finding the words he wanted.

' They might have blown you up as well as the dam,' he said. ' And that would have been much worse than merely blowing up the dam. Michael Gannon is quite capable of it. That's the worst of him. Celtic enthusiasm, always running into extremes and that sort of thing. However, I don't think you need be uneasy now. I spoke to Gannon very seriously this morning. He won't blow up anything else for a while. I can promise you that. In fact, he can't. He used up your entire stock of gelignite in last night's explosions. Did you notice the condition of the river bed ? '

' What do you want ? ' said Deissmann.

The words do not lend themselves to utterance in a hiss which is the way Deissmann would have liked to speak them and would have spoken them in his own language in which the question begins with ' Was.' But he managed by sniffing hard to convey the idea of hissing. Meldon smiled in reply.

' The Major and I—' he said, ' The Major is so upset about this unfortunate affair that he was quite unequal to coming round to see you this morning ; but he feels just as I do, and we both want you to understand that we sympathize with you deeply. Of course it's more or less your own fault. I don't want to rub that in but I can't help just pointing out to you that if you hadn't objected to my wading into the river the day we first met all this would never have happened. Michael Gannon is an old friend of the Major's, a sort of family retainer, if you know what that means. I've forgotten the German for family retainer for the moment or I'd

tell it to you in your own language. "Anhänger," I
fancy. Anyhow, I expect "Anhänger" will convey the
idea. Somebody who hangs on. That's exactly what
Michael Gannon used to do to the Major, so naturally he
felt aggrieved when you——'

'I am busy,' said Deissmann. 'You waste my
time.'

He spoke even more fiercely than before.

'No, I don't,' said Meldon. 'It's a thing I never do.
Simply never. You don't read the poet Longfellow,
I suppose. If you did you'd remember the beautiful
line in Evangeline, or if it's not there it's in Miles
Standish. It must be in one or the other, for it's an
hexameter.

'"Count not the moments lost which are spent
in cementing affection."

Forgive my using the word cementing. I know
it must suggest painful recollections of that dam of
yours. But it's the poet's word, and I don't feel
justified in altering it. That's what I'm doing or
trying to do, so I'm not wasting time. You see my
point, don't you? Here I am full of warm feelings of
sympathy for you, and the Major is in exactly the
same state, though he hasn't come to say so——'

Meldon had boasted that, though it might be a lengthy
and troublesome business, he could talk Deissmann into
a good temper. He had not, so far, succeeded in doing
that, but he had managed to take the edge off his
violent resentment. A feeling of confusion was coming over Deissmann. He was gradually becoming
bewildered rather than furious.

'If you've anything to say to me, say it, please.'

' I am saying it,' said Meldon. ' I've been saying it all along. But I'll begin again if you like. The Major and I—but tell me first, have you thoroughly grasped the meaning of that line of Longfellow's? Everything turns on that, and you won't be able to understand what I'm at, no matter how often I say it, unless you realize—" cementing affection." That's the central idea. Got it ? '

' Have you any business with me at all?' said Deissmann despondingly.

' Of course I have,' said Meldon, ' business of the most important kind. But before I start it I want to make sure that you're in what I may call a receptive mood. You weren't when I first came in. It's no use pretending that you were. You were in what I'd call a nasty temper. I hope and think that you're getting over it a little now. But you must realize that it would have been totally impossible to do business with you when you were scowling at me as you were at first. That's why I began by trying to pacify and reassure you. I mentioned the silver linings that clouds have. I told you I'd slanged Michael Gannon. Then I mentioned the Major's feelings and my own, all with the same object in view, to get you into a condition in which you could talk business.'

' What is your business ? '

' Sure you're quite fit to go into it ? ' said Meldon. ' Very well, then. I may as well begin by saying frankly that I don't know whether the Irish Free State has a law prohibiting the export of works of art from the country. Italy has, I know, and the French object to any one taking away old furniture. It's quite likely that the Irish Free State may have a law of that kind, but, as I say, I don't know. You perhaps do.'

'No, I do not,' said Deissmann, now thoroughly bewildered.

'You ought to,' said Meldon. 'There's a lot of talk about German thoroughness and method, but if you haven't taken the trouble to find out what the law is about an important point like that, all I can say is that you're either slack or entirely unsystematic. However, I mean to make inquiries myself at once, and I may say that if there isn't a law already there soon will be. There's nothing these new States like better than making troublesome laws, and I should say that the Irish Parliament, Dail, or whatever it's called, will simply jump at the chance of making a law of the kind. I don't suppose there's a single member of that assembly who owns a work of art, so there won't be any opposition. That's what I want to impress on you at the start: There either is, or very soon will be, a law forbidding the removal of works of art from this country. The penalties will be terrifically severe.'

'I do not understand what this has to do with me. I do not understand what your business is.'

'I am reluctant,' said Meldon, 'to think that you're not speaking the truth. But I'm quite unable to believe that you don't see the bearing of what I've just told you on your position. You're far too intelligent a man to miss a simple thing like that. But it's possible, just possible, that you don't regard candlesticks by Paul Lamerie as works of art. I can only assure you that they are, and I shall use my whole influence to see that when the new Bill is drafted they will be scheduled in a special subsection all to themselves. Now, I'm not accusing you of deliberate dishonesty. I'm quite willing to believe that you thought that anything you found in the bottom of the Shannon belonged to no one in particular, but——'

'The bottom of the Shannon!' said Deissmann, with a deep groan.

Mention of the river revived the recollection of what had happened to his works the night before.

'It's in a beastly state at present,' said Meldon. 'I quite admit that, and, as I said, both the Major and I deeply regret that. But that's not the point. What I want to get at is this: Are you prepared to return those candlesticks to their proper owner? I've explained to you what the law is or very soon will be. You haven't the slightest chance of smuggling them over to Berlin. But I hope, I sincerely hope, that feelings of common honesty, of which you cannot be entirely devoid, will prompt you to do the right thing at once, altogether apart from the difficulty and danger—I said the penalties were severe—of doing anything else.'

Deissmann pulled himself together with an effort. Anger at the destruction of his works revived in him. He believed that Meldon was more or less responsible for what had happened. He had never heard of Paul Lamerie. He had not the slightest intention of smuggling works of art out of Ireland. The suggestion that he was anything but strictly honest was an intolerable insult.

'You!' he spluttered. 'You! An impostor, who say you represent a company which does not exist. You! who incite my men to strike. You! who steal gelignite and blow up my beautiful dam. You come here to me and talk about art for which I do not care, about candlesticks of which I never heard before, of the rightful owner of I know not what. You ask me at once to return to a rightful owner— What? Who? Why? When? My God! But I see. I understand. It is—it is—' His English failed him suddenly. 'It is *Expressungsversuch*.'

'If that's the line you mean to take,' said Meldon, who had no idea whatever of the meaning of Deissmann's immense word, 'there's no use my talking to you any more. But I'll just say this. Kind words— I'm not alluding to that last word of yours, which sounded anything but kind——'

'Ah,' said Deissmann, 'I have it now, the English word. Blackmail.'

'Oh, that's what it means, is it? But I wasn't thinking of it when I said "kind words." I was alluding to the way in which the Major and I approached you. Nothing could have been kinder than the way I spoke and the way the Major would have spoken if he had been here. We believe in kind words, Herr Deissmann. At least, we did until you've shattered our faith with that horrible *pressung* word of yours which you say means blackmail. But kind words aren't the only way of getting back the Major's property.'

'The law,' said Deissmann firmly. 'You attempt to blackmail. I reply, the law.'

'I wasn't thinking of the law at the moment,' said Meldon. 'In fact—I like to be perfectly plain with you—we're not inclined to go to law with you, though we could, and we'd certainly win if we did. But owing to a little misunderstanding between the Major and an income-tax collector we'd rather not go to law, just at present, in Ireland. The means I intend to adopt, kind words having failed, are entirely unconnected with the law. That's all I need say; but I'd like you to think it over carefully, remembering what I said about the penalties for trying to smuggle away works of art. Not that you'll ever get as far as that. The Major will have his property back before you have even begun to make your arrangements.'

He left Deissmann's room. Jimmy Costello was waiting for him outside, and they drove cheerfully back to the hotel together.

Deissmann added an extra page to the report he was drawing up for his firm in Hamburg. In it he enlarged on Meldon's *Expressungsversuch*.

CHAPTER XVII

MELDON reached the hotel a little before two o'clock after his visit to Herr Deissmann. He went straight into the dining-room, expecting to find Major Kent there. The Major had fixed on half-past one as the proper hour for luncheon, and he particularly liked punctuality at meals. He also liked to eat slowly and linger a little afterwards over his coffee. Eileen Costello's coffee was seldom either strong or hot, for it was a drink which she did not understand. Most men would have either hurried over it or given up drinking it altogether. But the Major held the view that a self-respecting man ought to drink coffee after luncheon and ought to sip it slowly. The fact that it was bad did not absolve him from what he regarded as a duty.

Meldon, who knew all his friend's habits and most of his prejudices, fully expected to find the Major in the dining-room, probably sipping his coffee. The Major was not there, which was a very surprising thing. Almost equally surprising was the presence of a young man seated by himself at a small table in the corner of the room. This was Mr. Peter Jameson, the commissioner of the Free State Government, who had just arrived. Meldon nodded to him in a friendly manner.

Peter had satisfied himself the moment he reached the hotel that the dreaded Red Con Murphy was not in

Lisnamoe.   Eileen, his cousin, told him that, and it was
a great relief to his mind.   But she also told him that
Major Kent and Meldon were staying in the hotel.
Peter had never heard of either of them, and was
inclined to regard them as people of no importance.
But Eileen had information which she gave him in a
confidential whisper.   Major Kent was the Head of the
Irish Republican Army.   This, as Peter knew, could
not be true.   Red Con was the Chief of the Force.   But
he could not help feeling a little uneasy.   The Major
might very well be an intimate friend of Red Con's.
    ' It was him,' said Eileen, ' that set on Michael
Gannon and the rest of the boys to have a strike
and— Did you hear what they're after doing
last night ?   Blowing up all before them, so as you'd
hardly know the place if you saw it.   That's what
Jimmy tells me, anyhow.   I didn't see it myself, for
I've more to do than to be running to and fro to
Coolarrigan to look at every fire that any fellow
happens to light.'
    ' I heard of it.'
    ' Well, it was him that did that,' said Eileen, ' him
and the fellow they call Meldon that's along with him.
A nice enough sort of a man and easy to talk to and
fond of funning.   A bit too fond of funning, if you ask
me.'
    This made Peter very uneasy.   It was a great thing,
of course, that Red Con himself was not there, but he
could not help feeling that a man who was capable of
arranging for the blowing up of a whole tract of country
might be dangerous.   And he did not like what Eileen
told him about Meldon.   Fondness for funning may
be a sign of amiability, but it may be— People
have such different ideas of what fun is.   Meldon

might have a taste for grim kinds which would not strike a peaceful man like Peter as fun at all.

Meldon's friendly nod did nothing to reassure him. Meldon's appearance—at his best he looked anything but sleek, and that morning he had dressed very hurriedly and had not washed at all.

'Where's the Major?'

Meldon addressed the elderly and decrepit waiter.

'I didn't set eyes on him since breakfast.'

'Do you mean to tell me that the Major hasn't turned up for his lunch?'

The thing was incredible. Never before since Meldon had known him had the Major failed to be in the place where he ought to be at the appointed time—never, unless he happened to be under Meldon's guidance, and that morning he had been left by himself.

'Did you happen to see the Major?' said Meldon, to Peter Jameson. 'Military-looking man, grizzly moustache, spreading out a bit below the chest. A little slow in picking up the meaning of what's said to him, but reliable, absolutely reliable, and most tenacious once he gets hold of an idea.'

Meldon spoke with a breezy self-confidence, quite natural to him, but very unusual in Ireland, where everybody goes about in fear of what everybody else may be going to say or do. Such unguarded openness made Peter acutely uncomfortable.

'There was a gentleman,' he said, 'that might be him. He was smoking his pipe when I came in off the train, but I didn't see him since.'

Meldon hurried out of the dining-room in search of Eileen. He found her in the kitchen, and he found her in a bad temper.

'Oh, it's you, is it?' she said. 'Well, I wish you'd

be in time for your lunch. How am I to be keeping things hot for you half the day? Not that I would keep them hot for you, for it's my belief that you wouldn't know whether what you ate was hot or cold. But the Major's different. He's a quiet, easy sort of man that would give no trouble if it wasn't for you.'

' Where is he?' said Meldon. ' I distinctly told you to look after him while I was out. I told you to give him Pope's poems to read. Did you or did you not ? '

' I did not,' said Eileen. ' Was it likely I would ? '

' I told you to keep him amused. I told you to talk to him occasionally in a light and genial way. I told you not to flirt with him. Did you flirt with him ? If so, I don't wonder he's disappeared.'

' I did not. Why would I ? An old man like him.'

' Whether you flirted with him or not you didn't look after him properly.'

' Sure, I did look after him.'

' You did not. If you had he'd be here now. Did he rush off to the station and catch the one o'clock train ? '

This was what Meldon feared that the Major had done. He had been threatening to go home ever since they reached Lisnamoe. It was quite possible that he had seized the chance which Meldon's absence gave him to make an attempt to get back to England. Some exaggerated account of Michael Gannon's proceedings the night before might have frightened him, though it was difficult to see how an exaggeration of that affair was possible.

' He did not catch the one o'clock train,' said Eileen, 'for I seen him at quarter-past one and, what's more, I talked to him. I know what time it was, for my cousin Peter Jameson was just after coming in, and it was off the one o'clock train that he came. That's him in the dining-room. You might have seen him eating his lunch. He's a nice young fellow enough, and if he did go back on the Republicans and turn Free Stater it's hard to blame him, considering the salary he gets.'

' Stop talking about your cousin,' said Meldon. ' I don't in the least want to hear about him. Tell me what the Major said to you at quarter-past one. Was it anything about going home ? '

' It was not.'

' What was it, then?'

' What the Major said to me,' said Eileen, ' was this : " Who's that ?" My cousin Peter was just coming into the hotel. It was him you seen this minute eating his lunch.'

' Don't keep on talking about your cousin,' said Meldon. ' Talk about the Major.'

' Sure, how can I talk about the Major if you won't let me say a word about Peter ? It was him the Major was asking about. " Who's that ?" said he, looking after Peter who'd gone upstairs with his bag in his hand. " Who's that ?" said he, " and what is he ? and where does he come from?" Well, I told him the best way I could.'

' Told him what ? '

' I told him the truth, of course. I said Peter was a cousin of mine. I told him he'd been a Republican one time, but was a Free Stater now on account of his being in a Government office. " What office ? " says the Major. Well, I couldn't tell him that, for I didn't know what office it was. " What brings him here ? " said the Major. I didn't know that either, so I said it was likely the Government sent him down here to be doing some kind of business for them. The Major was upset about that. I could see he was terribly upset. But he didn't say another word, good or bad ; and that's the last I saw of him. Do you think now that anything would have happened to him ? '

' I'll try his bedroom,' said Meldon, ' before I send out a search party.'

The Major was in his bedroom with the door locked. It was only after he was quite sure who his visitor was that he allowed Meldon to enter.

' J. J.,' he said, ' I'm afraid I'm done. I always knew it would come to this. I'm not blaming you. I'm sure you acted for the best all along, or what you thought was the best. But I did warn you. You can't deny that.'

' Try to be coherent, Major. I've had an exhausting morning. First the excessive zeal of Michael Gannon. Then the obstinacy, the stupid and almost criminal obstinacy, of that German. Don't make things worse for me by being incoherent. Just say in as few words as possible why you've shut yourself up here instead of going down to lunch in the ordinary way.'

' Income-tax,' said the Major. ' I knew they'd get me in the end. But I won't pay. It's an utterly unjust demand, and I'd rather go to prison for the rest of my life than give in to that kind of legalized robbery. There's a man downstairs. He's just arrived from Dublin.'

' Eileen Costello's cousin,' said Meldon. ' His name is Peter.'

' He's an income-tax collector. She as good as told me so.'

' All she told you,' said Meldon, ' was that he's in a Government office in Dublin. Even if that's true— and most of what Eileen says isn't—but even if it is, it doesn't necessarily follow that he's in the Inland Revenue Office. There are dozens, probably hundreds, of other Government offices. I don't see the slightest reason so far to suppose that he's in any way connected with the income-tax.'

' He has all the look of it.'

' You can't go entirely by appearances,' said Meldon. ' It's a ridiculous thing to do. I might just as well argue that he can't be a tax collector because his name is Peter. If you knew your New Testament you ought to remember that so far from collecting taxes Peter was in trouble once through not paying up. An income-tax collector would be called Matthew if he had a New Testament name at all. I don't say that's a good argument. It isn't. I'm only using it to show you the foolishness of your own plan of deducing a man's profession from his appearance.'

' What brings him here, if he hasn't been sent down after my income-tax ? '

' He may have come to see his cousin. You may not think much of girls, Major. In fact, I know you don't. That's why I told her she wasn't to flirt with you while I was out.'

' You told her what, J. J. ? '

' Not to flirt with you. I said that quite distinctly.'

' I wish you wouldn't say things of that sort to her.'

' My dear Major, if I'd known you wanted her to flirt with you ! But how could I ? However, since you did it makes things much simpler. You will understand now that it's quite possible that Peter— whose other name is Jameson—may have come down here, not to collect income-tax from you, but simply to see her. That's apparently what you'd do if you weren't here already.'

' No, I wouldn't.   If I wasn't here I'd jolly well stay away.'

' Anyhow,' said Meldon, ' you appreciate the girl, so why shouldn't he ?   After all, even if she wasn't quite attractive, and you admit that she is, spending a few days with her, indeed, almost with any girl, would be a great deal pleasanter than collecting income-tax.'

' He may intend to do both,' said the Major.   ' Anyhow, the best thing for me to do is to lie low.'

' Lie low!   That's the idea, is it?   That's why you've locked yourself into your bedroom.   But you can't stay locked up until Peter Jameson chooses to marry his cousin.   It may be weeks before he even proposes.   Do you seriously propose to stay here, shut up in a frowsy room, fed on chance scraps by Eileen, until Peter Jameson goes off on his honeymoon ? '

' I only mean to stay here till to-morrow,' said the Major.   ' Then I'm going home, whether you've got those candlesticks or not.   By the way, how did you get on with Deissmann this morning ? '

' Deissmann,' said Meldon, ' turns out to be dishonest, and, what's worse, utterly unreasonable.   It has become necessary to deal rather drastically with him.'

CHAPTER XVIII

PETER JAMESON had finished his luncheon when Meldon entered the dining-room again. He had lit a cigarette and was eyeing with some suspicion the coffee which his cousin had provided, which old John Macmahon brought in a portentous silver-plated pot. Dublin is a city in which good coffee, remarkably good coffee, is obtainable, and Peter Jameson, since entering the Government service, had learnt what coffee ought to be. The brown liquid which his cousin Eileen provided was almost entirely without taste, and very far from being hot.

Meldon sat down at Peter Jameson's table with a cheery apology.

'Hope you don't mind my sharing your table,' he said. 'I hate eating by myself, and my friend the Major—I must introduce you to him later on. You're sure to like him. Unfortunately, he's feeling a bit off-colour to-day and is more or less confined to his room, so unless you let me lunch with you I shall be all alone.'

Peter Jameson murmured that he was smoking, and when Meldon brushed that excuse aside, said that he had finished his meal and was going away. He w̃ as a rule, a friendly man who welcomed company any sort, but his relations with the Irish Republi

Army were not cordial, and he could not help feeling a little afraid of Meldon.

'Oh, don't do that,' said Meldon. 'Stay here while I have my luncheon. Unless you're frightfully busy. But nobody could be really busy in a place like Lisnamoe. Perhaps you have an appointment of some sort?'

Thus Meldon began to feel about for some indication of what Peter Jameson's business was and why he had come to Lisnamoe. He took very little by this first effort.

'I have not,' said Peter Jameson, speaking cautiously and with some hostility.

'Well, stay here,' said Meldon, 'and talk to me. I don't mind your smoking in the least. Have a small brandy? You'll hardly be able to drink that coffee unless you take some brandy with it. Miss Costello is an excellent manager. You'd hardly meet a better anywhere. The man who gets her for a wife will be lucky. But she's weak on coffee. Macmahon——!'

The old man was hovering round with a dish of potatoes. 'Get a glass of brandy for Mr. Jameson, the same sort that the Major drinks. You'll have a glass of brandy, won't you, Mr. Jameson?'

'I don't mind if I do,' said Peter, still cautiously, but this time without hostility.

'Apart from its being dull,' said Meldon, 'eating by oneself is very bad for the digestion. Every doctor says so. Most diseases of the abdomen, colitis and duodenal ulcers, and nasty things of that sort, arise entirely from solitary eating. That is now an established fact. Sheep, for instance, don't get colitis. Why? Because they graze about in flocks. That's one of the reasons why every man ought to get married.

Once he's got a wife it's practically impossible for him to eat alone, and his digestion improves enormously. I daresay you've noticed that.'

'I have not,' said Peter. 'How could I when I'm not married?'

'Really? Never mind. You soon will be, and if Miss Costello is the lady I envy you. She's pretty well everything that a girl ought to be. Good-looking, competent, full of activity, highly educated—she wouldn't keep Pope's poems lying about the house if she wasn't. It isn't everyone that can read Pope. The Major goes to sleep every time he tries. But Pope's Miss Costello's favourite poet, in fact, the only poet whose works she cares to keep at all, which shows the highly-cultured condition of her mind. And besides, she has quite a nice little fortune, so they tell me.'

'Maybe you're thinking of marrying her yourself?' said Peter.

'I'm married already. Have been for years. If I wasn't— But there's no use talking about that.'

"I wouldn't say,' said Peter, 'but a man might do worse.'

'He could hardly do better,' said Meldon, 'and if I were you I'd seize the opportunity of being down here, at an off season, when there's nobody much in the hotel, and she's not particularly busy—but you know all that just as well as I do.'

'I do,' said Peter. And he did.

The fear of meeting Red Con Murphy had left him. He was beginning to feel that Meldon was not very terrible. He rather liked the thought of a few days in his cousin's company, a few days that might very well end in a formal engagement.

' But perhaps,' said Meldon, ' it was to see her that you came down here ? '

' It was not to see her I came,' said Peter, ' though, mind you, I'm willing enough to see her now I'm here. But, to tell you the truth, it was a different kind of business altogether that brought me down here.'

Meldon had not got the information he wanted. He had not found out what Peter Jameson's business was or why he had come to Lisnamoe. But he had made some progress in his inquiries. He had at least discovered that Miss Costello was not the first and principal cause of Peter's visit. He had also finished his luncheon. It seemed to him that it would be pleasanter to talk out of doors. The dining-room was stuffy and the sun was shining pleasantly outside. It might, besides, be easy to induce Peter Jameson to talk freely if he was able to talk without being conscious that old Macmahon was listening to every word he said.

Peter, who had very little to do and was in no hurry to do that little, agreed to take a walk. As Meldon passed Eileen's office he asked her to send up some luncheon to the Major.

' It's what I'm just after doing,' she said. ' He was ringing his bell something terrible, so I told old Macmahon to go up to him so soon as ever he'd done waiting on you. Well, it was lunch he wanted and lunch is what he'll get.'

' That rather looks,' said Meldon, ' as if his appetite was coming back to him, and if it is he's certainly better. I hope you sent up something wholesome, a milk pudding and a sweetbread.'

' I sent him up the same as what I gave you,' said Eileen, ' and the same as what I gave to Peter.'

' Boiled mutton,' said Meldon, ' a first-rate thing.   It was boiled mutton we had, wasn't it ? '

He turned to Peter with an inquiring smile.

' It was,' said Peter.

' Stupid of me to have forgotten,' said Meldon, ' but the fact is I never gave a thought to what I was eating. Too much interested in your conversation, my dear fellow.   Your cousin,' he turned to Eileen, ' has been talking to me in the most interesting way, all about his work, what he does in Dublin, and especially what he's come down here to do.   He hasn't told you yet, but he will.   All he wants is a little encouragement and I'm sure you'll give him that.   A man, especially a modest man, can't be expected to speak out unless the lady gives him a hint——'

Here he winked confidentially, and Eileen responded with a little blush.   Meldon took Peter by the arm and led him out of the hotel.

' I did you a good turn there,' he said, ' I suggested that you'd come down specially to see her.   If I were you I'd propose at once while she's in the mood for it. There's nothing so harassing as uncertainty, and girls simply hate a man who philanders.'

' I'd propose quick enough,' said Peter, ' if I thought she'd have me.'

' There's no question at all about that.   Didn't you see the way she blushed ? '

' It might not have been me she was blushing about. It might have been you.'

' Couldn't possibly have been,' said Meldon.   ' She regards me simply as an uncle, just as she does the Major.   If you knew the Major you'd see at once that no girl could possibly blush about him, and I'm just the same.   The poor Major, he's much more likely to blush than she is. A regular old bachelor. But you'll see what he is this evening, I expect. He's evidently getting over his little attack. To-morrow he'll be all right and quite up to doing business. You said you'd business with the Major, didn't you ? '

' I did not say so,' said Peter, ' but I might have without saying it.'

' Well, put it off till to-morrow,' said Meldon. ' Put it off altogether if you can. The Major's a highly-strung, sensitive man and it takes very little to upset him. You can see that for yourself. You must have seen it when he didn't come down to lunch to-day. I'm not suggesting that you should neglect your duty. Nothing would induce me to try to persuade you to deviate by as much as a hair's-breadth from the straight path. All the same you ought to remember that I did you a good turn to-day. Only for the way I winked at her, Miss Costello wouldn't have blushed, and if she hadn't blushed where would you have been ? In a condition of maddening uncertainty. You couldn't have been anywhere else. Whereas now, thanks to my tactful and at the same time vigorous action, you know exactly where you are. Remember that, won't you, when it comes to doing business with the Major.'

' I don't know have I business with him or have I not. It's a thing I might know later on, but I don't know yet.'

' If there's the slightest uncertainty about it,' said Meldon, ' make up your mind that you haven't and don't do it. My experience of life—and I've had a lot of experience, far more than most men—my experience has taught me that trouble very seldom arises out of not doing things. It's only when we're silly enough to do them that we get into trouble.

Take the late war, for instance. If nobody had done anything there wouldn't have been a war. Well, it's just the same with this affair of yours and the Major's. If you don't do anything, he won't. You can rely on that, and there'll be no trouble at all.'

' If I thought that——'

' You may be perfectly confident about it. If you let the Major alone he won't stir in the matter hand or foot. Then the whole miserable business will blow over, pass into the limbo of forgotten things, waters of Lethe and so forth.'

' I'd be willing enough to say no more about it,' said Peter, ' only I have my report to make which is what I was sent down here to do, and I'd like to know whether — What did you say your friend's name is ? '

' Kent,' said Meldon. ' I'm not attempting to deny that. The Major wouldn't like it if I did. He's an extraordinarily straightforward man, simply hates subterfuge of any kind.'

' How do you spell it ? ' said Peter.

' There's only one way you could possibly spell Kent, K-e-n-t. The same as the county in which the hops grow.'

Peter thought this over carefully. Then he turned to Meldon with a most unexpected question :

' Do you know Irish ? '

' No, I don't,' said Meldon, ' but I've given a subscription to the Gaelic League several times, and that's something. You can't blame a man for not knowing Irish so long as he subscribes to the Gaelic League, any more than you could blame him for not having appendicitis provided he gives his guinea to a hospital.'

' It's not hospitals I'm thinking of now,' said Peter.

' I know that ; but the principle is exactly the same.

Hospitals exist for the purpose of cutting out diseased appendices, other things, of course, but chiefly that. If you haven't got a diseased appendix you're not much use to a hospital, and the only thing you can do is to subscribe, which, after all, is the next best thing.   In the same way the Gaelic League exists for the purpose of talking the Irish language, but if you don't know any you can't do that, and you are more or less bound to make what compensation you can by subscribing.   You see the idea, don't you ? '

' I do,' said Peter.

But he did not speak the truth.   He supposed that there must be an idea behind Meldon's words, but it seemed to him an extremely elusive one.

' If you don't know any Irish,' said Peter, ' it'll not be much use showing you this.'

He pulled out of his pocket a copy of Michael Gannon's strike proclamation.   Meldon took it and a single glance showed him what it was.

' It's all in English,' he said, ' except one little bit at the end.'

' That's the bit I'd like your opinion about,' said Peter, ' but sure if you don't know Irish what's the use of asking you what you think of it ? '

' I know enough Irish for that,' said Meldon, ' though I don't know much.   " *Mise, le meas mór* " means, " myself, with great respect."   That's the literal translation.   It's practically equivalent to " yours faithfully," or "sincerely," or even "affectionately".'

' That's just what has me bothered,' said Peter. ' What name is it at all ? '

' It looks to me,' said Meldon, ' as if it might be a rather exaggerated form of Geoghegan, spelt with a C at the beginning instead of a G.'

'What I was wondering, was whether it mightn't be Kent.'

'Are you thinking of my friend the Major?'

'I am,' said Peter, 'for if it was him that signed that paper— Mind you, I've no objection to it myself— none in the world, and if I had the settling of things there wouldn't be a word said about it, not if he signed half a dozen more like it. Only there's others. There's fellows up in Dublin that has to be considered. If it was him signed that paper and if it was him that blew up the River Shannon last night——'

'If it was,' said Meldon, '—I don't admit it was, not for a moment, but if it was you must see that it's not much use trying to get income-tax out of him. Is it now?"

'Income-tax!' said Peter. 'Is it the like of him or any of the rest of them ones that would be paying income-tax? Sure, all ever they do is to burn down the offices where the taxes is paid in to.'

'Exactly. I thoroughly understood that, and I'm glad you take the same view that I do of the situation. If Ceagheanaght is the Irish for Kent, then it's not the slightest use your taking any further proceedings against the Major. In fact, if I were you I should not only be inclined to let the matter drop but I should——'

The little town of Lisnamoe stands divided into two by the Shannon; very much as Budapest is by the Danube. A picturesque bridge joins the half on the western bank to the half on the eastern. It is to this bridge, almost as much as to the Shannon fishing, that Lisnamoe owes its importance and the small measure of prosperity which it enjoys. There is no other bridge within six miles of Lisnamoe either up or down the stream. Every sort of traffic, therefore, tends to flow through the town. Farm carts go to fairs, cross the bridge and return the same way, to the great advantage of the Lisnamoe publicans. Carts laden with turf converge on Lisnamoe from various bogs. Drovers with their herds of store cattle and flocks of sheep must and do cross the bridge. Motor-cars pass through Lisnamoe if their owners want to get from Tipperary into Clare or from Clare into Tipperary.

It was on this bridge that Meldon and Peter Jameson stood and talked after they left the hotel. It was a pleasant place and quiet, very well suited for a serious and important conversation. Indeed, it was only at the end of their talk that they were disturbed at all.

Just when Meldon was explaining the futility of taking proceedings for the recovery of income-tax from a man who spelt his name Ceagheanaght, a motor cyclist appeared on the hill above the bridge. His machine was an unusually noisy one and could be heard a long way off. As it neared the bridge its explosions became disturbingly loud. Peter Jameson looked round. He caught sight of the machine and the rider while they were still some thirty yards from the end of the bridge. Without a word of explanation or without even an exclamation or cry of any so left Meldon and ran swiftly back towards the hotel.

Meldon, less disturbed than Peter was, by the noise of the motor bicycle, did not turn his head. He was intent, even while he talked, on watching a salmon which lay, head upstream, close beside one of the piers which supported the arches of the bridge.

' In fact, if I were you,' he said, ' I should write off that fifty pounds—it is fifty pounds, I think, or thereabouts, not a very large sum in any case. I should write it off as irrecoverable, what in commercial circles is, I believe, called a bad debt.'

At this point his eyes left the salmon and he looked round to see how Peter Jameson was taking his advice. He was surprised to find that his last words had been entirely wasted, unless the salmon heard and understood them. Peter was a long way off, running at top speed for the hotel. He could not possibly have heard what Meldon said. The motor cyclist, who by this time was crossing the bridge, could not have heard either. The explosions of his machine were the only sounds which could possibly have been audible to him.

Meldon, a little puzzled, watched Peter until he disappeared into the hotel. Then he watched the motor cyclist. He stopped at the door of his hotel and got off his machine. He walked, a little stiffly as a man does who has ridden far, into the hotel, leaving the cycle propped up outside.

Meldon, full of curiosity and a little excited, relit his pipe. Then he followed Peter and the cyclist to the hotel.

CHAPTER XIX

EVERY man has some self-respect and most of us have, in addition a little professional pride. We hate to be ignored. We hate to be pushed from positions which we have won for ourselves. When we are ignored in favour of outsiders and ousted by men who are not members of our trades union, then our feelings of resentment are likely to be both strong and bitter. The priest, however nearly Christian he may be, cannot bear to watch the activities of a successful heretic in his parish. Respectable women hate and affect to despise attractive courtezans. Doctors loathe unauthorized curers of disease, especially such as succeed in curing. It is hard to say just how much personal feeling—our natural self-respect—has to do with these hatreds, and how far they are the outcome of a loyalty to our union—a loyalty now recognized to be one of the very noblest virtues of the race. Probably the trade union feeling is the stronger of the two. At all events the dissenter, the courtezan and the quack are all very justly regarded as blacklegs. They refuse to accept the conditions under which the rest of us think it right to work. They are individualists and often amateurs. They are therefore detestable to those who see hope and salvation in the strict organization of all activity.

Red Con Murphy, the recognized leader of the active

wing of the Republican party in Ireland, was a remarkable man, of great originality of mind and force of character. He was looked up to, indeed, almost adored, by his followers. He was respected and, as in the case of Peter Jameson, feared by those who disagreed with him. But even he had some human weakness. No more than the rest of us did he like the interference of outsiders with his business. He particularly disliked such interference when it was successful and attracted the attention of an admiring public. For a long time he had organized and taken a prominent part in committing outrages of every kind. He boasted—and it was not idle boasting—that he had been active, usually the moving spirit, in every murder, every case of arson, every robbery of a bank or a post office, which had disturbed and delighted Ireland during the past two years. He heard of the strike at Coolarrigan with suspicion and disgust. At first he could scarcely believe that such a thing could have happened except at his instigation. He was profoundly annoyed because he realized that some amateur —some blackleg among outrage makers—had been interfering in his own proper business.

When the news reached him that the bed of the Shannon and several other things had been blown up he realized that he must take prompt and vigorous action. A plumber would not have been angrier at discovering that a carpenter had mended a leaky tap. A painter and decorator would have felt just as Con Murphy did if he had heard of an out-of-work miner who earned ten shillings by papering a room for a friend.

When the news of the doings at Lisnamoe reached him, Con Murphy was engaged in a series of light skirmishes with the Custom-house officers on the

Donegal frontier about the importation of a motor bicycle from Derry. It was not a serious affair. A few shots had been fired, but, as usually happens in Irish warfare, nobody had been hit. The Civic Guards were rambling about with an air of considerable self-importance, but it was well understood that they had not the slightest intention of arresting any one, least of all Con Murphy. The news from Lisnamoe put an end to these skirmishes, which, indeed, had never been more than an agreeable way of occupying a few idle days. Con Murphy informed the Custom-house officers, through a friend, that he really wanted the motor bicycle and wanted it at once. They gave him to understand that no difficulties would be put in the way of his getting it.

It was a good motor bicycle, powerful, swift and unusually noisy. Con Murphy had no hesitation in attempting a long journey on it. He started at dawn and reached Lisnamoe early in the afternoon without feeling seriously tired. He arrived, as has been said, just while Meldon was explaining to Peter Jameson and then to the empty air the folly of trying to collect income-tax from Major Kent.

Meldon followed Con Murphy into the hotel.

Peter Jameson, who had been the first of the three to reach the hotel, had completely disappeared. Con Murphy, when Meldon came in, was engaged in conversation with Eileen Costello. It was an earnest and absorbing conversation, but Meldon had no hesitation in interrupting it. Addressing himself chiefly to Con Murphy, but including Eileen with a glance, he remarked that it was a fine day. Con Murphy, who had had ample opportunity for observing the weather, made no answer. He did not even look round. Then Meldon told Eileen that he would be ready for tea at five o'clock. Eileen merely nodded. She seemed entirely absorbed in what Con Murphy was saying to her. It struck Meldon that she was uneasy, if not actually frightened. His curiosity was excited but he saw no way of satisfying it at the moment. Con Murphy stopped talking when Meldon spoke, and showed no sign of beginning again as long as Meldon stood beside him.

Meldon went upstairs and entered the Major's room.

'Major,' he said, 'I'm pretty busy. In fact, I've no time to spare at all. Things are simply crowding in on me. But I felt I ought to look in on you just for one moment to set your mind at rest about the income-tax. No attempt whatever will be made to collect that money from you. I've explained to Peter Jameson—he's the man you're hiding from, Eileen Costello's cousin, quite a nice fellow and a man you'll like when you get to know him. In fact, I was wondering whether we mightn't get up a game of bridge this evening. You and I and Peter would be three, and there's another fellow just arrived on a motor bike. I don't know exactly who he is yet, but I mean to find out, and if he seems to be all right we might rake him in as a fourth. You'd like a game of bridge, wouldn't you, Major ? '

' I won't play bridge with an income-tax collector.'

' Don't be narrow-minded, Major. You might just as well say that you wouldn't play bridge with a Christian Scientist or a Spiritualist. You may not believe in ghosts any more than you like paying income-tax, but you can't deny—at least you oughtn't to deny —that people who go in for being psychic or collecting taxes may be perfectly respectable members of society.'

' What I mean,' said the Major, ' is that it would be beastly uncomfortable to play bridge with an income-

G

tax collector to whom I owed a lot of money.   It would
be uncomfortable for us both.'

' What you've been saying all along,' said Meldon,
' is that you don't owe that money.   Now, just when
I've taken an enormous amount of trouble to see that
you haven't got to pay, you turn round and tell me you
do owe it.   I really think, Major, that you must be the
most difficult man in the whole world to help.   You get
into difficulties, but you never seem to be able to make
up your mind exactly what they are.'

' What did you say to that fellow about my income-
tax ? ' said the Major anxiously.

' I said very little.   I'm a man who seldom says
much about anything, and the little I did say he didn't
hear the whole of, for he ran away before I'd uttered
more than a couple of sentences.'

' Then how do you know he won't arrest me for not
paying.   If he wouldn't listen to what you said it looks
to me as if his mind was made up.   Not that what you
said would have made any difference, even if he had
listened to it.'

' Without saying anything very definite,' said Meldon,
' I allowed him to infer that you were the head of a
secret society of assassins.'

' Good God ! '

' And that any attempt to collect income-tax from
you would have the most unpleasant consequences for
him.'

' No wonder the poor fellow ran away,' said the
Major.

' Oh, it wasn't that which made him run away.   That
was no real surprise to him.   In fact he thought that
was what you were all along.   Eileen Costello may have
given him a hint, and he had a seditious proclamation in

his pocket with a signature which he thought was yours.'

' It wasn't.'

' My dear Major, need you assure me of that ? I've known you for over twenty years, and I've never once seen you sign a seditious document.'

' I suppose I'll be arrested for that, even if I'm not caught over the income-tax.'

' No, you won't,' said Meldon. ' You might have been arrested for not paying your income-tax. At one time I didn't regard that as possible ; but I'm inclined now to think that I was wrong. Peter Jameson evidently was sent down from Dublin to get the money from you. I gathered that from the way he talked. He knows now that he daren't even try, so he'll let you alone. It's no business of his whether you sign seditious documents or not. You may say what you like about income-tax collectors, Major, and I know you're prejudiced against them. But they have their good points. They don't go about the country arresting people for sedition.'

' Anyhow,' said the Major, ' I'm not going to play bridge with him. I couldn't. I really couldn't. He believes that I owe a lot of income-tax which I won't pay, and now, thanks to you, he thinks that I'm a murderer as well. I can't and won't play bridge with a man who has that sort of opinion of me.'

' Why will you talk in that exaggerated way ? ' said Meldon. ' It is such a pity. He doesn't think you commit murders. The leaders of secret societies hardly ever do. They simply organize them.'

' Besides,' said the Major, ' there's the other man, the fellow you mean to get as a fourth. He may have been sent to arrest me for sedition. How do you know he hasn't ? '

' I don't know yet,' said Meldon, ' but I mean to find out. In an hour from now I shall know exactly what he is and what he's come here for. I needn't say that if he's in the least bit fishy, in fact unless he turns out to be a perfectly satisfactory man in every way, I shan't ask him to play bridge with us.'

' Whatever sort of man he is,' said the Major, ' there'll be no bridge here, at least no bridge with me in it. I'm going away at once.'

' If you mean by that that you're going back to Weymouth, you can't. You've missed to-day's train. It went out just as Peter Jameson's came in. There isn't another till to-morrow.'

' I know that,' said the Major. ' You've told me about those trains every day since we came. All I mean is that I'm not going to spend the night in this hotel.'

' Don't calculate on getting even a shed to sleep in at Coolarrigan. There's not one left with a roof on it. I doubt if there's one with more than two walls standing.'

' I'm going to Gannon's,' said the Major. ' Gannon will put me up for the night. I'll be more or less safe there.'

' Gannon,' said Meldon, ' has a wife and nine children, and there are only two bedrooms in the house. I was talking to Mrs. Gannon the other day and she told me that. I don't know where you propose to sleep.'

' I shall sit up in the kitchen,' said the Major. ' I'd a great deal rather sit up in Gannon's kitchen than hang about here expecting to be arrested for fraud or sedition or murder every minute. That's what you've let me in for, J. J., with all the abominable lies you keep telling about me. For all I know to the contrary this man who's just arrived may be wanting to prosecute me for pretending to be an electrical engineer. That's another thing you said about me.'

'That's exactly what I said you weren't. Do try to be just. There's nothing worse than bringing false accusations against your friends. I never said you were an electrical engineer.'

'Well, an experimental chemist, or whatever you did say. Anyhow it was a fraud. Of course I'd rather be arrested for that than murder.'

'If you're arrested for anything,' said Meldon, 'it will be sedition.'

'Sedition, then, much the same thing. But I expect I'll be fairly safe in Gannon's cottage for to-night, and to-morrow I'll go home.'

'You shall,' said Meldon, 'with the candlesticks in a brown paper parcel under your arm. The end of our quest is very near now, Major. We've really nothing to do but to talk to Deissmann in a way that he'll understand. And that's what I've arranged to have done to-night. In the meanwhile it won't do you any real harm to spend the night at Gannon's. As you sit cramped and chilly in his kitchen after the fire has gone out, you'll hear the nine little Gannons snoring in one bedroom and Gannon and his wife snoring in another. That will make you wish there was a third bedroom in which you might be snoring, and then it may perhaps occur to you that it's your own fault that there isn't. You're Gannon's landlord, or you were before he burned down your house. It was your business to see that he had a proper number of bedrooms. Even if you had to sell a Paul Lamerie candlestick in order to build him another.'

'I wish I had sold them all,' said the Major. 'I wish I had given them away, to Gannon or anybody else. All this wouldn't have happened if I had.'

' If every landlord,' said Meldon, ' had to spend a couple of nights with each of his tenants there wouldn't be anything like the overcrowding there is, nor so many insanitary houses.'

This little homily had no effect whatever on Major Kent. He was no longer a landlord so it did not apply to him. Besides, he was not listening. He had left the room and gone to the top of the stairs. There he stood quite silent, peering down. In a minute or two he came back.

' J. J.,' he said, ' would you mind making sure that the coast is clear ? There's no use my trying to get away to Gannon's if either of those two men is waiting to arrest me as soon as I venture downstairs.'

' I've told you already,' said Meldon, ' that nobody has the slightest intention of arresting you. All you have to do is to walk out in the ordinary way, saying " Good evening, Eileen," as you pass her, and " Good evening, Peter," if you happen to meet him, and " Delighted to meet you, sir," to the other man whose name we don't know, if it turns out that he's standing about.'

' I won't risk it.'

' Very well. If you insist on being melodramatic and pretending to be a malefactor who's escaping in disguise I'll help you, of course. If the coast's clear —that is to say if neither Peter nor the other man is there—I'll whistle three times softly. Then I'll engage Eileen in conversation of a light but very interesting kind so that her attention will be diverted while you sneak past. I want to talk to her in any case, so that won't be sheer waste of time.'

CHAPTER XX

EILEEN was in a state of fluttered excitement when Meldon came down from the Major's room. It was not likely that she would take much notice of what was happening around her, and Meldon's task of diverting her attention from the Major's movements was an easy one.

A fashionable débutante who has just danced with the Prince of Wales will not, for some time afterwards, be in a position to give a detailed description of a sister débutante. A motorist who has run over a nursemaid, baby and perambulator, is not likely to notice whether the Morris car which passed discreetly on the other side is of the Oxford kind, or merely Cowley. All tremendous happenings obliterate small things which at calmer moments we should certainly observe. The Major might, just then, have run up and downstairs a dozen times, shouting as he went, and Eileen would scarcely have been interested enough to ask him why he did so.

'Did you see him?' she said, a little breathlessly, when Meldon slipped into her office through the side door.

'Do you mean the man who arrived on the motor bike?' said Meldon. 'Another cousin of yours, I suppose? You'll have to be a little careful, you know. I don't say the thing can't be done, but it's very difficult for any girl to keep two cousins on the hop at the same time, especially when one of them is as much in earnest as Peter is. What I advise you to do is to make up your mind which you want and then promise to be a sister to the other one on condition he gives you a really good wedding present.'

He took a chair and sat down as he spoke. He so placed himself that in order to face him Eileen must turn her back on the window which gave on the hall outside. He hoped that he had hit on a subject which would excite her and thus prevent her turning round to see what was happening behind her.

But Eileen was, for the moment, uninterested even in her own prospects of marriage.

' It's Con Murphy,' she said, in an awed tone.

Meldon had been out of Ireland for so long that he had never even heard of Con Murphy. There are some great men whose names are perpetually in the newspapers, whom, indeed, we count great just for that reason. If their names were not continually in the papers we should know nothing about them. But there are others who deliberately shun the publicity of print, preferring to be known only through the whispers which connect their names with striking deeds.

Con Murphy was one of these. Irish newspapers seldom, English newspapers never, mentioned him. He would have been greatly annoyed if they had. He would have taken vengeance, promptly and violently, on any editor who published an article about him, on any Irish editor, for he could not have got at those in England. The English editors, indeed, could not write articles about him, because for the most part they had never heard of him. They heard of his doings occasionally, but the confidential whispers which connected him with the deeds did not sound across the channel. It was only in Ireland that Con Murphy's greatness was fully understood. But in Ireland it was. Peter Jameson had fled at the mere sight of him. Eileen Costello spoke his name with a reverential awe which she would scarcely have felt in naming an archangel. Meldon was conscious of her feeling, but he put it down to another cause.

' Your cousin Peter,' he said, ' didn't seem to like the look of Con Murphy.'

' He did not,' said Eileen emphatically, ' and it's not to be expected that he would.'

Meldon, from his chair, could see the Major creeping downstairs very cautiously. He was most anxious, for his own credit as a conspirator, and for the sake of the Major's feelings, that Eileen should not turn round at that moment.

' Peter Jameson,' he said, ' is the better looking of the two. But Con Murphy seems to me to have more force of character. It's all a question of what you look forward to in married life. If you want to be boss of the house, then I advise you to take Peter. If you prefer being bullied—and I'm told that lots of women do—then I should say that Con Murphy is the man for you.'

That piece of advice, he calculated, would have the effect of completely engaging Eileen's attention. There is probably not a girl living who would turn away and go on with her ordinary business without answering a man who talked to her as Meldon did. But Meldon wanted to be perfectly certain. He went on :

' And stick to whichever you choose,' he said emphatically. ' I'm speaking plainly to you, Miss Costello, but entirely for your own good. There's nothing which leads to so much trouble as philandering in the early stages of love affairs. I said the same thing to your cousin Peter half an hour ago when he was talking about you.'

'Peter,' said Eileen indignantly, ' has the devil's own cheek to be talking about me that way or any other way.'

'Don't take things up wrongly,' said Meldon. ' Peter didn't talk about you at all until I introduced the subject, and very little even then.'

'And what right had you to be telling Peter that I'd marry him ? '

She was a good deal afraid of Meldon, whom she did not in the least understand. But, when sufficiently goaded, she was capable of speaking sharply to him.

'I didn't tell him anything of the sort. I merely told him that if he wanted to marry you—a very different thing from your marrying him—he ought not to philander. I don't expect I should have said anything on the subject at all if it hadn't been necessary to distract his attention for a little while from the Major's income-tax.'

Eileen stared at him. The bewilderment which often came on those to whom Meldon talked was affecting her.

'Income-tax,' she said slowly. ' The Lord save us ! '

The Major had slipped past the window of the office, tiptoed through the hall and reached the door. Meldon felt that he might safely drop Eileen's love affairs. They had served his turn and in themselves they did not interest him much. But it is not always easy to get away from a subject, however tiresome it becomes.

'I suppose now,' said Eileen bitterly, ' that you're after telling Con Murphy that I want to marry him.'

'As a matter of fact,' said Meldon, ' I haven't told

him that or anything else. I couldn't, for I haven't had the chance of speaking to him. But I will if you like.'

' You'd better not be talking to Con Murphy,' said Eileen, ' for he's not in too good a temper this minute, and it's you he's angry with. If I were you I'd get away out of this and not go near him.'

Her advice may have been good, but it was evidently not kindly meant. She spoke with a bitterness which showed that she hoped Meldon would go near Murphy and suffer for it. Meldon became interested. He knew of no reason why Murphy should either be pleased or displeased with him.

' Perhaps,' he said, ' Mr. Murphy may think that it's my fault that the Major hasn't paid his income-tax.'

' Income-tax!' said Eileen scornfully. ' You and your income-tax! It's not income-tax that Con Murphy will be talking to you about when he does talk.'

' I'm glad to hear that,' said Meldon. ' It would be a nuisance if all your cousins were income-tax collectors. The Major's income-tax affairs are rather complicated. All income-tax affairs are, but his unusually so. The fewer people that are mixed up with them the better. It would take me hours to explain the position to Con Murphy. And after all it's really no business of mine. The Major had made up his mind not to pay before he mentioned the matter to me. In fact, the first time I heard of the trouble was one day in Weymouth when —do you happen to know Weymouth?'

' I do not,' said Eileen. ' But there's one thing I do know. It's not to Weymouth that Con Murphy has gone now.'

Virgil has some important things to say about the tempers of ladies whose attractions have been undervalued. Meldon had not made that mistake in dealing with Eileen Costello. He had credited her with two lovers, which is more than most girls have at one time. Yet she seemed in just as bad a temper as if he had refused to admit that she had one.

' If ever he does go to Weymouth,' said Meldon, ' or if ever you go there, the Major's address is High Pines. You'll get a bus without the slightest difficulty which passes the door. The Major will have a warm welcome for you, and for Mr. Murphy, unless he comes about the income-tax. Tell him not to do that.'

' It's to Coolarrigan that Con Murphy has gone,' said Eileen. ' I hope that pleases you.'

It did not particularly please Meldon, nor did it in the least displease him. What it did was to make him more curious than before about Murphy and his doings. He made up his mind to get a little information out of Eileen if he could, but he was far too wise to ask her a direct question.

' I'm afraid he won't find Deissmann there,' he said. ' He's in his own house, writing reports about last night's outrage. At least that's where he was when I saw him this morning, and he can't have finished his reports yet. There's such a tremendous lot to say. You've no idea what a number of things were blown up. Perhaps Mr. Murphy's interested in explosives ? '

For the first time Eileen showed signs of returning good temper. She smiled slightly, but still rather grimly.

' You may say that,' she said.

' If so,' said Meldon, ' he'll find plenty to see at Coolarrigan. I don't suppose there's another spot in the whole British Isles so interesting to an expert in high explosives as Coolarrigan is at the present moment. Did he take your cousin Peter with him ? '

' He did not.'

' I haven't seen Peter anywhere since he ran away from me on the bridge,' said Meldon. ' That's what made me think that he might have gone to Coolarrigan with Mr. Murphy.'

' Peter wouldn't go to Coolarrigan with Con Murphy,' said Eileen. ' Nor he wouldn't go anywhere else with him. Peter has some sense. Sure, everybody knows that Con Murphy has it in against him this long time.'

Meldon was still inclined to think that Eileen herself might be the cause of whatever ill-feeling there was between the two men, but he did not want to start that subject again. Eileen was only beginning to recover from the effects of his last mention of it.

' Ah,' he said cautiously, ' I'd forgotten that.'

' Since ever he left the Republicans and took that job from the Free Staters,' said Eileen, ' Peter has been in terrible dread of Con Murphy, and small wonder.'

Then Meldon understood. Con Murphy was evidently a prominent Republican. Peter Jameson had once been a Republican, too, perhaps the trusted friend of Con Murphy. But he had accepted a post, with a salary attached to it, from the Free State Government, that is to say from the enemy. The position so far as Peter Jameson and Red Con Murphy were concerned was plain enough.

> ' Just for a handful of silver he left us,
> Just for a ribbon to stick in his coat.'

Con Murphy's dislike of Peter and Peter's fear of Con Murphy were accounted for just as satisfactorily as if they had been rivals for the kisses of Eileen Costello. The Frenchman who believed in seeking for a lady when investigating the cause of trouble would have been wiser if he had known Ireland. There it is far oftener a matter of ' *Cherchez la politique.*'

What Meldon did not yet see was why Con Murphy should have a grudge against him. Eileen had hinted pretty plainly that he had. Yet Meldon's conscience was perfectly clear. He had never been a Republican and so could not be accused of deserting that party. He had no hope whatever of getting the smallest salary or pension from the Free State Government. He was a married man and could not have been a rival for the hand and fortune of Eileen.

' It's a great pity,' said Meldon, ' that Murphy should take it that way. He ought to be reasonable. I'm always saying that to people, but it's very little use. I've said it to the Major scores of times. I've said it to Michael Gannon. I've said it two or three times to Deissmann. If Murphy had been what I call a reasonable man he'd have seen that Peter was bound to seize his chance when it came. It isn't every day that a man gets the offer of a regular salary, paid by a Government. It's what most of us want, and Peter couldn't possibly have been expected to refuse it.'

Meldon was still hoping for some light on the cause of Murphy's enmity against him. It did not, for some time, seem likely that he was going to get it.

' That's what I always say myself,' said Eileen, ' politics is all well enough, and there's nobody likes politics better than I do, but it doesn't do to let them interfere with your way of living, whatever that way of living may be. And Peter, poor fellow, never had any way of living till he got that job.'

Then suddenly and quite unintentionally she revealed to Meldon the nature of his offence.

' But sure Peter may make his mind easy for a while anyway,' said Eileen.   ' Con Murphy won't be bothering about him so long as he's as angry as he is this minute over what's been going on at Coolarrigan.'

' Michael Gannon's explosions ? '

' Them and the strike.'

' How odd ! ' said Meldon.   ' As a Republican leader I should have thought he'd have liked strikes and revelled in explosions.'

' And he does like them both,' said Eileen.   ' There's no man in Ireland is fonder of them than what he is, only he likes them better when he does them himself.'

' I must have a little chat with Mr. Murphy,' said Meldon, ' when he comes back from Coolarrigan.   When will he be back from Coolarrigan ? '

' I don't know when he'll be back,' said Eileen. ' But if you're intending to tell him that he's to marry me I'd as soon you didn't, if it's all the same to you.'

' I shan't mention your name at all.'

' Red Con Murphy wouldn't be seen on the same side of the street with a girl like me,' said Eileen with great humility.   ' Considering the high-up man he is these days it's not to be expected he would.   And, to tell you the truth, if I have to marry anyone, which seemingly I must, sooner or later, I'd as soon have a quieter sort of a man.   Heroes is all well enough, but I don't know would I like to be married to one.'

' Peter,' said Meldon, ' is certainly the man for you. Anyone who saw him running away from Con Murphy to-day would know that he hates rows and asks for nothing more than a peaceable life.'

' If I were you,' said Eileen, whose ill-temper had

completely vanished, ' I'd be mighty careful about talking to Con Murphy.   He's angry, so he is, terrible angry.'

' That's exactly why I want to talk to him,' said Meldon. ' He ought not to be angry, and he won't be once I've explained to him that professional jealousy, which seems to be what he is suffering from, is a most ignoble passion.   Really great men never give way to it and Con Murphy goes in for being a great man.'

' It's what he is.'

' Exactly.   And that's why he ought to rise superior to any feeling of annoyance over the part we took in getting up the strike and the explosions.   I quite understand his position.   He doesn't like meddling outsiders, especially when they're mere amateurs, and a little resentment is natural.   But when I put it to him in the proper way——'

' You'll do as you choose,' said Eileen, ' but if you'll be said by me you'll keep out of Con Murphy's way for a day or two.'

' My dear Eileen—you don't mind my calling you Eileen, do you ? Now that you're going to marry my old friend Peter Jameson I can't bear to be on formal terms with you.   My dear Eileen, you really ought to have a better opinion of human nature than you seem to have.   Con Murphy will be perfectly reasonable and friendly once I've explained the situation to him.'

CHAPTER XXI

'MR. MELDON, Mr. Meldon!'
Meldon looked round. He and Eileen were alone in the little office and the words certainly did not come from her.

They were repeated, hoarsely, as in a half-smothered whisper. The speaker, whoever he was, was anxious to be heard, but not to be heard by many people. He might have shouted. He preferred to whisper.

'Mr. Meldon, do you hear me?'

This time Meldon located the sound. At the back of Eileen's office, behind the desk on which she kept the books of the hotel, was a green curtain. It seemed to be covering part of the wall, quite needlessly, for why should walls be covered with curtains? It was from this curtain that the voice came. Meldon might have complained, as Hamlet did, of rats, but the curtain hung too flat to leave room for a human rat between it and the wall.

Meldon walked over to the curtain and drew it aside. In front of him was a door, shut. He turned the handle, vainly. The door was locked.

'Could I speak to you for one minute?'

It was Peter Jameson's voice, easily recognizable once it was not smothered by the curtain.

'If you want to talk to me,' said Meldon, 'you'd better open the door and come out.'

'Sure I can't get out,' said Peter. 'Eileen has the key.'

Meldon turned to her.

'Why on earth,' he said, 'have you locked up Peter Jameson in a cupboard?'

Eileen's face was crimson. She displayed every sign of extreme embarrassment.

'It's not a cupboard,' she said. 'It's the wine cellar.'

'Whatever it is,' said Meldon, 'you'd better let him out. His voice sounds to me as if he was smothering.'

Instead of doing what Meldon told her, Eileen began to upbraid Peter volubly.

'You're a low, mean fellow,' she said, 'and I'll never speak to you again for as long as I live. Not if I was to be a hundred years old, I wouldn't. It's not what I expected of you, though the Lord knows I didn't expect much. But such conduct is beyond the beyonds and I won't put up with it. To think of you standing there all the time listening to what Mr. Meldon was saying to me about—about—' Eileen sat down abruptly and began to cry. 'About me getting married.'

Both anger and grief were excusable. In the course of her talk with Meldon Eileen had made the sort of admissions which no self-respecting girl would make until she was quite sure of the man she made the admissions about.

'Peter,' said Meldon, 'were you listening at the keyhole of that door?'

'I was not,' said Peter. 'I was nowhere near the door, nor the keyhole either. I was down in the cellar, sitting on a case of whisky or it might have been rum. It's hard to tell what was in the case for there was no light. I didn't come near the door till a minute ago.'

'A minute may very well have been long enough,' said Meldon. 'Did you hear the advice I gave Miss Costello about getting married ? '

'What I heard was you saying that you'd give Red Con Murphy a talking to so as he'd mend his ways.'

Peter had, in fact, heard more than that. He had heard Meldon's excuse for addressing Eileen by her Christian name, but he thought it better not to confess that. Neither Meldon, nor Eileen, fortunately enough, remembered exactly how their talk had gone nor what Meldon's last words were.

'If that's all you heard,' said Meldon, 'there's no harm done. I don't in the least mind your knowing that I mean to have a talk with Murphy. But you haven't got it exactly right. Listeners at keyholes never do get anything right, but there's no harm in your knowing that that's what I'm going to do.'

'It was about that I was wanting to speak to you,' said Peter, 'but I can't if you won't let me out.'

'Before you're let out,' said Meldon, 'I'd like to know why you're in ? What are you doing locked up in the wine cellar ? You don't sound to me as if you were drunk, but if you're not why are you there ? '

Eileen, reassured by what Peter said, and no longer afraid that he had overheard her confessions, stopped crying.

'It was me put him there,' she said, 'and it was me locked the door on him. I did it so as he'd be safe out of the way of Con Murphy. Peter—' she smiled through the remains of her tears—' Peter does be in dread of Con Murphy, and small wonder.'

'I'm not sure,' said Meldon, 'that you chose the very best hiding-place. Con Murphy gives me the impression

of being a man who'd be very likely to take a look at
the wine cellar before he left a house, especially if he'd
any idea that there was a case of whisky in it. However, I daresay you were hurried and couldn't think of
anywhere better at the moment.'

' It would puzzle Con Murphy to get at him,' said
Eileen, ' for I have the key in my pocket.'

' If you have,' said Meldon, ' you'd better let him
out. Con Murphy is at Coolarrigan and he can't be
back again for a while. There'll be plenty of time to
lock Peter up again if necessary. That motor bike
that Murphy goes about on can be heard for miles.
There's not the slightest fear of his taking anybody by
surprise.'

Eileen got the key out of her pocket and unlocked
the door. Peter Jameson came out blinking helplessly.
The cellar, which was reached by descending a small
flight of stairs behind the door, was quite dark, and it
took his eyes some time to adapt themselves to the
light.

' Now,' said Meldon, ' you're out and you'd better
tell me what you want. Get to the point as quickly as
you can and don't waste time over unnecessary
explanations. I'm a busy man, and besides you may
have to bolt into that cellar of yours again at any
moment. Don't start off with a long story about why
Con Murphy wants to kill you. That has nothing to
do with me. For all I know to the contrary he may
have excellent reasons.'

' All the reason ever he had for trying to get me——'
said Peter.

' That,' said Meldon, ' is exactly what I told you not
to start talking about, and yet you immediately begin
to do it. I knew you'd want to. That's why I warned

you against wasting time. Can't you understand that all that doesn't matter ? '

' It matters to me,' said Peter.

' Peter,' said Eileen, ' will you talk to Mr. Meldon the way he wants you to ? Why can't you do as you're bid ? '

' I would do as I'm bid,' said Peter, ' only how can I if he won't let me tell him why Con Murphy has it in against me ? '

' You can tell me that some other time,' said Meldon, ' not that I ever want to hear it, but if you're like the Ancient Mariner and feel uneasy till you get your story off your chest— You know all about the Ancient Mariner, I suppose ? '

' I do not,' said Peter, and it appeared that Eileen knew no more than he did.

' Well,' said Meldon, ' all you need know at present is that he went to a wedding and when he got there behaved exactly as you're doing now. He button-holed one of the guests, who wanted to listen to a bassoon, and insisted on telling him a long story which he didn't want to hear. But you haven't got the kind of eye that he had, Peter. His was glittering and yours is mildly watery, so you can't hypnotize me however hard you try. You may just as well drop the Con Murphy story, whatever it is—and I don't mind telling you that the reason I won't listen to it is that I know it already. Con Murphy thinks you went back on him ; basely and treacherously deserted the cause for the sake of which he was sacrificing other people's lives in dozens. Whereas you walked out and took a salary.'

' Sure, what else could Peter do ? ' said Eileen, ' when they offered him a job under the Government ? '

' I'm not discussing the rights and wrongs of the

matter,' said Meldon. ' Peter may be perfectly
justified in what he did to Murphy. Murphy may be
perfectly justified in what he's going to do to Peter.
All that I'm trying to make clear is that I know the
facts and that it's mere waste of time going over them
all again. What I want to get at—what I would have
got at long ago if Peter hadn't insisted in trying to tell
long and totally irrelevant stories, is what he wants to
speak to me about. You clamoured to be let out of
that cellar, Peter, a place in which you were perfectly
safe and might have been happy if you'd had a cork-
screw with you—you clamoured to be let out because
you wanted to say something to me and now that you
are out you won't say it.'

' All I wanted to say to you was this.' Peter spoke a
little sulkily. ' If you're talking to Con Murphy there's
no need to mention to him that I'm down in Lisnamoe.'

' When I talk to Con Murphy,' said Meldon, ' which
I mean to do, I shall stick strictly to the business on
hand. You must not think that because you like
wasting time on desultory gossip every one else enjoys
it too. When I have anything to say I go straight to
the point and keep to it. There's not the slightest risk
of my trotting out all the social tittle-tattle of a place
like this, telling him who's here and who isn't.'

' You might not tell him straight out that I was here,'
said Peter, ' but he might draw down the subject
while you were talking to him about another matter
altogether.'

' If he's the least like you he'll try to,' said Meldon.

' If he does—' said Peter.

' If he does, I shall tell him the truth. That's one of
my fixed rules. Always, if at all possible, tell the truth.
Apart from the moral aspect of the question, which I

don't expect you to appreciate, it doesn't pay to tell lies. It simply leads to complications which become more and more confusing as time goes on.'

' And what truth are you thinking of telling him ? ' said Peter.

' There's never more than one truth,' said Meldon, ' except in theology. There the principle called economy comes in which means that there are several different kinds of truth, all equally true, but varying in accordance with the religious capacity of the people they're told to. People are invariably of different cultural levels, and so religion, if they are to receive it at all, has to be presented to them——'

' It might be better,' said Eileen, ' not to bring religion into it.'

' That,' said Meldon, ' is exactly what I'm explaining to you that I'm not going to do. Peter seems to think I ought to. If your question about truth means anything, Peter, it means that, and I decline to treat the matter in any such way. When I say that I'm going to tell Con Murphy the truth about you—in the unlikely event of my having to tell him anything at all about you—I mean the truth in the ordinary, irreligious sense of the word.'

' And what will you tell him ? '

' I'll tell him that you're here for the purpose, the nefarious purpose of trying to terrify the poor Major into paying income-tax which you know perfectly well he doesn't owe.'

' If you tell him that,' said Peter, ' it'll be all right, supposing he believes you.'

' And is that what you're here for, Peter,' said Eileen. ' Why did you never tell me that before ? '

' It's not what I'm here for.'

' He didn't tell you,' said Meldon, ' and he won't admit it to you even now because he feels himself bound by the code of morals adopted by men who occupy high positions in the civil service. It's called official reticence, and that means that nobody ever tells anybody anything. The principle is carried so far that if you ask the secretary of a diplomat what time it is he'll reply that it's not in accordance with the traditions of the service to give that kind of information to the general public.'

' It's not what I'm accustomed to,' said Eileen. ' I like to be told what's going on, and I may as well tell you, Peter, that your official—what did you call it, Mr. Meldon ? '

' Official reticence,' said Meldon. ' That's the regular name for it.'

' Well, whatever the name of it is,' said Eileen, ' it'll not suit me.'

' But it isn't that at all,' said Peter. ' It's——'

' Explain all that afterwards,' said Meldon, ' not now. What I'd like to know now is whether you're good for a game of bridge this evening. The Major would like it and so I'm sure would Mr. Murphy.'

' Is it me play bridge with Con Murphy ? ' said Peter. ' Sure, how could I do that ? '

' You can do it perfectly well if you try,' said Meldon. ' Of course I shall have made everything all right with him long before evening, and he'll have quite forgotten any grudge he may have had against you. In fact, I expect he's forgotten it already. At the present moment he's far angrier with me than he is with you. I suppose you've no objection to playing with the Major ? '

' I have not,' said Peter. ' Why would I ? '

' He thinks you have,' said Meldon. ' His idea is that so long as you regard it as your duty to dun him for income-tax you might not care to sit down to bridge with him. I told him that was all nonsense and that you weren't that kind of man at all.'

' Peter,' said Eileen, ' why did you not tell me about the income-tax ? How do you expect me to go on being friends with you if you won't tell me things like that ? '

' Sure, it isn't true at all,' said Peter. ' And how would I be telling you what isn't true when I know well that you'd be mad with me after if I did ? '

' There you are,' said Meldon. ' Exactly what I said. Official reticence. An extreme form of it ; but not very unusual. I've known cases quite as striking, but it doesn't do to pay much attention to it. If you take my advice, my dear Eileen——'

Here he turned to Peter with an apologetic smile.

' You don't mind my calling her my dear Eileen, do you ? I seem to have known her so long and so intimately.'

' What you said a minute ago,' said Peter, ' was that you were calling her Eileen on account of her being going——'

Here he stopped abruptly. Eileen was blushing again, an angry red. She had suddenly remembered Meldon's last words to her, spoken just before Peter made his first appeal for release. Meldon remembered them, too, but not very accurately. ' You don't mind my saying " Eileen," do you ? Now that you're going to marry my old friend Peter Jameson I can't bear to be on formal terms with you.'

' You said you weren't listening,' said Eileen, angrily to Peter.

' I was not listening,' he said, ' but how could I help hearing ? '

It was the time-honoured excuse of all listeners, made no doubt by Rebecca when she overheard her husband's conversation with his elder son, made probably long before her time, certainly made over and over again through all the following centuries. It failed, apparently, to pacify Eileen. Once more her blush seemed likely to be drowned in tears. Meldon intervened to save her from that disaster.

' These affairs,' he said—' I'm not now talking of the Major's income-tax or Con Murphy's activities, past or future, I'm talking about you and Peter—these affairs cannot really be satisfactorily settled by outsiders. I've done my best for both of you. I've told Peter what he ought to say to you. I've told you—or almost told you—what you ought to answer when he says it. I don't see what more I can do for you except go away and leave you to settle the little that's left for yourselves. I'll keep Con Murphy away from you if I can, but if I can't and you hear him coming into the hotel I advise you to go into the cellar, both of you, and lock the door behind you. If you can't settle things there in the dark when there's nobody to see you and you can't see each other, you'll never be able to settle them at all.'

CHAPTER XXII

MELDON was standing at the door of the hotel when Con Murphy came along the road from Coolarrigan, his motor bicycle making a rattle of sharp explosions. He was in a thoroughly bad temper. A mere glance at his face showed that, and he had very good cause for anger. Never before in all his experience of outrages—an experience greater than that of any other man in the whole world—had he seen anything so complete as the devastation wrought at Coolarrigan. If the strike had been a failure, if the men had dribbled back to work in twos and threes, Murphy might have found it easy enough to forgive the organizers. If a paltry fire had injured a couple of wheelbarrows and a shower of stones had broken a few panes of glass, he would have regarded the amateurs who had thus displayed their incapacity with perfectly friendly feelings. But the strike had been a complete success and the explosions extraordinarily effective. Con Murphy realized that a serious and dangerous rival threatened his supremacy in his own particular business. He was as angry as an Admiral might be if some one of whom he had never heard were suddenly to seize part of the Fleet under his command and achieve a naval victory while the Admiral himself was dining quietly. That, of course, could not possibly happen, but if it did the Admiral's feelings would be very like those of Con Murphy.

The simple and obvious thing to do was to shoot Caegheanaght, whoever he might be, and afterwards pin a label to his chest warning other traitors that the same fate waited for them.   But there were some difficulties about this, and Con Murphy realized very clearly what they were.   In the first place he did not know who Caegheanaght was.   The name puzzled him precisely as it had puzzled Peter Jameson, as it had puzzled Peter's friends, as it had puzzled the Free State Government. For the first time in his life Con Murphy wished that he knew Irish better than he did.   He would very much have liked to be able to translate that name into its English equivalent.   But he was not wholly in the dark about who his rival was.   Eileen Costello had mentioned Meldon to him.   She had also mentioned Major Kent. Con Murphy thought that Caegheanaght must be one or the other.   The fact that he did not know which troubled him very little.   He would have had no hesitation about shooting them both if it had not been for a horrible doubt which assailed him.   Here was his second difficulty.   It was possible that Caegheanaght, that is to say Meldon, or the Major, or both, might be an American sent over on a special mission to see how the Irish Republic was getting on.   Con Murphy was almost entirely dependent on the ' greater Ireland beyond the seas'—the Irish-Americans in New York and Boston—for the funds with which he carried on his work.   He had read, as a boy, the story of the man who killed the goose which laid the golden eggs.   He was very much afraid that he might be doing the same foolish thing if he shot either Meldon or Major Kent.

He was therefore in a mood of anger mixed with perplexity as he rode back from Coolarrigan to the hotel. Meldon greeted him with an entirely friendly waving of his hand. He stopped his bicycle and dismounted.

' Mr. Connemara Murphy, I think,' said Meldon, ' or is Con short for Connemara ? I've often wondered.'

Anger, for the moment, overcame both perplexity and prudence in Con Murphy. He clutched the butt of the revolver which he carried in his coat pocket.

' Look here, my fine fellow,' he said, ' if you think you can get off by making jokes you're damned well mistaken.'

' I wish you wouldn't swear,' said Meldon. ' It gives you an unfair advantage over me, for, being a clergyman, I can't swear back. Just look at my collar if you want to make sure what I am.'

Con Murphy looked at the collar. Prudence and perplexity, a strange pair of allies, got the better of anger. He loosed his grasp on the revolver. Religion still keeps its ancient hold on the Irish people. They regard it as unlucky to shoot priests.

' But, perhaps,' said Meldon amiably, ' it's short for Cornelius. Anyhow, whatever Con stands for, I'm extremely pleased to meet you. I've heard such a lot about you that I've always wanted, absolutely longed, to make your acquaintance. So has the Major. Michael Gannon is always talking about you. So is Eileen Costello. So is——'

He remembered his promise to Peter just in time. ' So is the Government up in Dublin. I can't tell you what a lot they think of you. But, of course, it would be affectation to pretend that they actually like you.'

This was flattery of a subtle kind. Con Murphy was a man who thoroughly enjoyed his notoriety and had never sought the affections of the Free State Government. He began to feel a little less angry with Meldon. He took his hand out of the pocket where the revolver lay.

' It's scarcely to be expected,' Meldon went on, ' that they would be very fond of you, considering all you've done, but I wouldn't go so far as to say that they actually hated you. Their feeling is that of an aunt towards a grown-up niece—affectionate but hostile. Michael Gannon, of course, feels no hostility. Nor does Eileen Costello. Nor do I. Nor does the Major. Our feeling is respectful admiration. Not that we actually approve of everything you do. It would be too much to expect that from us, especially from the Major, who is an old-fashioned Conservative, and I, as a clergyman, am more or less bound to disapprove — officially, you understand, merely officially—of unauthorized executions. Do you play bridge ? '

' From what I've heard of the way you've been going on at Coolarrigan,' said Con Murphy, ' and from what I've seen with my own eyes, I'd say that there was very little in the way of outrages that you disapproved of, or the Major either.'

' Ah, Coolarrigan ! ' said Meldon. ' How odd that you should have mentioned Coolarrigan ! As it happens, that's the exact subject I want to talk to you about. But do tell me, before I begin, whether you play bridge ? '

' What business had you meddling in Coolarrigan ? ' said Con Murphy.

His anger was beginning to rise again. The mention of Coolarrigan, the very word ' outrage ' which he had used himself, reminded him that Meldon and the Major had been interfering in a totally inexcusable way with his business.

' Interference,' Con Murphy went on, ' is what I won't stand from you nor from any one else.'

' I'll explain the whole Coolarrigan business to you in a few words,' said Meldon, ' though I'd rather you'd tell me first whether you play bridge. However, if you'd rather not, I'll begin at once. The Major and I——'

' It's my belief,' said Con Murphy, ' that you and the Major is spies in the pay of the English Government, and that you're getting up outrages for the purpose of bringing discredit on the Irish people.'

This was not really his belief. It was a convenient way, constantly adopted in Ireland, of accounting for doings which few people liked to approve and every one feared to condemn. That was very nearly Con Murphy's position. He could not possibly approve of violent explosions set off without his consent and help. At the same time he could not very well condemn outrages which—he was still uncertain on this point—might have been planned in America.

' So far from being paid by England,' said Meldon, ' the Major is at this moment liable for a large sum of income-tax, fifty pounds, I think. It's due, though the Major doesn't admit that, to the Irish Free State, not to England. But that does not affect the general argument. Would any State—I put it to you as a man of experience in these things—would any State charge income-tax, or even try to, on the money it paid out to spies for the purpose of getting up outrages? You know just as well as I do that money of that sort is always regarded as tax free. But the Irish Free State is worrying the Major day and night, even threatening him, to force him to pay. I wish you'd seen some of the letters they've written him. If you had you wouldn't suspect him of being a spy. A man who's dunned for income-tax can't possibly be a spy. You see that, don't you ? '

' In the name of God, then,' said Con Murphy desperately, ' who are you, and what are you at ? '

' That is what I'm trying to tell you. I'd get on quicker if you wouldn't keep interrupting me with perfectly ridiculous suggestions of your own. I understand your feelings quite well. You don't like us chipping in and blowing up things like the River Shannon, which you always intended to blow up yourself. What you think is that we're sneaking round behind your back and taking the bread out of your mouth. You're furious, naturally. I don't blame you in the least, but I want you to understand what the position really is. Then you'll see that there's nothing to be angry about. The simple fact is that the Major and I—or, strictly speaking, the Major, for I'm merely helping him, out of a feeling of friendship—the Major had a little business of a private kind with that fellow Deissmann.'

' If that's the way of it,' said Con Murphy—' and of course there's no reason in the world why one gentleman shouldn't have private business with another nor why the business mightn't end in burning a few things which belong to the other gentleman, or, for the matter of that, blowing up a river or anything else— but if that's the way of it what call had you to be acting in the name of the Irish Republic ? That's what has me annoyed.'

He put his hand into his pocket, not the pocket which

contained the revolver, and drew out a copy of the original strike proclamation.

'Look at that,' he said, 'and tell me what's the meaning of it.'

'Oh, that!' said Meldon. 'That was simply meant —Look here, Murphy, the Major and I have behaved badly to you. We don't deny it for a moment, and we're both sorry. We'll apologize to any extent you like. We know perfectly well that we ought not to have done what was really your business. We understand all about professional etiquette, thoroughly, and we have the greatest respect for it. As a matter of fact, we're both professional men ourselves. But we couldn't help doing what we did. If Deissmann had been a reasonable man, the sort of man it's possible to persuade, we'd never have done a single one of the things which have annoyed you. But he wasn't, so we had to take a strong line with him. That's a thing which may happen to any one. It must have happened to you, lots of times. There must have been plenty of men that you've been practically forced to deal with rather sternly simply because they would insist on behaving outrageously.'

'There's a fellow called Peter Jameson——'

'I mean to speak to you about him,' said Meldon, 'and I will later on. But, first, I'd like you to realize what our position is, the Major's and mine.'

'Sure, I'd have no objection to your shooting Deissmann,' said Murphy, 'none in the world, but what right have you to be saying that it was the Irish Republic that did it?'

Again he held out the strike notice to Meldon.

'Don't go on waving that paper at me,' said Meldon. 'It's dirty. It's unpleasant. It's positively

H

insanitary. I've seen quite as much of it as I want to.'

' Is that your name at the bottom of it ? '

' Mine ! ' said Meldon. ' Certainly not. It's yours.'

' It is not.'

' I'm not very good at Irish,' said Meldon. ' Nor is the Major, but——'

' It's nothing like my name.'

' It's nothing like anybody else's,' said Meldon. ' Now do be reasonable, Murphy. The Major and I wanted to give Deissmann an uncomfortable half-hour or so, on account of his selfishness and obstinacy, but we didn't want any credit for what we did. Our wish was that you should have all the credit that was going. In fact, we wanted the public to believe that you worked the whole thing—as you would have if it had occurred to you. We meant, and we still mean, to keep entirely in the background. That's why we signed your name to the proclamation so that all the glory and honour should be yours. Surely you see that ? '

' If it's that way it is——'

' It is. All the Major wants—all I want—once we've settled with Deissmann, is to slip quietly away to England leaving everything here in your hands. All the credit, all the profit, if any, all the satisfaction of goading the Government to desperation, in fact everything—it's all yours.'

Con Murphy was mollified. Meldon was behaving with unexpected generosity.

' So now,' said Meldon, ' we can go on to talk about the future. Now that you're here—and I can't tell you what a relief it is to the Major and me that you've arrived—now that you are here you will of course take full command and everything else that is done to Deissmann will be done by your orders.'

' Unless we shoot him,' said Con Murphy, ' I don't see what else there is to do to him.'

' I'd hardly care to go as far as shooting him,' said Meldon, ' at least not just yet. What about burning down his house ? It's not a very big one so it won't make much of a blaze. Still it will be very annoying for him.'

' We could do that, of course.'

' Letting him get clear away first,' said Meldon. ' We might give him five minutes, longer if you like. I am quite willing to be guided by you in matters of detail. The Major, as well as I recollect, was given ten minutes, but his was a much larger house.'

' Five minutes will be plenty for him.'

' Very well,' said Meldon. ' You and I and perhaps Michael Gannon—I don't think we'll take the Major. He has a habit of arguing at critical moments. You and I and Michael Gannon will go to-night, starting about—now what is the recognized hour for a job of this sort ? '

' Between one and two in the morning is the best time.'

' Capital,' said Meldon. ' Jimmy Costello can drive us over. If we start at half-past twelve it will be quite early enough. That will give us comfortable time for our bridge after dinner. Let me see—did you say you played bridge ? I know I asked you but I can't remember what you said.'

' I do play bridge,' said Con Murphy, ' but I'd sooner play spoil five if I'm to play anything.'

' I am not at all sure,' said Meldon, ' that the Major knows how to play spoil five. However, we can teach

him.   And if he's not very good—well, that'll be all the
better in one way.   You'll be much more likely to take
a little money off him than if you were playing bridge
He plays an uncommonly sound game of bridge—all
retired Majors do—but spoil five, which he can't play,
is another thing altogether.   You'd like to make a bit
of money in the course of the evening, wouldn't you,
Murphy ? '

' I would,' said Con Murphy, ' anybody would.
But what I wouldn't like would be to be taking money
off a man that couldn't afford to lose it.'

Thus unexpected virtues appear in the worst of us.
Con Murphy would have had no hesitation about
burning down Coolarrigan Castle if it had not been
burnt down already.   He would have quite willingly
shot the Major or Meldon for reasons of a purely
political kind.   But he was genuinely unwilling to take
advantage of his skill at a particular game of cards
in order to win money from a poor man.   Meldon
reassured him at once.

' The Major has plenty,' he said.   ' In fact—and this
brings me to a thing I particularly want to say to you
—at the present moment the Major is being dunned
by the Free State Government for fifty pounds arrears
of income-tax.'

' Let him not pay.'

' He won't if he can help it,' said Meldon, ' but he
has the money.   That's what I want you to grasp.   He
has the fifty pounds and if he isn't forced to pay it over
it will be, so to speak, found money for him, money to
play with.   I mention this so that you need have no
hesitation about winning a little from him to-night.'

' It would be better in my pocket than the Government's.'

' Exactly, but not the whole of it. I couldn't agree to your fleecing the poor Major to that extent. Say ten pounds. He won't mind losing that much if he gets off paying the tax. It'll be clear gain of forty pounds for him. You see what I'm getting at now, don't you ? '

' I do not.'

' How odd ! I thought you'd have been sure to see that at once. We want you to put a stop to this persecution of the Major by the income-tax people. In fact, we're relying on you to see that no further demand is made on him for the money.'

' I'd do it if I could,' said Con Murphy, a good deal puzzled. ' I'd do it with the greatest pleasure in life, but how can I ? '

' Don't make yourself out stupider than you really are,' said Meldon, ' stupider than any one could possibly be. There's a young man called Peter Jameson. You know him, don't you ? '

' I know him. It might be better for him if I didn't.'

He spoke with a grim ferocity which showed Meldon that Peter Jameson's fears were not entirely groundless.

' He's come here,' said Meldon, ' straight from Dublin to get that fifty pounds out of the Major. You have a good deal of influence with him, so I understand.'

' You may call it influence if you like.'

' Very well, then, use it. That's all I want. See to it that Peter stops dunning the Major. Then—well, you see how it all works out. If he doesn't have to pay the tax the Major will be delighted, simply delighted, to lose ten pounds to you at spoil five or any other game, and we shall all have an extremely pleasant evening together.'

' You may make your mind easy about Peter

Jameson,' said Con Murphy. ' It's not collecting taxes in Lisnamoe he'll be in an hour and a half from now, but collecting sticks in hell so as the devil will be able to make up the fire as hot as it should be for the roasting of fellows like Peter Jameson.'

' Thanks,' said Meldon. ' I knew you'd be willing to do what you could once you grasped what was wanted. But I don't think we need actually kill Peter.'

' That fellow deserves what he gets and more.'

' I know,' said Meldon. ' He deserted the sacred cause of the Republic. He sold himself to the Free State for a salary. He went back on his principles and all that sort of thing. Still, it's not right to be vindictive, especially at the present moment. You know that he's just got engaged to be married to Eileen Costello, or perhaps you hadn't heard that. Anyhow he has. At least I expect and hope he has. I left them together in a pitch-dark cellar, and I'm practically certain that they have it all settled by this time, even the date of the marriage. And she's a nice girl. It really won't do to shoot the man she's just going to marry.'

' She'd be better marrying some other fellow, not him.'

' I daresay you're quite right about that, but she doesn't think so. You and I know what girls are once they've made up their minds to marry a particular man. We may think he's a rotter who ought to be shot, but that doesn't make it a bit pleasanter for the girl if he is shot. Besides, in this case it isn't really necessary. Peter Jameson isn't what I call an obstinate man. He'll be amenable to reason. All I want is for you to use your influence with him.'

' Influence ! What influence is there with a fellow like him only to shoot him ? '

' I can't and won't have Peter shot in that offhand
way,' said Meldon firmly. ' Get that clearly into your
head once for all, Murphy, and don't start arguing about
it.   Have you no sense of decency ?   You can't shoot
a man who's actually on his way to be married.   But
if you don't see that—and apparently it's beyond you
—think of the matter this way.   If you shoot Peter
he'll be dead afterwards, won't he ? '

' He will.'

' And if he's dead he can't play spoil five this
evening.   That seems obvious.   Eileen, assuming that
Peter is dead, will be in deep mourning, and while in that
condition can't, or at all events won't, spend the evening
playing spoil five.   No nice girl would.   Then there'd
be nobody left but you and me and the Major, and
three isn't enough for spoil five.   Therefore we shan't
be able to play.   That'll be a disappointment to me and
a disappointment to the Major.   But it'll be a worse
disappointment to you, because you're looking forward
to winning ten pounds, a thing which you won't be able
to do if Peter Jameson happens to die, in any way,
before evening.'

' In the name of God,' said Con Murphy, ' will you
tell me straight and plain what you want me to be
doing ?   I'm a man who's willing to do what I can to
please any one, but how can I if I don't know what it
is ? '

' I've been telling you all along what's wanted,' said
Meldon, ' but I don't mind telling you again if you like.
Make it clear to Peter Jameson—you can write him a
letter if you like, or send him a message through Eileen,
or I don't mind taking a message myself.   You won't
be able to say it to him yourself because he's sure to
hide if he sees you coming.   Send him a message to say

definitely that if he makes the slightest attempt to collect the Major's income-tax before to-morrow evening —I don't mind what he does after that for we'll be on our way back to England, but if, either to-day or to-morrow morning, he so much as hints that the Major owes a penny, he'll be shot at once.   You can do that, can't you ? '

' I can, easy.'

' Very well, do it.   That's what I meant by using your influence with him.'

CHAPTER XXIII

EILEEN COSTELLO, who thoroughly understood her business as manageress of an hotel, made excellent arrangements for Meldon's spoil five party. In the centre of the smoking-room she set a table and on it two unused packs of cards. On a side table were two bottles of whisky, several siphons of soda-water and a row of tumblers. Two boxes of cigars, the best which she kept for her fishermen, and a quantity of cigarettes, were on another table in a corner of the room. There were ash trays wherever ash trays could be put, though Eileen had small hope that the smokers would use them. Meldon, she knew, scattered his tobacco ashes about with no regard for carpets, and Con Murphy was almost equally careless. But ash trays, most of them with advertisements of mineral waters upon them, looked well, and gave an air of finished luxury to the room. A turf fire burned cheerfully in the grate. Even in high summer a fire is pleasant in the west of Ireland. That evening it was particularly desirable. The wind was rising, a west wind, warm and moist from the Atlantic, and there was promise of much rain before morning.

Meldon and Con Murphy dined together, waited on by the aged Macmahon. They dined well, for Eileen had done her best with the cooking.

Meldon apologized for the Major's absence.

' Silly of him, of course,' he said, ' missing an excellent dinner. But that's the sort of man the Major is ; brave as a lion in any sort of battle, doesn't mind machine-guns in the least, but an utter coward when called upon to face an income-tax collector. However, he'll turn up later on. I've sent Jimmy Costello down to him— he's in Gannon's cottage—did I tell you that ? Well, he is. He's probably eating bacon and drinking stewed tea, with the nine little Gannons crawling round him, all for the want of a little moral courage. However, I've sent Jimmy Costello down there, with a written guar-antee, signed by Peter, that the subject of income-tax won't be mentioned for the evening. If I'd only thought of doing it sooner we might have had him for dinner. Peter himself prefers a quiet dinner with Eileen. We can't blame him for that. After all it isn't every day that a man gets engaged to be married to a really attractive girl. I can't tell you what a comfort it was to me to find out that your little differ-ence of opinion with Peter was merely political. If you'd wanted the girl too, it would have been much more serious.'

' It's serious enough,' said Con Murphy, ' and that's what Peter will find out when you and the Major have gone home out of this.'

' But not to-night,' said Meldon, ' or to-morrow. You've promised me that. It would utterly spoil our evening if you shot Peter at the card table. Eileen would weep and leave damp pocket-handkerchiefs about, just as if she had a cold in her head. Most unpleasant things, damp pocket-handkerchiefs. The Major would be horribly upset. He's accustomed to corpses, of course, on battle-fields and other suitable places ; but he would—you don't know him, so you'll have to take my word for this—he would simply refuse to play cards in this room if Peter Jameson's body was lying on the hearthrug in a pool of blood. That's the kind of man the Major is, full of old-fashioned prejudices.'

' I'll not touch him to-night. I promised you that and I'll be as good as my word.'

' I don't expect you ever will. When you see him and Eileen together, holding hands under the table and playing wrong cards because they're so busy making eyes at each other that they don't know what's trumps ; love's young dream, and so forth—you won't have the heart to do anything really drastic to Peter. However, that'll be a matter for future consideration. The great thing is to keep your promise and do nothing to-night. After all—I know you're one of those men who count a day wasted in which something definite hasn't been done. But after all we're going to burn down Deissmann's house and that's something. You oughtn't to try to crowd too many good deeds on one day. Even the most enthusiastic boy scout wouldn't do that. Not that I want to commit myself to the opinion that shooting Peter Jameson is a good deed. From my point of view it isn't, and the Major would call it murder. But I quite see that you look at it in a different light. You'd rather think of it as an execution, a disagreeable necessity but perfectly right.'

Con Murphy nodded. He had eaten a great deal and drunk freely. He began to feel benevolent, as men often do after good dinners. It seemed to him possible that he might forgo the pleasure of shooting Peter Jameson, and—another consequence of a good dinner —he felt disinclined to argue. Indeed, if left to himself, he would probably have gone to sleep. That was why he merely nodded in reply to Meldon's appeal for clemency.

' I wonder,' said Meldon, ' if Eileen is giving us anything more to eat.'

The elderly Macmahon had left the room and stayed out of it for an unusually long time.

' We've had six courses,' said Meldon, ' counting the sardines on toast, and a savoury is usually the last thing. I hardly think there can be anything more. Suppose we trot into the smoking-room and see that everything's ready there.'

In the smoking-room Con Murphy secured a glass of whisky and a large cigar. Then he stretched himself in the most comfortable chair he could find. Meldon wandered about, noting with approval all the arrangements which Eileen had made. He broke the cover of one of the packs on the card table. He stood shuffling the cards with very rapid motions of his fingers while he talked.

' I think everything's satisfactorily arranged for to-night's expedition,' he said. ' Jimmy Costello has nine tins of petrol ready in the back of the car. That ought to be enough for a small house like Deissmann's. Michael Gannon's to meet us at eleven-thirty. That's a bit early, I know, but a steady, systematic, hard-working man like Deissmann is sure to go to bed about ten, so half-past eleven will be just as convenient as two in the morning for him.'

The wind gave a dreary moan outside. A puff of smoke blew out into the room from the chimney. Con Murphy snuggled deeper down into his chair. The burning of houses in the middle of the night was a favourite amusement of his ; but the most ardent sportsman does not always want to be forced out into a gale of wind and a downpour of rain, late at night after a good dinner.

' And I'd like to be in good time,' said Meldon, ' because I want to have a look round the house before it's actually burned. Deissmann has some property of the Major's hidden there. I told you that, didn't I ? '

' You did not.'

' Stupid of me not to have mentioned it before. He has a candlestick or two which belong to the Major and he won't give them up. My idea is to find them. They'll very likely be hidden, but we'll get them if we make a thorough search, and after that we can burn the house. There's no sense in destroying what belongs to the Major. The only object in burning anything is to annoy Deissmann, and so far as the candlesticks are concerned, it will irritate him just as much to have them given back to the Major. In fact, I expect he'd rather see them burnt.'

Again Con Murphy nodded, took a draught of whisky and soda and stretched his feet out towards the fire. The first drops of the coming rain rattled sharply against the window-panes. He began to hope that perhaps Meldon and Michael Gannon, if they really wanted no more than to annoy Deissmann, would manage the affair without his help.

Then Eileen Costello came in. She was wearing a pink silk dress in honour of the party. She had found time to put it on and to give a few extra curls to her hair after sending up the sardines on toast which ended the dinner. It was a very pretty dress, covered with flounces. It billowed out below the waist in the very latest fashion. Her stockings matched the dress, and she had shoes which looked as if they were made of gold. She ought, therefore, to have been a very happy girl, but it was plain from the look in her eyes and the down-drooping corners of her mouth, that she was in trouble. She walked straight over to Meldon, glancing doubtfully at Con Murphy as she passed his chair.

' Where's Peter ? ' said Meldon.

' It's about him I want to speak to you,' said Eileen in a whisper.

She looked round at Con Murphy. His eyes had closed. If he had actually fallen asleep—and he looked like it—there was a good deal of excuse for him. He had ridden his motor bicycle far and fast. He had suffered an annoying shock at Coolarrigan. He had been reasoned with by Meldon for more than an hour. He had dined. He had, since dinner, drunk a tumbler full of whisky and soda, chiefly whisky. He had consumed half a cigar.

' Do you mean to say,' said Meldon, ' that Peter hasn't proposed to you ? If he has backed out at the last moment it's one of the most disgraceful things I've ever heard of. I left him there alone with you. I practically put the words into his mouth. I told him that he needn't be the least afraid of your refusing him, and yet he's had the nerve to slink away somewhere without committing himself. Well, all I can say is that— Here I've been pleading for the life of that fellow, saying that he might improve if once he was married to you, and he turns out after all to be the sort of worthless swine who plays fast and loose with a girl's affection.'

' Sure, it's not that at all,' said Eileen. ' He did what you told him right enough.'

' Then he must have done it in the wrong way,' said

Meldon. ' If he'd done it properly you wouldn't be looking as unhappy as you are. I suppose he simply suggested some unemotional business partnership with you. If so I don't wonder you're vexed. That sort of cold-blooded fish of a man ought never to be allowed to speak to a girl at all. I'm disappointed in Peter. I thought he'd have done what any young man of decent feeling would have done, that is to say, seize you in his arms, press you to his chest, and rain kisses, long, clinging kisses on your upturned lips, while murmuring more or less incoherently words like "darling."'

Eileen blushed. The red spread from her cheeks, where, it started, to her forehead, round each side of her face to the tips of her ears, past her ears over her neck. Her arms were flushed. Her very hands glowed. She was like all Irish girls, modest. Meldon, seeing what had happened to her, realized that Peter Jameson had not been a tepid lover after all. He had evidently done all that in Meldon's opinion was proper to the occasion.

' Oh, he did all that, did he ? ' said Meldon. ' I'm glad to hear it. But if he did, if he really kissed you properly and often, what on earth are you looking so glum about ? You ought to be warbling about all over the place like a skylark. Why aren't you ? '

' It's on account of him,' said Eileen, glancing quickly in the direction of Con Murphy, who was now quite unmistakably asleep in his chair.

' Peter's in dread to come into the room with Con Murphy,' said Eileen, ' for fear he might be shot.'

' I told him,' said Meldon, ' that I'd settle that all up and that he needn't be afraid.'

'Sure, I told him that. But where's the use of talking to a man when the fear of death is on him?'

'He ought to have believed me,' said Meldon. 'If he'd known me better he would have believed me. When I promise to do a thing I invariably keep my promise. I undertook to pacify Con Murphy and I have.'

'Sure, I told him you would.'

'And in spite of all that—what a wretched creature Peter is! For the sake of his own miserable terror, which is perfectly groundless, he's going to leave us one short in our game of spoil five. I wonder if he'd believe Con Murphy if he promised not to shoot him.'

'He might.'

She spoke hopefully. A promise from Red Con himself might well carry conviction even to Peter's mind.

Meldon fumbled in his pocket. He brought out first a stump of pencil, then a bundle of old letters. From among these he selected a blank half sheet and wrote rapidly on it.

'I declare to goodness,' he said, 'I've never had so much trouble over a game of cards in all my life. First the Major refuses to play unless I get a written promise from that young man of yours that he won't rag him about income-tax, and now Peter won't play unless he has it in writing that Con Murphy won't shoot him. I suppose the next thing will be a demand from Murphy for a guarantee that you won't try to marry him. How much simpler it would all be if you'd all behave rationally and trust each other a little, or, if you can't do that, at all events trust me.'

He finished writing while he spoke. He went over to Con Murphy and shook him into wakefulness.

'Sit up and sign this,' he said.

Con Murphy grasped the pencil which was thrust into his hand, signed his name and immediately dropped off to sleep again.

'Now,' said Meldon, 'take this back to Peter and tell him— But perhaps you'd better read it first.'

Meldon's writing is never very legible. When he writes hurriedly it is extremely difficult to read. Eileen stumbled, but the document was short. She got through it in the end.

'ARTICLES OF AGREEMENT

Between Red Con Murphy (hereinafter called the Avenger) of the one part, and Peter Jameson (hereinafter called the victim) of the other part.

Whereas the Avenger has been and still is desirous of killing the said victim.

It is hereby agreed as follows :

The Avenger will not shoot or otherwise slay the Victim (except by accident, such accident to be bona fide, to the satisfaction of arbitrators hereafter to be appointed) during the present evening or to-morrow up to the hour of twelve noon (Greenwich time. One p.m. Sun time) or hereafter without full twenty-four hours' notice, such notice not to be valid unless sent to the Victim or his authorized agent by registered letter.

Signed, Con (Red) Murphy.'

'I hope that satisfies you,' said Meldon.

' It does,' said Eileen.   ' And it'll satisfy Peter, so it will.'

' I don't expect Murphy would have signed that last clause if he'd been awake,' said Meldon.   ' But there it is now and he can't get out of it.   So Peter is safe for life if only he remembers never to allow a registered letter to be delivered to him on any pretext whatever.'

CHAPTER XXIV

EILEEN, with the guarantee in her hand, went to
look for Peter. She found him sitting in her
office with the key of the cellar beside him,
ready at any moment to make a bolt for safety. He
read the guarantee through carefully, but seemed
doubtful whether he could rely on it. It was not until
Eileen had assured him that Con Murphy was sound
asleep, that he ventured to follow her towards the
smoking-room.

On their way, as they crossed the hall, they came on
Michael Gannon, who had just entered the hall. He
was wet, for the rain was falling heavily, and he had
walked all the way from his own house.

' It's Mr. Meldon I'm looking for,' he said. ' I have
a message for him from the Major.'

He was led into the smoking-room, where Con
Murphy still slept and Meldon was impatiently shuffling
the second pack of cards.

' Ah, there you are, Peter,' said Meldon. ' Now, if
we only had the Major we could wake up Murphy and
get started at our game.'

Then he caught sight of Gannon, who stood near the
door, unwilling to bring his dripping clothes and muddy
boots into the room.

' Hullo, Gannon ! ' he said. ' What brings you here ?
Surely there's no hitch in the arrangements for our

little fire to-night ? Have a drink. You look as if you wanted a drink. Don't attempt to tell me what's gone wrong until you've had a mouthful of whisky. There it is, on that table in the corner. Help yourself.'

Gannon helped himself.

' Now,' said Meldon, ' what's wrong ? Have you come to tell me that you want to back out of this business of Deissmann's house to-night ? I'm disappointed in you, Gannon. There's nothing more disgraceful than failing to keep an engagement which you've once made, and few things which cause greater annoyance to other people. Take the historic case of the Earl of Chatham and Sir Richard Strahan, who agreed to fight a duel. Neither of them intended to back out of the engagement as you're trying to back out of yours, but——'

' Sure, it's not that at all,' said Michael Gannon. ' I'm ready to start this minute if you like.'

' If you're not trying to back out,' said Meldon, ' and I'm extremely glad to hear that, what have you come here to say to me ? Has Deissmann found out what we intend to do, and fortified his house, or laid in a couple of machine-guns ? If so we shall have to proceed cautiously. It won't do to have a man like Red Con Murphy losing his life in a paltry scrimmage with a German engineer. It doesn't so much matter about you and me ; but a man like Con Murphy, who has defied whole Governments—it would never do for him to perish, like Richard Cœur de Lion, from a more or less chance shot fired by a fellow like Deissmann.'

' You needn't trouble about Diessmann shooting anyone,' said Gannon, ' for he has no gun.'

' Then for goodness sake go on with whatever it is you do want to say. It's most unreasonable to expect

me to stand here all night listening to a long list of
things which you don't want to tell me. The Major
may be here any minute, and, as soon as he arrives,
we shall wake up Con Murphy and start our game of
cards. Unless you manage to say whatever you want
to say before the Major comes you'll never get the
chance of saying it at all, for I shan't listen to you.'

' If you're going to wait till the Major comes,' said
Gannon, ' you'll wait long enough, for he's not coming
at all.'

' What ? '

' He's not coming,' said Gannon. ' That's what he
sent me to tell you, and that's what I would have told
you long ago if you hadn't had so much to say about
machine-guns in Deissmann's house, and earls fighting
duels, and some fellow called Richard that was shot.'

' Why isn't the Major coming ? '

' How would I know why he isn't coming ? ' said
Gannon. ' What he bid me say was that there was
some paper which wasn't satisfactory on account of
its being signed by a man he didn't trust, some fellow
that was trying to rob him of his money. That's the
best I could make out of what the Major said, but I
didn't see the paper he was talking about.'

' That's your guarantee of immunity, Peter,' said
Meldon. ' The Major says he can't rely on your
promise. That's the sort of reputation you income-
tax collectors seem to have.'

' I'm not an income-tax collector,' said Peter. ' I'm
tired telling you that.'

' After listening to that statement,' said Meldon,
' which, as you say, I've heard before, I don't wonder
that the Major doesn't trust your written guarantee.
If you're not an income-tax collector, what are you ? '

'I'm a special commissioner,' said Peter. 'Anyhow, that's what they told me, up in Dublin before I left.'

'I do wish,' said Meldon, 'that you wouldn't treat me as if I were an imbecile. Give me credit for some intelligence, and try to lie plausibly even if you can't speak the truth. Nobody who had ever seen you could possibly believe that you are a special commissioner. And even if you looked like one, which you don't, it wouldn't explain your being here. No Government would send a special commissioner down to a place like Lisnamoe. Special commissioners are the sort of men who are sent to settle fishing disputes off Newfoundland, or boundary questions in Venezuela, or how much coal Germany ought to send to France. Lisnamoe is no place for a special commissioner. You might just as well send a Lord Chancellor to weed the strawberry bed in a kitchen garden. Come now, Peter, if you're a special commissioner, what are you supposed to be doing here?'

'What I'm doing here—' said Peter. 'What I was sent here to be doing——'

He got no further than that. Eileen seized him by the arm and hissed a tense 'Whisht!' into his ear. As she did so she glanced at Con Murphy, who was still sleeping in his chair. Peter's eyes followed hers and he abruptly stopped speaking. Written safeguards are all very well, and Peter had one in his pocket, but neither he nor Eileen was prepared to take the risk of admitting, in the presence of Red Con Murphy, that the Irish Free State Government had sent a special commissioner to investigate the outrages at Coolarrigan.

'There you are,' said Meldon. 'You've totally failed to give a plausible account of yourself. No wonder the Major doesn't believe a word you say and refuses to trust that written guarantee of yours. The poor Major ! Just because you can't or won't tell the truth he's condemned to sit all evening in Gannon's kitchen, tortured by nine children who are climbing all over him, dragging at his watch-chain, pulling his hair, incessantly asking him to wipe their noses for them— a thing which the Major would hate to do for any child, and simply loathes in the case of filthy brats like those nine of Gannon's.'

This attack on his family roused Michael Gannon to a mild protest. He could not go so far as to assert that his children were clean, but he did defend them against the charge of tormenting the Major.

' It's not climbing on the Major them childer is,' he said, ' but playing house, quiet and easy, in the corner of the kitchen.'

' And do you really suppose,' said Meldon, ' that the Major can possibly enjoy playing house with your children ? I can't imagine anything he'd hate more except blowing their noses.'

' The way of it with the childer is this,' said Michael Gannon mildly, speaking as a man who offers an entirely satisfactory explanation of some troublesome facts. ' They did be playing house in the pig-sty most of the time until I bought a new pig, a bonham it was, out of the money that the Major is to give me for blowing up the pier. And of course when I bought the pig I had to put the childer out of the sty.'

' You might perfectly well have left them,' said Meldon. ' They'd have got on quite contentedly with the pig, and certainly not annoyed it nearly as much as they do the Major.'

' So they cleared out the bits of things they had in the sty,' Gannon went on, ' what they did be playing

house with, old china and the like, and what tins they
might have picked up and any rags they'd begged off
their mother. They had pretty nigh a barrow full
gathered there ; but they're good childer, though I say
it that shouldn't, and they took the lot out of the sty
when I told them to. They were in dread the pig
might eat them, so they took them out and they
brought them into the kitchen, so that they'd be able
to play with them there. That's what they were doing
when I left; and they were doing it contented enough,
without interfering with the Major, either good or bad.
To the best of my belief it's what they're doing still.'

The door was flung open as Michael Gannon was
finishing his apology for his children. Major Kent
walked in. He was very wet, for it was raining heavily.
He looked tired, for he had been battling with a strong
wind. But there was a light of jubilant triumph in his
eyes.

CHAPTER XXV

WHEN he walked into the smoking-room of the hotel Major Kent had a parcel in his hands, a large parcel wrapped up in brown paper. He went straight to the card table and laid it down there in front of Meldon, who was still standing with a pack of cards in his hands.

' There they are ! ' said the Major.

There was no mistake about the satisfaction, even the jubilation of the tone in which he spoke.

' There what are ? ' said Meldon. ' Don't ask me to guess riddles, Major. I've had a trying time, a very trying time, persuading Con Murphy not to shoot Peter, which was hard enough, and persuading Peter that he wasn't going to be shot, which was harder still. Don't make things worse for me than they are, by asking me conundrums. Do try to make your meaning plain.'

The Major dragged the wrapping off his parcel, a thing which was very easily done for the brown paper was soaked, like the Major's clothes and everything else about him.

' The candlesticks,' he said.

He disentangled them from the string which still clung round them. He set them upright in a row in the middle of the table. They were a good deal battered and scratched. They were horribly discoloured. But there were seven of them and Meldon saw at once that they were the long-lost masterpieces of Paul Lamerie.

' I congratulate you, Major,' said Meldon. ' I congratulate you heartily. Not only on the recovery of your property but on having had the nerve to burgle Deissmann's house all by yourself. I never imagined that you'd have done it. I didn't think you could. Of course I know that you're a brave man, as brave as anybody could possibly be. No ordinary peril would daunt you in the least. But burglary requires a special kind of courage, a kind which I really did not think you possessed. How did you get into the house ? Did you force a window or pick the lock of the back door ? Or did you simply ring at the door and then hold a pistol to Deissmann's head ? Did he put up any kind of fight ? '

' I don't know what you're talking about, J. J.,' said the Major. ' I didn't burgle any house. What happened was this——'

' Do you know,' said Meldon, ' I half hoped all along that that would happen. I couldn't help feeling that Deissmann was fundamentally an honest man, in spite of his objectionable manner and his almost insane conceit. After the way I talked to him—and I put things pretty plainly as well as persuasively—I hoped he'd see that the only proper thing for him to do was to send the candlesticks back to you. Well, he has, and I'm glad of it. It restores one's faith in human nature to see a man behaving as Deissmann has in the end, though he certainly didn't at first and didn't seem inclined to when I was with him. Did he send any note of explanation or apology along with the candlesticks ? '

' Deissmann didn't send me back the candlesticks,' said the Major. ' He——'

' My dear Major, either you took them from him, which I called burglary for the sake of brevity and convenience, though you may perfectly well argue that it wouldn't have been burglary when the things you took were your own. But whatever name you give to your action it comes back to the same thing : Either you took the candlesticks from him, more or less by force, or he gave them up to you of his own accord. There is no other possible hypothesis.'

' Yes, there is. Deissmann——'

' I see,' said Meldon. ' You're quite right, Major. There is another hypothesis. I see that now. Deissmann sold them to you. I hope, I sincerely hope that you didn't give him more than ten pounds for them at the outside. They're worth more, of course. I've always said they're worth one thousand pounds at least, but not to Deissmann. He couldn't have got them out of this country on account of the law against exporting works of art. I should have given the tip to the custom-house people and he'd have been caught to a certainty. He couldn't have sold them in London without our finding out. They were therefore practically valueless to him. I do hope you didn't give him more than ten pounds.'

' I didn't buy them,' said the Major. ' Deissmann never had them.'

' If he hadn't,' said Meldon, ' who had ? Gannon, had you those candlesticks ? For if so——'

' I had not,' said Gannon, ' but I don't deny that I knew where they were. The childer had them. And what's more,' here he turned to Major Kent, ' I know where another of them is. I have it myself and I've had it ever since the night I took it off the sideboard in Coolarrigan before the house was burnt.

Sure, if I'd had any notion, Major dear, that it was them things you wanted I'd have told the childer to give them to you long ago and I'd have given you back the one I have with a heart and a half, for it's little use it ever was to me. It was in the pig-sty the childer had them along with the rest of the rubbish that they did be playing house with.'

'Major,' said Meldon, 'do you mean to say you've been grubbing about the recesses of a pig-sty with the Gannon children?'

'I don't know anything about the pig-sty,' said the Major. 'All I know is——'

'Amn't I after telling you,' said Michael Gannon to Meldon, 'that I bought a new pig this morning and the childer had to clear whatever belonged to them out of the sty before I brought the creature home.'

'They were playing with them in a corner of the kitchen when I saw them,' said the Major.

'To the best of my belief,' said Gannon, 'it was out of the river they got them the time Deissmann cleared away the old boat-house. Anyhow that was the last time—up to the day of the strike—that the childer was near the river, for it was after that that Deissmann hunted them away.'

'And now, J. J.,' said the Major, 'I hope you'll come straight home to-morrow before anything else unpleasant happens to us.'

'There are one or two small matters,' said Meldon, 'that I must settle before I go. But I think I can manage them all this evening. Then, I need scarcely say, I shall be ready to start at once. I haven't the very smallest wish to stay here. I never wanted to come here. It was entirely for your sake, and in order to help you out of a difficulty that I took all the trouble

I have taken.   I assure you it hasn't been a pleasure to
me.   Now that the object of our expedition is accom-
plished—and you must remember, Major, that I always
said it would be—you were the person who steadily
said it wouldn't.   Now that we've got what we wanted
there's no reason for not going home by the next
train.'

He walked over to the chair in which Con Murphy
still slept.   He took that hero-patriot by the arm and
shook him vigorously.

'Murphy,' he said, 'to-night's expedition is definitely off.   There's no longer the slightest necessity
for burning down Deissmann's house.'

The wind was howling dismally and the rain beat
fiercely on the window-panes.   Murphy nodded his
complete agreement with what Meldon said, refilled his
tumbler, took another long drink and then went to
sleep again.

'It's a pity now about Deissmann's house,' said
Michael Gannon, 'for we have the petrol and everything ready.'

'Don't you fret about that, Gannon,' said Meldon.
'You'll get the price of your pig just the same.   Major,
pay Michael Gannon the price of the pig he bought this
morning.'

'Why should I pay for his pig?' said the Major.
'Did I promise to?   How much is it?'

'What the fellow that sold him to me asked for him,'
said Gannon, 'was four pounds.   But I told him
straight and plain that he wasn't worth the half of it,
so in the latter end I got him for three pounds two and
six, with half a crown back for luck.'

'Make it a fiver, Major,' said Meldon.   'You can
afford it perfectly well now you've got the candlesticks.

You must remember that poor Gannon's been disappointed about the fire to-night. He was looking forward to seeing Deissmann's house burn. Have you got the money on you, Major? Very well, then, hand it over. Now there's just one thing more. Peter, I shall rely on you to see that this ridiculous income-tax claim against the Major is quashed at once and finally. There musn't be another word said about it or another letter written. Eileen, I hope that you'll see to it that Peter does that. Major, you'll have to send Peter and Eileen a wedding present, not simply a silver-mounted blotter, but something really substantial. A fairly fat cheque would, I think, be the best thing. Say twenty-five pounds. When the income-tax claim is withdrawn you can afford to do that easily, especially after getting back your candlesticks. But remember, Peter—and you remind him, Eileen, if he forgets—that he must wipe the Major's name clean off the Free State income-tax books.'

' But how can I do that,' said Peter, ' when I've nothing in the wide world to do with the income-tax one way or the other? It's not in that office I am at all.'

' Whisht, now, Peter, whisht,' said Eileen, ' don't you know that if Mr. Meldon says you're to do a thing you'll have to do it in the latter end? '

' He will,' said the Major.

PRINTED BY
WYMAN AND SONS, LIMITED
LONDON, FAKENHAM AND READING